RAVANOK THE UNMAKER

SINGULARITIES BOOK 4

ANTHONY JAMES

Illustration © Tom Edwards
TomEdwardsDesign.com

Sign up to my mailing list here to be the first to find out about new releases.

ONE

No more than ten minutes had passed since Captain William Lanson's crew on the Aral vessel *Ragnar-3* had rescued him from the Ravrol facility. The mission had been tough – they all were – but the outcome was a success.

Against the odds, Lanson, aided by Sergeant Evander Gabriel and his squad of soldiers, had survived the onslaught of a Sagh'eld fleet, and, in addition, they'd inflicted potentially grave damage on the monstrous Ixtar warship *Tyrantor*.

Perhaps of even greater significance, the *Ragnar-3* had combined with the *Ragnar-2*, creating a vessel which Lanson expected would have greater capabilities than either warship acting alone. What those capabilities might be, Lanson didn't yet know, though he intended to find out just as soon as he made it back to the bridge.

With his mind racing, he hurried through the cold, dim corridors of the warship, while the steady thrum of the propulsion pressed against him as the alien vessel tore its way across space at a high multiple of lightspeed.

Soon, Lanson found himself standing at the bridge

entrance, and, given everything which had gone before, it felt like a lifetime ago that he'd passed through this same doorway at the beginning of his journey to the Dalvaron space station.

A touch of his fingers on the smooth, glassy surface of the access panel, was enough for the warship's security systems to authenticate him, and the dense alloy door slid aside with hardly a sound.

The bridge was an enclosed space, too cold, and the lights too dim, and the overall effect was that this was a small room buried deep underground, rather than the command station for a vessel with colossal destructive power.

"Welcome to the *Ragnar-L*, sir," said Commander Ellie Matlock.

"*Ragnar-L*?" said Lanson. "So that's what it's called now?"

"Yes, Captain. The software updated as soon as we combined with the *Ragnar-2*."

Lanson didn't know if his warship's new name had any specific background or meaning. He gave a mental shrug. "It's good to be back," he said. "For a time, I thought I'd never make it." He turned so that he was addressing the other four members of the crew. "Thanks for the rescue, folks. And thanks for keeping the *Ragnar-L* in one piece."

"From what I've heard of your time on Dalvaron, it sounds like we had it easy, Captain," said lead propulsion officer Lieutenant Gus Abrams. "Are you going to fill us in on the missing details?"

"Soon," said Lanson. "Commander Matlock, I'm ready to resume command of this warship."

"It's all yours, Captain."

Lanson nodded. He approached the left-hand console at the forward end of the bridge and lowered himself into the command seat. "What's our destination?" he asked.

"Nowhere in particular, Captain. The journey time will be twenty-four hours unless we cancel it earlier," said Matlock.

"And the lightspeed scatter?" asked Lanson.

"We left nine false trails when we entered lightspeed," said Matlock. "If the Ixtar have a mind to follow us, they have a ten percent chance of picking right."

"I'm not so sure, Commander," said Lanson. "Neither the *Ghiotor* nor the *Tyrantor* seemed to have too much difficulty locating Ravrol. Either they have access to the Infinity Lens, or they have other technology which allows them to filter out the false trails."

"Both of those Ixtar warships arrived at Ravrol ahead of the *Ragnar-3*," said Matlock. "The *Ghiotor* left Dalvaron after we did, so it must have a higher lightspeed multiplier."

"Maybe not any longer," said Lieutenant Abrams. "Our maximum propulsion output has increased by more than a hundred percent since we linked to the *Ragnar-2*."

"I felt the extra thrust as we were lifting off," said Lanson.

"We'll need to do some field testing to determine the effect on our velocity and manoeuvrability," said Abrams. "I'm sure we'll see significant improvements in both."

Opportunities to test the *Ragnar-3* had been thin on the ground, otherwise Abrams would have been able to provide estimates on how the *Ragnar-L* would perform. Those tests would have to wait, since Lanson wasn't ready to cancel the lightspeed transit just yet.

For the next couple of minutes, he scanned the output data on his status displays. The joining of the *Ragnar-2* and the *Ragnar-3* had resulted in the combined vessel having more firepower than the *Ragnar-3* alone, though not by an enormous amount. Already, Lanson suspected the *Ragnar-2*'s intended purpose was to be the main propulsion module for the final vessel which would be created when all six of the Singularity class warships were joined.

Which reminded him...

"Let's see if I have access to the Singularity menu," said Lanson.

He hesitated with his hand poised over the console touchpad which would bring up the weapons systems. In the adjacent seat, Commander Matlock was watching carefully. This was the moment of truth – the primary reason for the mission to Dalvaron had been to elevate Lanson's security level within the Aral systems from Tier 1 to Tier 0 in order that he could utilise the *Ragnar-L*'s locked down weapons systems.

I might be the only living being with Tier 0 access.

Tapping with a finger to open the top-level menu, Lanson then touched the Singularity menu. The words on his screen changed. He read them once, twice and then for a third time.

"Damnit," he said.

"What's wrong, Captain?" asked Matlock.

"*Singularity Cannon – missing component.*" Lanson read from his screen. "Beneath that are three other options, all of which are unavailable for the same reason – *missing component.*"

"So the Ragnar warships aren't able to fulfil their main function unless all six are combined," said Matlock.

"That's what it looks like, Commander," said Lanson. "Maybe some of these Singularity weapons will become active if we combine with one or two of the other vessels, but I guess we'll need to find the other four before the Ragnar's full capabilities are available."

"What the hell is this spaceship's main function anyway?" asked comms Lieutenant Becky Turner.

"I don't know," said Lanson. "When we first captured the *Ragnar-3*, I thought it was nothing more than a warship from an alien fleet. It's clear now that we stumbled upon something that's a whole lot more."

"Are you going to tell us what happened on Dalvaron and Ravrol, Captain?" asked Lieutenant Abrams for the second time.

For the next few minutes, Lanson spoke, describing the events he and the other mission personnel had survived. The crew asked questions, and he answered them. Once Lanson was finished, Commander Matlock recounted the experiences of the *Ragnar-3*'s crew during the time at Dalvaron, though there wasn't much to tell.

"We watched and we waited," she concluded. "Then, at what we believed was the right time, we set a course for Ravrol."

"What happens next, sir?" asked propulsion officer Joe Massey.

"I haven't had a chance to think ahead," said Lanson. "Lieutenant Turner, do we have any additional entries in our star charts since the *Ragnar-3* combined with the *Ragnar-2*?"

"No, sir," said Turner.

"So we have no way to return home," said Lanson.

"Not unless we can obtain the coordinates of a Human Confederation planet," Turner confirmed. "We can't send a comm either."

"We have to press on," said Lanson, confronting the ugly truth. "The Infinity Lens is currently only activated for what the Aral defined as Sector 3. As far as we know, there are five other sectors still to activate, and one of those sectors will contain Human Confederation worlds."

"Where do we go, sir?" asked comms Lieutenant Fay Perry. "The *Ragnar-L*'s star charts contain many entries for other Aral worlds, and not just those in Sector 3."

"The problem is picking the right destination, Lieutenant," said Lanson.

He grimaced and tried to follow the threads in everything he knew so far. Locating the Infinity Lens was vital, though, since Lanson couldn't conceive what form this device had taken, he had no idea how to deal with it. Having seen the Aral hardware on Scalos collapse an entire star, he greatly doubted the Infinity Lens would be something trivial to destroy.

The Singularity warships are the key.

Lanson didn't know if there was any truth to this thought and, in fact, it didn't seem likely the Aral would have created a device like the Infinity Lens, but then required a six-component warship to destroy it. No, he was missing something, and he lacked the information to understand what the Aral had intended.

"What do you think happened to the Aral, Captain?" asked Commander Matlock. It was as though she were reading his mind. "You mentioned that when you were in the Ravrol facility, all the final time stamps on the facility hardware were identical."

"That was another thing I didn't have a chance to investigate," said Lanson. He felt a sudden shiver just from thinking about his discovery, as if he'd caught a distant hint of momentous events. "At the time, I thought that something had happened so abruptly it had taken the Aral completely unawares."

"The base was intact when you arrived, sir," said Matlock. "Whatever took place, it didn't involve an attack with explosives."

"I know," said Lanson. He paused for a moment. "The Ixtar death weapon might have been enough to kill everyone on Ravrol."

"Except it doesn't affect an area anything like the size of the

Aral facility," said Matlock. "And you said the base was well defended."

"It was," said Lanson. "Yet those defences had been disabled."

He cursed everything he didn't know. The situation was messy enough already, with the Sagh'eld and the Ixtar both hunting for Aral technology, and yet Lanson couldn't shake a feeling that there was far more to this than he was currently aware. He hated being in the dark, especially when the future of humanity might well be at risk.

"We don't have the answers, so the only option is to keep looking," said Abrams. "Even if it is damned frustrating."

"I don't want us to spend weeks, months, or years visiting every known Aral planet or military facility in the *Ragnar-L*'s databanks," said Lanson. "We don't have the time for that. Our next target we have to choose well."

"While you were on Dalvaron, Lieutenant Perry and I spent time searching through the *Ragnar-3*'s databanks, sir," said Turner. "We already knew how to filter by tier – that's how we located Dalvaron – but then I noticed that Ilvaron doesn't appear when I apply the highest-level filter. In fact, it doesn't appear at any level of filter."

The cogs in Lanson's brain turned quickly. "What about Ravrol?"

"That facility doesn't appear either, Captain."

"The *Ragnar-3* was at Ilvaron, and the *Ragnar-2* was at Ravrol," said Lanson. "They must be Tier o facilities."

"You're the only one with Tier o access, sir," said Turner.

"Let me take a look."

Lanson felt the stirrings of excitement as he called up the charts on his main screen. The *Ragnar-L*'s database of known places contained a vast number of entries, many of which he guessed would require months of lightspeed travel to reach.

The moment he accessed the charts, he checked the available filters.

"I can apply a Tier 0 filter," Lanson said.

"What are you waiting for, sir?"

Lanson applied the filter and watched his screen for the outcome.

> *Tier 0 Locations [14]. Display?*

As soon as Lanson entered his confirmation, several entries on the star chart became highlighted. Straightaway, he spotted that something was wrong.

"Only eight highlights," he said. "Not fourteen."

Just to be sure, he removed the filter and reapplied it. The result was the same – only eight of the fourteen reported Tier 0 sites became highlighted.

"Six missing," Lanson said. "Do you have any theories as to what happened to those entries, Lieutenant Turner?"

"If they aren't showing on the charts, they aren't in the backend database, sir. Unless there's some corruption in the database itself."

"This isn't corruption," said Lanson. He couldn't remember the last time he'd heard of data being corrupted on a Human Confederation array, and he was sure the Aral storage tech was equally robust.

"I don't think it's corruption either, sir, I was just offering you a possibility."

Lanson sat back and stared at his screen. His elevation to security Tier 0 on Dalvaron had allowed him to identify the most critical locations within the Aral empire, and yet six of those entries were missing.

The cynic in Lanson had a powerful suspicion that the missing entries would be exactly the ones he would most need to investigate.

TWO

Calling up the descriptions of each available Tier o location, Lanson searched for something – anything – which would make his coming decision easier. The only familiar names were Ravrol and Ilvaron.

"How many of these sites fall within the range of the Infinity Lens?" he asked.

"I'm just taking a look at that, sir," said Perry. A moment later, she had the answer. "Only Ilvaron."

"That's not going to help us," said Lanson.

Although he was disappointed, Lanson also felt an inner relief. If the Infinity Lens had reported the existence of light-speed tunnels at a site other than Ilvaron or Ravrol – places he'd already visited - then he would have been obliged to set an immediate course for the new location in order to prevent the enemy from making off with whatever technology would be found there.

He wasn't keen to fight – not having seen the commitment of warships the Sagh'eld had made at Ravrol, and the over-whelming power of the Ixtar vessels *Tyrantor* and *Ghiotor*.

The *Ragnar-L*'s data arrays did not hold much information about the eight Tier 0 facilities, beyond their names and locations. However, the main functions of each facility were provided. Six of the bases were described as *research and readiness*, a seventh was described as *research and construction*, while the last Tier 0 facility had no listed function, though its entry did contain the word *Error#*.

"What's up with this error code?" said Commander Matlock, who was also studying the Tier 0 entries.

"It's the same response that appeared on Ravrol when I tried to activate the local defence systems," said Lanson, remembering his frustration at the time. "The code wasn't documented in the Aral systems."

"Meaning?"

"I don't know, Commander." Lanson half-turned in his seat. "Do you have any ideas, Lieutenant Abrams?"

"If the *Error#* response wasn't in the documentation, then the coding which generated the error was added after the documentation was written," said Abrams. "Shit like this happens, but I'd expect it to be a rare occurrence in a military change control system."

"Except I've seen this error response twice now, on discrete systems," said Lanson. "I can accept that the Aral made one screw up when they were updating their coding, but for it to happen twice strikes me as more than coincidence."

"What's your theory, Captain?" asked Abrams, with his eyes narrowed.

"We have six missing entries and an additional entry which has been tampered with," said Lanson. "This is deliberate sabotage." He cast his mind back a short time. "The Ravrol defence systems were disabled at the same time as the last commands were issued to the local hardware. Then all the Aral disappeared."

"That's what you *believe* happened, sir," said Abrams. "There's no proof of it."

"I know, but nothing else fits." Lanson drummed his fingers. "If you accessed the back-end code for the tier database on the *Ragnar-L's* data arrays, would you be able to find out what was deleted or updated?"

"I shouldn't need to access the code, Captain. There'll be a revision list on the same data array that will show any changes which were made, and when they happened."

"Check it out, please," said Lanson.

"Yes, sir."

Lanson pursed his lips as he stared at his screen. "We have six entries described as *research and readiness*, including Ilvaron and Ravrol. It's my belief that the remaining four Singularity class warships are located at these other four places."

"*Research and readiness?*" asked Turner. "That doesn't sound like a place the Aral would have built their warships."

"The Ravrol base had extensive shipbuilding facilities, but construction is not mentioned in its purpose," said Lanson. "I think the Singularity warships were all built at—" he peered at the name of the one location which contained the word *construction* in its description, "Tarafon."

"Then why not combine them at the place they were built?" asked Lieutenant Perry.

"I don't know," said Lanson. "Just because we don't understand why, it doesn't mean the Aral didn't have their reasons."

"I've entered the coordinates for every Tier o facility into our navigation system, Captain," said Lieutenant Massey. "The nearest is three days' travel from our current location and the farthest is nine hundred days."

"Nine hundred?" said Lanson in disbelief. "Which of the sites is that one?"

"Site eight – the one with the error code, sir."

"Send me the travel time data for the other locations," said Lanson.

"Yes, sir, it's with you now."

Lanson cursed inwardly as he read down the list which Lieutenant Massey had provided. The Tier 0 locations were widely spread, the distances between them unimaginable. Suddenly, Lanson was struck by the magnitude of the Aral territory. Trillions of stars lay within its bounds.

And now the Aral are gone.

It was hard for Lanson to believe that the Aral – a species which evidence suggested had populated thousands of different worlds, and created wonders like the Dalvaron space station – could have allowed themselves to become extinct. And yet, he couldn't shake the belief that something had befallen this unknown species.

Sitting back, Lanson's head spun as he tried to grasp the enormity of everything. The Aral facilities he'd visited since escaping from Cornerstone - what seemed like a lifetime ago - gave no indication that the aliens had been involved in war. Their bases were intact, except for the more recent damage inflicted by the Ixtar.

"What's chewing you, sir?" asked Matlock.

"The Aral," said Lanson. "My lack of knowledge bothers me. Where is their fleet? Why did they create the Infinity Lens? Were they planning to launch an offensive against another species we know nothing about? Were they already fighting the Ixtar five thousand years ago?"

"Maybe it's for the best that the Aral are gone," said Matlock. "I can buy the idea that having a strong defence is the way to deter attackers, but the Galos cubes—" She shook her head. "They're something else. Who needs the power to collapse a star?"

"I have a feeling that if we learn more about the Aral, we'll be better placed to force a good outcome – not only for us, but for the Human Confederation too."

"You might be right, Captain, but would the time we spend searching through history be better utilised on picking up the other four Singularity class warships and then doing what we can to destroy or take full control over the Infinity Lens?"

"I don't see why we can't accomplish both tasks at the same time, Commander," said Lanson. "Wherever we go next, there'll be Aral hardware. Perhaps we'll find some data that will fill the gaps in our knowledge," said Lanson.

"I hope so, Captain," said Matlock.

"You don't sound convinced, Commander."

"I'm torn, sir. My brain is telling me that our best shot at success is to ignore everything else and destroy the Infinity Lens as soon as we locate it. Our enemies are too strong – we lack the means to deny them access to the capabilities of the Lens."

"For what it's worth, I'm also torn," Lanson admitted.

Matlock smiled. "But we're still going to look through those history books."

"Damn right." Lanson raised his voice. "What have you found in that database revision list, Lieutenant Abrams?"

"I'm just looking at it now, sir." Abrams went quiet for a few seconds. "There's no revision entry corresponding to a coding change that would have produced this error code, and there are no entries for the missing six Tier o locations."

"What does that mean?"

"The revision list should update automatically, so it's not as if this was an oversight," said Abrams. "I'll leave you to draw your own conclusions."

"Like I said before – we're seeing the results of sabotage," said Lanson.

"I'm sure you're right, sir," said Abrams. "But the motive behind it isn't clear, nor are the means by which it was accomplished."

"Maybe the Aral were at war amongst themselves," said Perry.

"It's possible," said Lanson.

"You're not convinced?"

"Not nearly. Lieutenant Abrams, would there be any value in reading through the code?"

"Probably not, sir. If I had to place a bet, I'd say there'll be some deleted lines, with no indication of what they were."

"Take a look anyway," said Lanson. "Treat it as a high priority."

"Yes, sir."

Lanson felt anger like the faintest of touches in his mind. He wanted answers now, damnit, and it wasn't just to assuage his own curiosity. Taking a deep breath, Lanson calmed himself – there was a decision to be made and he wanted a clear head.

"We either go looking for other components of the *Ragnar*, or we head directly for location six – Tarafon - and find out what else the Aral were building there."

"It's a twenty-one-day journey to Tarafon, Captain," said Matlock. "On the other hand, it's a three-day journey to location two – the Baltol facility on Tetron. Neither of those places are within the Infinity Lens' range - we'd be going in blind."

"So we'd follow the usual procedure of exiting lightspeed at distance and scanning until we know what we're facing," said Lanson.

"Locations four and five – Landrol and Indeston - are ten and eleven days' travel time respectively," said Matlock. "Aside from these two locations, we have the Avristol facility on planet Gotarus, which is forty-two days' travel time."

In the end, the decision was an easy one. A forty-two-day

transit was out of the question, given that Lanson needed to make quick gains to bring the *Ragnar-L* up to parity with its opponents. He ordered Lieutenant Abrams to end the current lightspeed transit.

With a faint shudder, the *Ragnar-L* re-entered local space. Given past experiences with the Ixtar, Lanson was on edge, half-expecting the enemy to exit lightspeed right on his doorstep.

"Set a course for Tetron," he ordered. "We're going to find another *Ragnar*."

The combined *Ragnar-2* and *Ragnar-3* benefitted from having more processing cores than either vessel alone, and the lightspeed warmup time was reduced by fifteen seconds from its previous three minutes. It was an improvement, though not one which Lanson could bring himself to be excited by.

After a tense two minutes and forty-five seconds, during which the area scans detected nothing more than stars and darkness, the warmup completed. The *Ragnar-L*'s propulsion created a burst of incredible energy, and the warship entered lightspeed.

In three days, it would arrive at Tetron. There, Lanson hoped to make a fast pickup of a third Singularity warship from the Baltol facility, without interference from either the Sagh'eld or the Ixtar.

Sometimes, Lanson got lucky and things went his way. This time, he wasn't about to start counting his chickens.

THREE

A three-day journey was not overly long in comparison to many transits Lanson had undertaken over the course of his years in the military. Even so, he became agitated, and filled with nervous energy after only a short time. He was itching to find out the secrets of Baltol and to gain a position from which he might challenge the Ixtar and the Sagh'eld. Although the recovery of the *Ragnar-2* was a great success, Lanson couldn't help but feel disappointed that the Singularity menu functions were still unavailable.

On the other hand, the one-sided engagement with the *Tyrantor* at Ilvaron had reduced the *Ragnar-L*'s Galos reserves down to three, so even with access to the Singularity weapons and defences, the warship would run out of ammunition quickly. Since the *Ragnar-2* had not been carrying any Galos cubes, Lanson hoped to gather some of the devices from Baltol. How they were loaded onto the *Ragnar-L*, he didn't know, but when it came to warship functionality, he could usually figure things out.

Having excused himself from the bridge, Lanson explored

the passages of what had until recently been the *Ragnar-2*. He soon discovered that the personnel areas were hardly more extensive than those on a Human Confederation destroyer – a vessel class which was completely dwarfed by the Aral spaceship.

Cold passages with low ceilings cut through the *Ragnar-2*'s propulsion modules. Intersections were few, and Lanson came across only the occasional room. These rooms contained monitoring panels and little else, reinforcing his opinion that the *Ragnar-2* had never been intended to carry passengers.

After twenty minutes of exploration, Lanson ran into Sergeant Gabriel and Private Davison at the intersection of two passages.

"How's the search going, Sergeant?" asked Lanson, having given the soldiers orders to hunt through the *Ragnar-2* for whatever they might find.

"We're almost done, Captain," said Gabriel. "You've probably already noticed there isn't much here."

Lanson nodded. "Does that mean no handheld Galos launchers?"

"No armoury and no Galos launchers," Gabriel confirmed. "And nothing which looks remotely like a bridge."

"From what I've seen of the *Ragnar-2*, it was most likely piloted remotely. I'm sure the Aral had their reasons for making it so."

"Does that mean we lucked out when we found the *Ragnar-3*, Captain?" asked Private Davison. "Since it's got a bridge and everything."

"It gave us something to work with, Private." Lanson turned his gaze towards Gabriel. "Have my comms officers told you about our next destination, Sergeant?"

"Baltol," said Gabriel, speaking the word like he was

chewing on a bitter-tasting insect. "We're going to find part three of the puzzle."

"It's more than just a spaceship we're looking for," said Lanson. "Someone deleted information from the *Ragnar-L*'s star charts – information that might tell us where to find the Infinity Lens."

"You'll need us to deploy and find out if we can extract the data from one of the ground consoles," said Gabriel. He didn't miss much.

"It's a possibility," said Lanson. "What happened to the Ezin-Tor?" he asked, referring to the huge Galos-powered hand cannon which the mission team had recovered from Ravrol.

"It's in the *Ragnar-3*'s armoury, sir," said Gabriel. "Carrying it around these passages would have been a pain in the ass."

"Do you and your soldiers have enough ammunition for another deployment, Sergeant?"

Gabriel's face twisted. "It's touch-and-go. Some of my squad will likely have to switch to the Aral weaponry in the armoury."

"You have three days to become familiar with those guns," said Lanson.

"It won't be a problem, sir."

Lanson took his leave and continued on his way, leaving Gabriel and Davison to head in the opposite direction. Another hour and he was done with the exploration, having located nothing of particular interest. Lanson had discovered a handful of maintenance tunnels, which vanished into the depths of the warship. These, he'd left alone, having located similar passages on the *Ragnar-3* and decided they led nowhere he needed to go.

Having returned to the bridge, Lanson offered Matlock,

Turner and Massey a six-hour break from bridge duties. They left at once.

With little to say, Lanson contented himself by watching the *Ragnar-L*'s monitoring tools, while he allowed his brain to work through recent events. There were times when his mind functioned better if it was left to its own devices.

"Captain, I've finished checking the database code," said Abrams. "It was an ass of a job."

"What did you find?"

"Deleted lines, with no sign of how the deletion took place. The Aral systems are extremely well audited, and with numerous backups, and yet the same lines of code have disappeared from every single one of those backups – even the write-once versions."

Lanson frowned. "The way you describe it, that shouldn't be possible."

"Well, it's happened so I know it *is* possible, sir," said Abrams. "However, I'm damned if I know how. The best I can think of is that an advanced infiltration system was used – a system that was able to completely evade the Aral's data protection."

"If the Aral were at war with themselves—" Lanson began.

"There may well have been a schism," said Abrams. "But if the Aral had split into rival factions, they'd have certainly modified their data protection systems to prevent the other side from gaining access."

"What about the Ixtar? Could they have broken the Aral security to this level?"

"I'd need to know more about the enemy hardware and software before committing to an answer, sir."

"The Ixtar seemed efficient enough at breaking the Aral security on Dalvaron," said Lanson.

"But not so efficient if they've had five thousand years of

technological development between now and the construction of the space station."

"Good point," said Lanson. "So if it wasn't the Ixtar and it wasn't the Aral themselves, we're looking at interference from another as-yet unknown species."

"I didn't say it wasn't the Aral, sir," said Abrams. "But I wouldn't rule anything out."

"It's a big universe, Lieutenant," said Lanson with sudden bitterness. "And, through no fault of our own, we're being exposed to parts of it which I would have preferred remained hidden - at least until the Human Confederation develops the hardware that will allow us to defend ourselves."

"We can't fail this mission, Captain."

"No," said Lanson. "It's not an option."

The conversation died off and he sank into his thoughts. Lanson found himself burdened by worries – so much remained unknown, and he was left chasing answers from a species which had almost certainly become extinct millennia ago.

Before he knew it, the six hours were over, and, when the three members of his crew returned, Lanson excused himself, along with Abrams and Perry.

A short time after, Lanson was in the mess area, eating replicated mush and drinking a bright purple concoction with a taste reminiscent of tomatoes. Sergeant Gabriel was here, along with most of his squad. It didn't escape Lanson's notice that everyone was carrying an Aral rifle.

"I thought you were planning to stick with your HC guns," said Lanson.

"That was the initial plan, sir," said Gabriel.

"And I remember you telling me that the Aral rifles weren't noticeably better than your own AR-50s."

Gabriel's expression became pained. "That was true until we discovered the explosive ammunition."

He picked his gun up from the floor and laid it on the table. The Aral rifle was mid-grey in colour and it possessed a longer barrel than a Human Confederation AR-50, and with a fractionally larger bore. The stock was moulded in such a way that it could be held comfortably, and the magazine was a six-inch cube which jutted out from the weapon's underside just in front of the pistol grip and trigger.

With deft fingers, Gabriel ejected the magazine, and then pressed a tiny switch on top, which caused a single projectile to spring out. The bullet was streamlined and, when Lanson took it out of Gabriel's palm, he discovered it was heavier than he was expecting.

"It's a larger calibre than the projectiles we fire from an AR-50, Captain," said Gabriel. "The head of the bullet is soft, so they already have huge impact. And then they explode."

"How effective will they be against an Ixtar energy shield?" asked Lanson, handing the bullet back.

"I can't give you a definitive answer until we've shot a few of those bastards, sir," said Gabriel, using his thumb to push the projectile back into the magazine. "But I reckon these guns with this ammo will be a big upgrade over both our AR-50s and our RAHDs."

"They have more stopping power than a RAHD?" asked Lanson in surprise.

"More stopping power, greater effective range, and the Aral rifles fire faster than a RAHD as well, sir," said Gabriel. He slotted the magazine back into place. "And they hold sixty bullets rather than the fifty capacity of an AR-50."

Lanson trusted Gabriel enough that he didn't bother asking if the soldier was making the right call in adopting the Aral weapons while there was enough AR-50 and RAHD ammunition for a few members of the squad to hold onto the more familiar HC guns.

"What about Private Damico's Kahn-3?" asked Lanson.

"I was coming to that, Captain," said Gabriel. "Private Damico only has a mag-and-a-half left for his repeater. Luckily, we found a replacement for that as well."

"A repeater with explosive shells?" asked Lanson, half-joking.

"Yes, sir," said Gabriel. "Private Damico's new repeater is something else."

"I'm going to have to find an excuse to order your deployment," said Lanson.

Gabriel smiled. "And then there's the question of the Ezin-Tor. Is it safe to use?"

"I've asked myself the same question, Sergeant," said Lanson, remembering how the Aral cannon had punched several huge Ixtar shuttles out of the Ravrol skies, but also how it had caused Gabriel and those nearby to shimmer, like their ties to reality had been weakened.

"If I'm forced to use the Ezin-Tor in order to save my squad, I'll do so without hesitation, Captain," said Gabriel, his gaze intense. "Whatever the consequences."

"I don't doubt it for a moment, Sergeant," said Lanson, trying to read what the other man was thinking. "Would you prefer me to give you an order, or should I leave it to your discretion?"

"I—" Gabriel looked suddenly uncertain.

"Leave the Ezin-Tor behind, Sergeant," said Lanson. "You've lived this long without it, and the rest of your weapons received an upgrade."

"Yes, sir," said Gabriel, trying to hide his relief.

He knows the power of the Ezin-Tor and he's fearful he

won't be able to resist the urge to use it at every opportunity, thought Lanson.

The matter was settled, though Lanson found himself gripped with a sense of longing to see what would happen if the Ezin-Tor was fired without restraint. Perhaps the Galos power source within the gun would imbue him with a new potency, like that which he'd absorbed from the device on Cornerstone.

"Hell no," muttered Lanson, struck by the unexpected feeling that he was being manipulated by an outside source. It was a most peculiar thought and one which made him experience a fleeting giddiness.

"Captain?" asked Gabriel.

"I'm just talking to myself, Sergeant," said Lanson.

"Private Davison does a lot of that, sir," said Corporal Hennessey, who'd joined the table mid-way through the conversation about the Aral weaponry. "That's when he's not getting himself shot."

Having taken a couple of bullets during the mission to Dalvaron and Ravrol, Private Davison had earned himself a reputation as a man with targets painted in various locations about his person. It was all in good humour, of course, and Davison's Galos-enhanced constitution ensured he'd completely healed from his injuries.

Just thinking about it made Lanson flex his leg under the table. Not even a memory of the pain lingered from the time he too was shot, and he was fully recovered from an injury that might have led to his death in other circumstances.

Lanson stayed in the mess room for a time. He finished his mush and drank another cup of the purple fluid, while listening to the soldiers talk. Although he felt most at home on the bridge of a warship, Lanson also enjoyed being part of the camaraderie of these soldiers, albeit he was only on the fringes of it owing to his rank.

Eventually, he headed for his room. Five hours remained before he was due back on duty, though Lanson's body was accustomed to irregular sleep.

Four hours and fifty minutes later, he awoke, still dressed in his flight suit. Grabbing his helmet and his AR-50, he set off for the bridge, belatedly wondering if he'd be better off with one of the Aral rifles.

Having taken his seat, Lanson listened to Commander Matlock's report. No incidents had taken place while he was away.

The remainder of the journey passed in a similar fashion. Lanson decided he would prefer to be equipped with an Aral rifle and he had Sergeant Gabriel show him how the weapon was operated. After a couple of hours' practice, Lanson was entirely comfortable with his new gun, though he hoped he wouldn't be required to use it so soon after the last mission. He was back on the *Ragnar-L* and that was where he wished to stay.

By the time the *Ragnar-L* was an hour from planet Tetron, Lanson and his crew were completely rested and as ready as they'd ever be for whatever was to come. The last minutes on the lightspeed timer counted down slowly in a way that Lanson was familiar with, and which brought a wry smile to his face.

At last, the digits on the timer changed to zeroes. A split second later, the *Ragnar-L* shuddered with the trauma of re-entry to local space. Leaning forward, with his hands on the control bars, Lanson waited for the sensors to come online.

FOUR

The sensor feeds appeared all at once, and Lanson gazed upon the usual canvas of endless nothingness. At the same time, he commanded the *Ragnar-L* into motion, utilising a quarter of its maximum propulsion output. The warship accelerated and he sensed the increased eagerness from the engines - a result of them gaining many billions of tons of additional mass from the joining with the *Ragnar-2*.

"Running the local scans," said Perry.

"I'll obtain a sensor lock on Tetron," said Turner. "We came in at a ten-million-klick distance, so it shouldn't be too hard to find."

In only a few seconds, the *Ragnar-L*'s velocity gauge was showing three hundred kilometres per second, and the propulsion didn't sound at all strained, like the engines were running at not much above idle. Lanson cut the acceleration and allowed the warship to coast.

"Local scans clear," said Perry.

"Expand the sphere diameter and keep scanning," said Lanson.

"Yes, sir."

"I've located a planet, sir," said Turner. "It's at ten million klicks and heading away from us on its orbital track. I'm working on the enhancement."

"Show me it when you're done," said Lanson.

His grip around the controls was too tight, and he recognized the stress he was feeling. Taking a slow breath, Lanson felt the tension diminish, if only a little.

"I've put the enhanced feed on your screen, Captain," said Turner. "There's more enhancement to be had, but you'll need to reduce velocity first."

"Acknowledged," said Lanson, drawing back on the controls. The velocity readout tumbled.

He turned his eyes to the feed. Tetron was a cold-looking sphere of whites and pale blues, with a diameter in excess of forty thousand kilometres. At the current level of enhancement, the details were lost except for the colours, though Lanson thought he detected atmospheric movement, as if the planet were ravaged by storms.

"I've managed to clear up the feed some more, sir," said Turner.

The planet suddenly snapped into much greater focus, such that Lanson was able to increase the zoom. His initial impression of the planet didn't change. Tetron looked as inhospitable as they came.

"If there's a surface facility, will you be able to detect it from here, Lieutenant Turner?" Lanson asked.

"The answer to that is a *maybe,* Captain," said Turner. "It depends on the size of the facility and if there are any emissions of a type which the sensor arrays are sensitive to."

"I'll bring us to a halt," said Lanson, drawing back on the controls again until the *Ragnar-L*'s velocity was at zero. The propulsion hummed quietly and soothingly in the background.

"How long will you need to be sure one way or another, Lieutenant Turner?"

"Not long, sir – a few minutes."

"You'd best get on with it."

"Yes, sir."

Lanson's earlier tension hadn't entirely vanished, but the mundanity of protocol had helped him settle. Tetron – and the Baltol facility he expected to find here - might turn out to be a place of danger, but at least he had this opportunity to scan ahead, in order to maximise his chances of controlling any engagement with possible enemy forces.

"I think I've located something," said Turner after a short time. "There's a storm over the area and the surface is covered in ice, which makes me—" She went quiet for a moment. "I'm sure of it – there's definitely metal beneath the ice. A lot of metal."

"Highlight the area," said Lanson.

"Adding the overlay."

A red circle appeared on the planet's central belt, where the whites and blues seemed even colder than elsewhere. The area enclosed within the circle was huge, with a diameter of about a hundred kilometres.

"It's a mountainous region, Captain," said Turner. "Though there are no mountains within the circle itself."

"Is that significant?" asked Lanson, peering at the feed. A range of high peaks started far to the north, widening as it snaked south. The circled area was in the middle of where the range was at its most extensive.

"I don't know, Captain. If this were naturally occurring, it would be geographically unusual, but if an advanced species like the Aral wanted to level a hundred-klick area, I doubt it would have been difficult for them."

"I'm sure," said Lanson, staring at the centre of the circle.

Without being certain, he thought he detected a grey tinge to the white. "Assuming this is an Aral facility, how deeply buried is it?"

"I can't give you an exact number, sir. Some parts appear to be deeper than others."

"I'd expect the facility to have structures of different heights, Lieutenant," said Lanson.

"Yes, sir, but—" Turner cursed. "I don't think those are buildings beneath the ice."

"What do you mean?"

"Give me another few minutes to run some additional scans, Captain. We're at the extremes of range and I don't want to give you incorrect information."

"Take the time you need," said Lanson, trying to sound like he wasn't impatient for immediate results.

Turner didn't keep him waiting. Two minutes later, she spoke once more. "I'm ninety percent sure it's a dome buried beneath the ice, Captain."

"A hundred-kilometre dome?" asked Lanson. Having seen the three-hundred-metre wonder that was the Dalvaron space station, he knew he shouldn't be surprised, and yet he couldn't help himself.

"It's not quite a hundred kilometres, sir. More like eighty in diameter. I think it's likely to be a perfect hemisphere, though again I'm only ninety percent certain."

"Why would the Aral make such a commitment to a planet like this?" asked Lanson. "Resources? Strategic value?"

"I don't think the reasons are important, sir," said Matlock. "If you're right about the Aral, they became extinct five thousand years ago, so all we have to worry about is finding out what's inside that dome."

"You know I like answers, Commander," said Lanson.

He grimaced as he continued looking at the feed. No

matter how hard he stared, he couldn't discern the shape of a dome within the red circle on his screen.

"Our next step should be to approach the planet, sir," said Matlock.

Lanson nodded. "Lieutenant Turner, at what range would you be confident you could detect the presence of enemy vessels?"

"Two million klicks, sir."

"Two million it is," Lanson confirmed. "Lieutenant Abrams, prepare us for lightspeed."

The timer appeared and soon fell to zero. Such a short transit barely registered in Lanson's brain. The sensors went offline for three seconds and then the feeds resumed.

"Running local area scans," said Perry.

"Our portside arrays are already locked on Tetron," said Turner. "I'm working on the focus."

Before Lanson could say anything, he noticed a high-priority alert which had appeared on his central screen in red letters.

> *Combination request received. Combination not available.*

"Commander Matlock, have you received a notification on your console?" asked Lanson. He read out the message on his screen. "This more or less confirms there's another Singularity class warship here."

"In that dome," said Matlock.

"As possibilities go, that one's the frontrunner."

A moment later, the feeds from the array targeted on Tetron sharpened appreciably. Now, the dome was clearly outlined, deep beneath a layer of ice which appeared dull grey, rather than the whites and blues from when it was viewed at ten million kilometres.

"Lieutenant Turner, scan for entrances which are not

buried underneath the ice," said Lanson. "The Aral might have bored through the mountains."

"Yes, sir," said Turner.

"Local area scans clear, sir," said Perry.

"Run a receptor sweep, Lieutenant," said Lanson. "Find if we can make a comms link to whatever transmitted the *combination request received* message."

"Receptor sweep running," said Perry. "Receptor found. Requesting data link. Data link request accepted!"

"Find out what you're connected to, and then dig out whatever information you can."

"I've just sent a request for the receiver's asset number, Captain," said Perry. "No response has been offered."

"Keep trying," said Lanson.

"Will do sir."

Lanson flexed his fingers. The tightness in his gut hadn't gone away. In fact, it was intensifying, such that he wondered if his instincts were giving him a warning of danger. Added to the tension was a growing excitement – a third Singularity warship might well be within his grasp, and, with no sign of enemy vessels, this could turn out to be an easy mission.

Fat chance.

For several minutes, Lanson did his best to project an outward calm, while Turner scanned the planet's surface and Perry attempted to extract some information from the linked receptor.

"I can't find any sign of an entrance anywhere in the surrounding mountains, Captain," said Turner. "However, our viewing angle prevents me from scanning certain areas. And then we have to consider that an entrance might be deliberately hidden."

Lanson cursed inwardly and realised he was allowing his impatience to get the better of him. Rarely did success come without hard work and preparation, and here he was, expecting a Singularity warship to fall into his lap.

"Add a course overlay to the tactical," said Lanson. "I'll reposition and you can continue the surface scans from the new location."

"Yes, sir," said Turner. "Overlay added."

The new position was almost a quarter of a million kilometres away and Lanson banked the *Ragnar-L* onto the route line.

"Let's see how the new propulsion works," he said, pushing the control bars to the end of their guide slots.

At first, the engines rumbled, and then the sound quickly became a howl. The velocity gauge surged upwards and Lanson felt the accelerative forces push him into his seat, before the life support system caught up and stabilised the interior.

"Fast," said Matlock.

"Hell yes," said Lanson, a smile frozen on his face.

The velocity needle surpassed five hundred kilometres per second and climbed without any apparent decrease in its rate.

"We're above the highest velocity of an Ex'Kaminar," said Lanson as the gauge reading went past seven hundred kilometres per second.

"Eight hundred kilometres per second," said Matlock soon after. "We could outrun a Gorlan missile."

As the *Ragnar-L*'s velocity surpassed nine hundred kilometres per second, the rate of increase began to slow, though Lanson didn't back off on the controls. When the needle finally breached the thousand-kilometres-per-second mark, he relented. The *Ragnar-L* had more to give, though Lanson could tell this was close to the warship's limits.

"A good result," said Abrams. "A *damn* good result."

"We're way faster than anything in the Sagh'eld fleet," said

Lanson. "I'm not sure I'm ready to test the *Ragnar-L* against something like the *Tyrantor* or the *Ghiotor*."

When the time came to decelerate, Lanson hauled back on the controls and the velocity gauge tumbled to zero.

"Commencing scans," said Turner.

"Have you managed to extract anything from the receptor, Lieutenant Perry?" asked Lanson.

"No, sir, and I don't think that's going to change."

"Run the local area scans and then try again."

"Yes, sir."

Less than two minutes went by before Turner declared that she'd been unable to locate anything resembling a tunnel through the mountains.

"Should we reposition again?" asked Lanson.

"There are a couple of smaller areas where the scan results are inconclusive, sir," said Turner. "Those areas make up less than ten percent of the total scan zone."

"We won't reposition," said Lanson. "But I'd like you to scan for enemy warships. You have ten minutes."

"Yes, sir."

Once again, Lanson endured the wait. Logic said it was the right thing to do, though it didn't stop him wanting to head straight in towards the dome.

"Assuming there are no enemy vessels in the vicinity, what's the plan for accessing the dome, sir?" asked Matlock.

"We might have to force an entrance, Commander."

"Missiles?"

"It's not the subtlest of approaches, I'll give you that. Maybe another way will present itself when we're right on top of the dome. We might spot a way in that isn't apparent from two million klicks."

Ten minutes after she'd started, Lieutenant Turner

announced that she'd been unable to detect any warships either close to the planet's surface, or within its atmosphere.

"There's too much scan volume for me to guarantee there're no enemy vessels in the two million klicks between here and Tetron, sir, and that's a risk which will take me longer to eliminate."

On balance, Lanson didn't believe there was much chance Turner had missed anything of importance. Besides, there was always a point when necessary caution became timidity. It was never possible to completely eliminate risk and he decided that the time for action was now.

"Lieutenant Abrams – ready us for lightspeed. Our target is a half-million klicks, directly above the dome."

"Yes, sir. Coordinates entered. Lightspeed warmup commencing."

As the *Ragnar-L*'s processing cores worked on the calculations for the lightspeed jump, Lieutenant Turner continued her scans for enemy warships. She found none.

Less than three minutes after the commencement of the warmup, the *Ragnar-L* entered lightspeed. If there were any nasty surprises waiting, they would likely present themselves in the very near future.

FIVE

The sensors came online, Perry completed the local area scans without detecting anything of significance, and Turner focused the underside arrays onto the target area.

From half a million kilometres, the view was a breath-taking example of bleak desolation. The mountains were clad almost entirely in snow and ice, but here and there, patches of dark grey showed. Many of the peaks were higher than anything found on Earth, and they stood defiant against the blizzards which blew from east to west and which covered at least half of the planet's visible side.

Just looking at it was enough to make Lanson shiver. The universe held many places of wonder, and, despite the beauty to be found, almost every one of those places was utterly hostile to life. Tetron was as harsh and lonely as anywhere.

Focusing his attention on the half-hidden dome, Lanson's eyes traced the edges of its circumference. The dome's apex was at a lower altitude than most of the peaks, which meant the structure was sunk many kilometres into the planet's surface.

Given the size of the dome, the excavation works would have required an extensive use of resources.

"I've scanned the dome again, sir," said Turner. "The ice is about 150 metres thick across most of its surface – that's far more uniform than I'd have expected. There's plenty of snow piled up on the dome's eastern side, which gives the appearance of a heavier ice layer, but it's all loose and likely blown in by the wind."

Looking again, Lanson could see that Turner was right. There was something unnatural about how the ice had formed over the dome, and he couldn't quite put his finger on what it was. Then, it came to him.

"It's like the source of the cold is coming from within the dome," said Lanson. A chill of fear lanced into him, and he suddenly didn't want to contemplate what the source of so much cold might be.

Matlock said it. "Galos cubes?"

"That's what I was thinking," said Lanson.

"If that dome is full of Galos, it's going to make a missile strike on the ice a bit more of a gamble," said Abrams.

"Understatement of the year, Lieutenant," said Lanson. He twisted around in his seat. "Lieutenant Turner, I want you to run another scan of the dome and the area around it. If there's a way in, we need to find it."

"Yes, sir," said Turner. "I've already spotted a twenty-klick seam running across the dome's centre, so the usual method of entry was through its upper doors."

"Keep looking anyway."

"Yes, sir."

Lanson found himself at a loss as to how he should approach the situation. Given the likely presence of Galos tech within the dome, he was reluctant to force an entry, though he might not have a choice if no alternatives materialised.

"Why is there only one visible receptor?" he wondered aloud.

"All the others could be hidden, sir," said Perry.

"In which case, why leave this single receptor open, when its backend hardware isn't responding to our requests for information?" asked Lanson. "We're a Tier 0 vessel. The Aral hardware will recognize us as a friendly."

"I don't have an answer for you, Captain."

"Unless..." Lanson continued. "Unless the receptor isn't meant to receive verbal information requests, and it's just part of a sensor array – an array which detected our presence and transmitted details of our arrival to somewhere else."

"Which then triggered the attempt to combine us with the Singularity warship which we thought was in the dome," said Matlock.

"But which might be somewhere else," said Lanson. "We found this dome and assumed our target was inside, without completing a full surface scan of the planet."

Lanson cursed himself for a fool. Perhaps he was wrong to think there was another Aral facility elsewhere on the planet, but for the sake of a rapid scan, it made sense to check out the possibility.

I'm being ruled by my impatience. I can't let it jeopardise the mission.

He reminded himself that the Ixtar had already shown themselves competent at lightspeed pursuit, so it wasn't as if his impatience was without good cause. Still, he couldn't allow any more mistakes to creep in.

"We're going to resume our scans of Tetron," said Lanson.

"At our current altitude, that's a three-point-three-million klick circuit, Captain," said Turner. "That'll take us fifty-four minutes to complete at a thousand klicks per second, but at such a high velocity, there's a chance Lieutenant Perry and I will miss something."

"What's your recommendation, Lieutenant?"

"Approach to ten thousand klicks, sir. At that altitude, we'll require more circuits, but the overall time to complete will be much lower."

"Ten thousand klicks it is," Lanson confirmed.

He aimed the *Ragnar-L* towards Tetron and requested power from the engines. Soon, the warship was racing towards the planet. Lanson found himself mesmerised by the storms whipping across the wide plains and through the mountains. It was almost like Tetron held a seething hatred for all things living, and Lanson didn't want to imagine what it would be like to stand on the planet's surface and experience the full extent of its natural fury.

"Levelling out at ten thousand klicks," said Lanson.

"If you could hold a velocity of four hundred klicks per second, that should be low enough to ensure we don't miss anything, sir," said Turner. "And each circuit will be just less than eight minutes."

"How many circuits?" asked Lanson.

"Two should be enough, but let's go for three – just to be on the safe side."

"If there's a Tier o Aral facility on Tetron, it'll be hard to miss, Lieutenant."

"I'm sure you're right, sir."

For a little more than three minutes, Lanson held the *Ragnar-L* on the same heading. Far below, the storms of Tetron raged with a ferocity which seemed to build with each passing moment, until he couldn't imagine how anything could possibly survive in such conditions. Of course, it wasn't naturally occurring life he was interested in finding. The Aral might have been inconvenienced by storms such as these, but it clearly hadn't prevented them from constructing the enormous dome.

"There's something on the horizon, Captain," said Perry. "It's directly ahead."

Lanson's eyes searched the feeds and then he saw it too. A structure of dark grey loomed high above the surface. Even from this distance, Lanson could tell that it was colossal. For the sake of caution, he resisted the urge to increase the *Ragnar-L*'s velocity.

For several seconds nobody spoke. Soon, other buildings were visible on the feeds, clustered below the main structure, and dwarfed utterly by it.

"A cube," said Turner. "A hundred-klick cube, sitting on the planet's surface."

"Is it a Galos device?" asked Lanson. It was time to reduce velocity and he did so, decelerating until the *Ragnar-L* was travelling at less than a hundred kilometres per second.

"I'm scanning for energy readings, Captain," said Abrams. He swore softly. "The cube is generating power, but only at a low level. I have no idea what we've found."

Lanson shook his head slowly, trying to make sense of the sights before him. At first, he'd thought the cube was featureless, but Turner had made some adjustments to the sensor feeds, which allowed him to see that slender lines had been scored into its surface. These lines were a mixture of straight and curves, and they formed no discernible pattern.

Otherwise, the cube was just another example of the Aral's technological capabilities, and with no purpose that was immediately apparent.

Turning his attention to the buildings at the cube's base, Lanson studied them for a time. They covered an area approximately ten kilometres by twenty and were surrounded by a twenty-metre wall. Beyond the wall, the planet's surface was uneven and thickly covered with both snow and ice.

Within the walls, the architecture was anonymous and reminiscent of that which Lanson had seen on Ravrol. Most of the structures were flat roofed squares or rectangles of various heights, and some would likely be impressive in size were they not cast in such inescapable comparison with the enormity of the cube.

Aside from the buildings, Lanson noticed that, although snow came down thickly within the perimeter wall, nowhere had it settled, and he guessed that the exterior of every structure was heated, to ensure the installation didn't become clogged and unusable.

"I guess this must be Baltol," said Matlock.

"I reckon," said Lanson. "There's no sign of a landing field from here."

"The transmission we received stated that a combination was not available, Captain," said Matlock. "Wherever the next Ragnar is located, it's unable to complete its automatic linking routine, so it's probably not sitting on a landing strip."

"Even so, let's eliminate the possibility, Commander."

Lanson had an idea where the target vessel was most likely to be located, though he didn't say it out loud since none of his crew would have missed anything so obvious.

"I'm going to take us around the cube," he said at last. "There might be a landing field on the far side."

"With a Singularity warship chained to the ground," said Abrams. "Just waiting for us to come and cut it free."

"I know it's a long shot, Lieutenant," said Lanson, putting the *Ragnar-L* once more into motion. "And if you have a better proposal, I'm all ears."

"Let's go look for that landing field, sir."

"Captain, should I scan for ground receptors?" asked Lieutenant Perry.

"Go ahead, Lieutenant."

"Scanning...no receptors found."

"That's a big facility down there," said Lanson. "Why might there be no receptors?"

"Either they're all hidden – which is unlikely, given that we're piloting an Aral warship – or the ground comms systems are offline," said Turner.

"Then how did we receive the transmission about the failed combination?" asked Lanson.

"It's possible there's a functioning hard link between Baltol and the dome, sir."

Lanson wasn't yet alarmed, but he was starting to believe there'd been some interference with the facility hardware. Of course, it could have failed naturally over the course of the centuries, but he expected the advanced systems created by the Aral would have an effectively unlimited lifespan.

So, with caution in mind, Lanson took a steady approach. He reduced the *Ragnar-L*'s altitude to 120 kilometres and maintained a velocity that would give his sensor team plenty of time to scan ahead. Everything about this situation was distinctly unusual, so rushing in would be foolish.

"Captain, I don't know how significant this is," said Perry. "The cube is on the exact opposite side of the planet to the dome."

"How exact?"

"Down to the metre, sir."

"Damn," said Lanson. "That's got to be more than coincidence."

"What the hell were the Aral doing here?" wondered Matlock. "The resources needed to construct that cube and the dome would be monumental."

"That's why this is a Tier o location, Commander," said Lanson.

He was already asking himself if this would turn into a mission that involved more than simply recovering a Singularity class warship. The Aral had built all of this for a reason, and Lanson felt a strong urge to discover exactly what that reason was.

By now, the cube was not far ahead, and it dominated the skyline. Wind-hurled snow pelted the structure without cease – nature and technology locked in a battle that so far technology was winning.

"There's no sign of a way into the cube, sir," said Turner. "At least not on the two visible faces."

"Keep searching," said Lanson.

His gaze dropped to the smaller facility buildings far below. Perhaps entry and exit to the cube was controlled from a command centre somewhere amongst those structures. Not for a moment did Lanson consider that the cube had no accessible interior. There was space inside – he was sure of it.

"I'll take us westwards around the cube," said Lanson, banking the *Ragnar-L* and reducing velocity.

Soon, the west-pointing face of the cube became visible. This was the lee side, yet the shelter was not enough to prevent the snow from swirling in ever-changing patterns. At the base of the cube, Lanson saw only rough ground, layered in ice.

"I can't find an entrance on this face either, Captain," said Turner. "I have a feeling that the door seam is hidden by the surface etchings, but I can't pinpoint any imperfections that might indicate the presence of a way in."

"If there's an opening, I'm sure you'll find it, Lieutenant," said Lanson.

He held the *Ragnar-L* on a circular course around the cube. Despite the size of the warship, it was insignificant in comparison to the Aral structure and Lanson found it hard not to feel dismay at the disparity between Human Confederation technology, and the technology of every other species he'd encountered so far.

The northern face of the cube was etched like the others, again with no obvious way to gain entry. No buildings had been constructed at its base, and the snow blew unrelenting towards the west. That snow had not formed drifts anywhere along the cube's lower edge, making Lanson believe that this structure was heated in the same way as the buildings to the south.

"One more face to go," said Matlock. "I don't think we're going to find that landing field."

"I'm sure you're right, Commander," said Lanson, guiding the warship around the north-east corner of the cube.

No surprises lay in wait. The wind blew and the snow fell. No further buildings lay at the base of the cube, and Lieutenant Turner identified no apparent way to gain entry. Lanson experienced a surge of irritation. Nothing was ever straightforward.

He piloted the *Ragnar-L* once more to the south face of the cube, and brought the vessel to a standstill at the same 120-kilometre altitude, directly over the smaller facility buildings below.

Somehow, Lanson had to figure out a way to enter the cube – ideally without having to order a ground search. Baltol was much too expansive for that to be a practical solution, though he was sure Turner and Perry would be able to identify a few likely target structures.

Pursing his lips in thought, Lanson considered the best approach. At the back of his mind was a constant whispering reminder that the Ixtar might show up at any moment.

Lanson knew he had to make progress before that happened.

SIX

"There are at least thirty structures down there which might house the facility's main comms hardware," said Lieutenant Perry.

"If all the receptors are offline, wouldn't that suggest there's an issue with the base power supply?" asked Matlock.

"There's no problem with the power, Commander," said Abrams. "I'm reading emissions from every building, and I can even pinpoint the location of the installation's four generators."

"How are you progressing with your scans of the cube, Lieutenant Turner?" asked Lanson.

"I've run a molecular-level sweep of the south face, sir, which has failed to detect an entrance seam."

"Is it possible the door was created so perfectly that even the molecular-level scan wouldn't detect its location?" asked Lanson.

"In theory it's possible, Captain," said Turner. "However, neither the *Ragnar-2* nor the *Ragnar-3* were constructed with such precision. I'm not saying the Aral didn't have the skill, but they haven't demonstrated it on their warships."

"Damnit!" said Lanson, curling the fingers of his left hand into a fist. "We don't have enough personnel to conduct a rapid search of thirty ground structures."

He weighed up the limited options. Aside from ordering a ground deployment, he could either attempt a brute-force entry into the cube, or he could return to the dome and try to crack it open with the *Ragnar-L*'s Gradar repeaters. However, Lanson didn't require years of experience to understand that the use of weapons wasn't the answer to his problems – not this time.

He was on the brink of ordering Sergeant Gabriel and his squad to one of the shuttles, when something completely unexpected happened. The sensor feeds darkened and, when Lanson looked for the cause, he saw to his shock that an object had appeared in the skies above. Such was the immense, unbelievable size of the object, that it blotted out the stars in every direction.

"What the hell?" said Lanson.

His first instinct was to run, though he instinctively knew it was no use. He thrust the control bars as far as they'd go, expecting to hear the thunder of the warship's propulsion. Instead, the engines died and went quiet, as if they'd been turned off with a switch. The bridge lights almost went out, and the screens on Lanson's console flickered rapidly.

"Our power generation has dropped to zero percent, Captain," said Abrams.

"Can you get the engines back?" asked Lanson.

"I'm checking it out, sir. Gut feel says no. We're switching to backup power."

Lanson didn't know what kind of technology allowed the backups to keep running when the main propulsion had failed, but he was glad it was unaffected by the shut-down attack. The bridge lights strengthened and the images on his console screens stabilised.

Unfortunately, the backup power wasn't intended to provide thrust, and the *Ragnar-L*'s controls were still unresponsive.

"Commander Matlock, whatever the hell that thing is up there, target it with our weapons."

"Our missiles won't lock, sir," said Matlock. "Shit, neither will the Gradar turrets."

"What if you switch the repeaters to manual targeting?" asked Lanson in desperation.

"We don't have the firepower to defeat an opponent of that size, Captain."

Lanson knew it too and the feeling of powerlessness was as painful as a kick in the balls. To have his warship neutralised like this, without warning and without a chance to fight back, was almost more than he could bear.

"We need our engines, Lieutenant Abrams," Lanson growled.

"I don't know what has caused the failure, Captain," said Abrams. "The monitoring tools are all giving the same warning and it's one I don't understand."

"What does the warning say?"

"Ravanok nullification detected, sir."

"What the hell does that mean?" asked Lanson angrily.

"You'll know as soon as I know, Captain," said Abrams.

Lanson scraped his teeth together at the lack of answers. With the greatest of efforts, he shut his mouth and let his crew get on with their work. Meanwhile, he called up a dozen status readouts, and tried to understand what was happening to the *Ragnar-L*.

"We aren't falling," said Lieutenant Perry. "We have no thrust, but we're staying at the same altitude."

With each new piece of information, Lanson became progressively more lost as to what was happening. His mind spun as it tried to come up with a solution, even though he had no idea what was causing the problem.

"Captain, there's been an energy spike from the cube," said Lieutenant Massey. "Crap...what the—"

"Tell me, damnit!" snapped Lanson.

"The cube must have been dormant, Captain, and the arrival of that object must have brought it out of sleep," said Massey, talking so fast he was almost babbling. "Now it's generating so much energy that the numbers hardly make sense."

Something calamitous was about to happen, and the helpless *Ragnar-L* was trapped in the middle of it. Lanson's hands darted across his control panel as he frantically hunted for a way to bring the warship's engines back online. Nothing responded to his inputs, and his frustration grew until it threatened to overwhelm his conscious thought.

Out of nowhere came a booming reverberation, originating deep within the *Ragnar-L*. It was a sound Lanson recognized immediately.

"Our negation shield activated," he said.

Lanson was sure the attack originated from the object in the skies above, rather than the cube, and it was proof – had it been needed – that the immense alien vessel was hostile.

"We've only got two activations remaining on the shield, sir," said Matlock.

A second booming, almost before the first had died away, made the *Ragnar-L* shudder with the force of barely repelled energy. Lanson's eyes jumped of their own accord to the warship's weapons panel, just in time to see the Galos reserve number drop to one.

"We can only soak one more attack," he said.

Usually when things came down to the wire, Lanson would have a chance – however slim - at pulling off an escape if he played his cards right. Here, his hand was empty and he couldn't begin to think of a way to extricate himself from what looking increasingly like a preordained loss.

"The output readings from the cube are totally crazy," said Massey. "I think something's about to—"

Before he could finish the sentence, a hemisphere of hazy darkness, centred on the cube and with a radius of two hundred kilometres, sprang into being. The *Ragnar-L* was within the bounds of the hemisphere and straightaway, the warship's propulsion fired up again, producing a vibration that made Lanson's vision blur for a moment. Grabbing the control bars, he watched for developments.

A message appeared at the top of Lanson's centre screen. He read it once, though he couldn't spare any time to consider its origins. The meaning was clear enough.

> *Ravanok nullification cancelled.*

"Captain, there's an opening in the cube!" yelled Turner. "Almost dead ahead!"

Hoping for salvation, Lanson checked the feed. The cube's surface had parted in the centre, and two rectangular doors slid rapidly out of sight. How those doors had remained undetected by a molecular level scan, Lanson didn't know, but he wasn't about to start pondering this engineering masterpiece. Instead, he rotated the *Ragnar-L* as rapidly as he could and aimed it for the ten-thousand-metre entrance.

What lay beyond the opening, Lanson didn't know, since the feeds showed only an impenetrable darkness. He didn't hesitate and held the warship on course. With its engines rumbling, the *Ragnar-L* sped through the black curtain and into the cube. The moment the sensors began gathering a feed, Lanson pulled back on the controls, to slow the vessel before its rapid entrance resulted in an unwanted collision with whatever else was inside.

The feeds showed that the *Ragnar-L* was inside a square

tunnel with featureless black walls. Fifteen kilometres ahead, the tunnel opened into a larger space and Lanson peered at his screens to see what lay within. The sensors had no trouble with the darkness, but they identified no features other than the far wall of the cube's internal bay.

Without warning, the controls stopped responding to Lanson's input and the *Ragnar-L* accelerated steadily. A new message appeared on his screen.

>*Ragnar-4, linking routine initiated.*

The *Ragnar-L* exited the tunnel, allowing the sensors to gather information about the internal bay. To Lanson's shock, the bay cut deep into the surface of Tetron. A shaft, sixty kilometres across went down and down, opening into yet another space approximately a thousand kilometres below. The walls of the shaft weren't stone – instead, they'd been lined with what he suspected was the same material which had been used in the construction of the cube.

"There's a vessel heading our way from below," said Lieutenant Turner.

"I see it," said Lanson. "The *Ragnar-4*." He couldn't spare the incoming warship his full attention, since other matters were pressing. "Lieutenant Turner, are there any open receptors now that we're inside the cube?" he asked.

"The hardware won't let me run a sweep, Captain," said Turner. "When the *Ragnar-3* combined with the *Ragnar-2* on Ravrol, both the comms and the sensors shut down. I think the same thing is about to happen here."

Turner's words were prophetic. The sensor feeds went offline, leaving Lanson to stare at blank screens. In his head, he pictured the *Ragnar-4* as he'd seen it approaching up the shaft. The vessel didn't resemble a warship in any way – rather it was a bulky shape, flat on one end and with a kind of elongated curve on the other. Lanson could think of only one place the *Ragnar-4* could link to the *Ragnar-L,* and that was on its stern.

"How long did the sensors remain offline last time?" asked Lanson.

"As soon as we exited lightspeed in Ravrol's solar system, the sensors and comms were unavailable. It was a total of about eight minutes," said Turner. "Lieutenant Perry and I believed it was in preparation for the hardware of the two vessels to tie in."

It seemed as logical a suggestion as any, though Lanson wasn't pleased that he might have to wait as long as eight minutes – not with that alien object which had appeared above the planet.

"What've we got ourselves into?" asked Lanson.

"I've been analysing some of the readings I took before our sensors went offline, Captain," said Abrams. "The energy signature from the cube was almost identical to that produced by a Galos device."

"The cube created a shield of some kind that protected us from attack," said Lanson. "What the hell was that out there? Was it a spaceship, or something else?"

"I've just finished analysing the feeds we gathered when we were outside," said Perry. She drew in a breath, making it clear her next words weren't going to be anything resembling good news. "It's a sphere, Captain. A sphere with an eight-thousand-klick diameter."

"You're shitting me?" said Lanson. He tipped his head back and closed his eyes. "That must be what the nullification warnings called the Ravanok."

"Why was it interested in us?" asked Massey. "And how did it find us?"

Several pieces fell into place in Lanson's head and, though he didn't know if he'd guessed right, he had a strong feeling he was on the right track.

"We've always asked ourselves why the Aral developed the Galos tech," he said. "Why they would need anything so destructive."

"They were fighting against the Ravanok," said Matlock.

"It has to be," said Lanson.

"And now it's found us," said Abrams.

Lanson nodded. "And now it's found us."

For the first time since he landed on Cornerstone, so long ago, he experienced a hint of regret that he'd pushed and kept on pushing for answers. Perhaps, Lanson reflected, some things were best left in the shadows.

SEVEN

The sensors had been offline for less than two minutes when Lanson felt a collision. It wasn't a high-velocity impact, though he sensed the colossal weight of it happening. Then, he heard distant clunking and thudding sounds. Something groaned like it was under enormous stress, and then all Lanson could hear was the idling propulsion.

"The combination must be finished," he said, glancing at the sensor feeds. They remained blank. "We need our control back."

"And what happens then?" asked Matlock. "Even if this cube is filled with Galos energy, I can't see it being enough to hold off the attacks of an eight-thousand-klick warship for long."

Lanson could only nod his agreement. "We might have enough time to complete a lightspeed warmup," he said. "Once we're away from Baltol, we should have some breathing room."

"I'll pick a destination, Captain," said Lieutenant Abrams. "Somewhere chosen at random, and with a transit time of twenty-four hours."

"Please," said Lanson. "Don't commence the warmup until I give the order."

"Yes, sir."

The seconds ticked by and Lanson breathed deeply to keep himself calm. Another message appeared on his centre screen.

> *Baltol defence energy at thirty percent. Galos ejection initiated: Infinitar.*

No sooner had Lanson finished reading the words than the sensor feeds came back online. At once, he spotted the changed shape of his spaceship – he'd been correct to think that the *Ragnar-4* would link to the *Ragnar-L*'s existing stern, though the sensors didn't give him a perfect external view.

Aside from the new addition to his warship, Lanson also noticed that the sensor arrays were struggling to pierce the darkness within the cube. He could just about make out the far walls, when he'd have expected the view to be clear. For a moment, Lanson stared, and he couldn't help but think that the cube was being steadily overcome by an energy that was different to anything he'd encountered before – an energy that even the Galos couldn't resist.

Testing the controls, Lanson discovered he was still frozen out. "The combination has finished," he said. "Why can't I pilot the damn ship?"

"All the onboard systems came back immediately on Ravrol, Captain," said Matlock. "I don't know why it's different this time."

"I have full access to the sensors and comms," said Turner. "So partial control has been returned."

Partial control wasn't going to be enough. Lanson's eyes went back to the message on his screen. "Galos ejection initiated," he said.

As if his words were a trigger, the *Ragnar-L* began accelerating vertically down the shaft. Faster and faster it went, until it seemed as though it would crash into the floor of the open space at the bottom. Lanson told himself there'd be no impact, though part of his mind believed otherwise.

The *Ragnar-L* raced into the bay, which turned out to be a vast space. Hundreds of warships were parked here in rows and columns. Such was the velocity of the *Ragnar-L* that Lanson could hardly take in the details.

"We're going to hit the floor," said Matlock tightly.

Even though Lanson had faith in the life support systems, he braced himself. However, the impact didn't come. Two doors in the bay floor, unseen until now, slid open with tremendous speed, revealing a continuation of the shaft, though here it was circular rather than square.

As the *Ragnar-L* sped through the opening, Lanson noticed that a dark, seething, miasma clung to the walls of the shaft, reminiscent of that which he'd seen in the higher of the two bays.

He didn't have long to stare. In the blinking of an eye, the *Ragnar-L*'s velocity gauge went all the way to the right. Then, the numbers started recalculating so rapidly that Lanson's eyes and brain couldn't keep up. He remembered how Perry had discovered that the Baltol cube and the ice-clad dome were on exact opposite sides of Tetron.

We're heading right through the middle of the planet.

Lanson didn't know if the Baltol flight control computer intended to hurl the *Ragnar-L* out through the dome, but he'd seen the thickness of the ice and he wasn't at all sure the doors would open.

Outside, the walls of the shaft had become blurred, as though they occupied a different reality to the *Ragnar-L*. When Lanson glanced at the velocity gauge, the reading was unbelievable, and yet, he knew it was accurate.

I know what's going to happen.

Even as the thought formed, the sensor feeds went offline. The warship convulsed, and the propulsion howled louder than anything Lanson had heard before. He felt a thumping in his back and then came a feeling of dislocation, as though his consciousness and physical form had been torn apart and then forced back together.

The howling of the propulsion suddenly lessened, and the digits on the velocity gauge began to recalculate downwards, though the sensors remained offline. Lanson was sure the *Ragnar-L* was undergoing savage deceleration, yet he felt none of it. He was tempted to find out if the control bars were responding, but he kept his hands away – just in case.

"What just happened?" asked Lieutenant Perry.

"The Baltol facility sent us somewhere far from Tetron," said Lanson.

A moment later, the sensors came online, and he wasn't surprised to find that the *Ragnar-L* was inside a circular shaft, with walls cloaked in dark energy. Visually, it was identical to the shaft on Baltol, though Lanson remained convinced he and his crew had been transported elsewhere.

"I wonder what we're going to find here," he said, watching the forward feeds. "Wherever *here* is."

"It looks like there's another bay ahead of us," said Turner.

The warship was approaching the bay at much too great a velocity and Lanson wrapped his fingers around the control bars, even though he knew they wouldn't accept his input. Still the engines roared, and the velocity gauge reading dropped like a stone. Guided with the precision of a computer, the *Ragnar-L* entered the bay and then came to a standstill. An experimental movement on the controls told Lanson he was back in charge. Already, he could see that something was wrong.

"Scan the bay," he said. "It looks like we weren't the first ones here."

The bay itself was a cavernous space, forty kilometres by forty and with a height of ten thousand metres. At some point in time, a massive hole had been blown in the twin overhead doors, and the metal around the opening was ragged and sharp. It was dark outside, though Lanson could see the pinpoints of stars.

Otherwise, the bay was empty.

> *Infinitar: Welcome to Avristol.*

Lanson read the words on his screen and then glanced towards Matlock. "We finished a forty-two-day journey in a handful of seconds," he said.

"And it seems like our warship is onto its third name, Captain. The headings on my control screens updated. Now, we are in command of the *Infinitar.*"

To Lanson, the name sounded complete, like it was intended for the finished product when all the Singularity class spaceships were combined. He gave a mental shrug. Perhaps the combination of only three was sufficient for the warship to gain its final name.

"I like it," Lanson said. "It sounds as if it has meaning."

He resolved to check out the name in the warship's databanks if he ever got the chance. It wasn't important, but he liked to know.

For the moment, Lanson had more to worry about than the origins of a warship's name. He and his crew had been taken to a place a long way from any of the other Tier 0 locations. In addition, Avristol – on planet Gotarus - was one of the places he expected to find another of the Singularity warships. So far, he'd seen no indication that the automatic linking routines had activated.

"Scan for receptors," snapped Lanson, his mood already becoming foul.

"Receptor scan running...and complete," said Perry. "No receptors found."

"Damnit!" said Lanson, again wondering why a Tier 0 warship like the *Infinitar* was unable to initiate communications with a Tier 0 facility. Maybe the Baltol and Avristol control systems hadn't been created with any kind of autonomy. It was the only explanation Lanson could think of.

It was time to take stock.

"Our warship has three parts out of six," he said. "I want to know if and how the *Infinitar* is more capable than the *Ragnar-L*. In addition, I would like to hear theories as to what has taken place in this bay."

"The *Ragnar-4* was nearly all propulsion, Captain," said Lieutenant Abrams. "Our output readings have climbed significantly."

"I was hoping for more than just engines, Lieutenant."

"I haven't had longer than a couple of minutes to look into this, sir," said Abrams. "I think there's more to learn."

"Let me know what you find."

"Yes, sir."

"Captain, the scans of the overhead bay doors indicate they were subjected to an extended missile attack – you can tell by the distortion on the alloys," said Turner. "There's only minor damage inside the bay itself, which suggests the attack was stopped as soon as the doors were sufficiently breached."

"How wide is the opening?" asked Lanson.

"A little over three thousand metres, sir."

Lanson drummed his fingers. "So whoever wanted access to the bay, they were expecting to find something valuable inside. Something valuable, like a Singularity class warship."

"And now it's gone," said Matlock.

"Gone or destroyed, Commander. Let's hope it's the former."

"The Ixtar and the Sagh'eld are playing the same game as we are, sir."

"I reckon the Ixtar would have disintegrated the bay doors," said Lanson. "Which makes me believe it was the Sagh'eld who got here before us."

"Those bastards seem to have plenty of intel on Aral planets," said Massey.

Lanson nodded. "I wonder if they stumbled across a data array somewhere – an array containing the locations of Aral facilities."

"This is the third Aral planet the Sagh'eld have visited – that we know about," said Matlock. "And we saw on Ravrol the kind of progress they've made into researching Galos tech."

"Aren't we forgetting about the Ravanok?" asked Turner. "What role does that sphere play in all of this?"

"I wish I knew," said Lanson. "Having seen the Ravanok, it's clear that neither the Human Confederation, the Sagh'eld, nor the Ixtar are anything more than insects in comparison." He shook his head at the memory. "What secrets the universe holds."

Lanson was distracted from his thoughts by an excited shout from Lieutenant Abrams.

"Captain, I've found out the *Ragnar-4*'s main function!"

"Tell me," said Lanson.

"Galos tech, sir. The *Ragnar-4* is made up from hundreds of Galos modules – and some of them are huge."

"What is their purpose?" asked Lanson.

"Propulsion, sir. Our sub-light output has increased and so has our lightspeed multiplier. I haven't had a chance to fully analyse the data, so I can't give you figures yet." Abrams cleared his throat. "There's more - the Galos tech is going to let us execute an instant lightspeed transition."

Lanson cast his mind back to the warship *New Beginning*,

which had also been capable of an ILT when it was charged with Galos energy. However, each activation of the instant transit had produced critical instabilities on the vessel's propulsion, threatening the lives of everyone on board.

"Is it going to be safe this time, Lieutenant?" Lanson asked.

"I can't offer you a guarantee, sir, but I'm confident the Aral knew how to make this work."

"I have the same confidence," Lanson admitted. He looked at his control panel. "How do I activate an ILT?"

"I'll have to bind the command to one of the buttons on your control bar, Captain. It'll take me a few minutes. When I'm done, you should be able to choose a destination on the tactical and execute the ILT by pressing the button."

"Any limitations on the tech?"

"I don't know, sir." Abrams cleared his throat. "There's more."

"What else?" asked Lanson.

"The Ravanok was able to shut down our normal propulsion modules, but it didn't accomplish the same feat with the Baltol cube. Now the Infinitar is carrying Galos tech, we shouldn't be vulnerable to the shutdown kill switch."

"I'm sure you're right, Lieutenant," said Lanson. "However, I don't think we're equipped to handle the Ravanok, with or without Galos engines."

"It's better than having nothing, sir."

"That it is," said Lanson. He shifted his attention to the efforts of his sensor officers. "Lieutenant Turner, have your scans turned up anything else?"

"Yes and no, sir. There's faint residual heat in the bay door alloys around the opening. From that, I've estimated that the breach was created three or four days ago."

"The Sagh'eld will be long gone," said Lanson.

"Maybe, sir. Remember, the enemy would have to break

into the Singularity warship, and experience suggests the Sagh'eld hardware isn't great at the task. It might have taken them many hours before they were ready to pilot it out of here."

"Or they could have hauled the vessel straight into the hold of a superheavy lifter," said Lanson.

"Maybe," said Turner. "The lifter's crew would have a tough job bringing a large warship through that hole in the bay doors. If the Sagh'eld had a lifter with them, I'm sure they'd have made the opening bigger."

Lanson wasn't convinced. He reckoned a competent lifter crew would be able to haul a *Ragnar*-sized vessel out of the bay. At the moment, it didn't matter one way or another. The Singularity class vessel from Avristol had been stolen and he had to think of a way to get it back.

EIGHT

"It would be damned useful if the Infinity Lens had visibility on this planet," muttered Lanson.

He cursed under his breath. Despite the incredible potential of the Infinity Lens, it was only partly activated. Five sectors out of six were not yet monitored, and that meant Lanson and his crew were blind to the movements of any spaceships which might have visited this planet in the recent past. In fact, it was possible that enemy vessels remained at Avristol, though he doubted it was so.

The seed of an idea crept into Lanson's mind, and he tapped his fingers on the edge of his console while he considered it.

"Whenever we're close enough to another Singularity warship, the linking routine triggers automatically," he said.

"Yes, sir," said Abrams.

"Which means the two vessels communicate across a certain range."

"You're wondering if we can increase that range," said Abrams.

"I am," said Lanson. "We know the range at which the routine is triggered can vary – on Ravrol it happened at millions of kilometres, whereas on Baltol the activation occurred at only thousands of kilometres."

Abrams made a *hmm* sound. "I looked at the code during our transit to Baltol and the routine can't be deleted – at least not without some major changes to the control system."

"The activation range might be a modifiable variable," said Lanson.

"It might," Abrams conceded. "I didn't spend a lot of time checking the code – once I saw how deeply it was intertwined with the control systems, I left it well alone."

"Take another look," said Lanson.

"Yes, sir."

Lanson's gaze fell on the topside feeds, which were locked on the opening in the bay doors. He wondered what lay beyond and asked himself if he even needed to find out. Dangers could be waiting, and Lanson didn't want to fight if he didn't need to. The *Infinitar*'s defensive ammunition was still lacking.

"Captain, the range variable can be changed," said Abrams. "I haven't tested it, but I think I can set it to be effectively unlimited."

"Enter a high value, Lieutenant."

"Yes, sir." It only took a moment. "That's done."

"If the target vessel is at lightspeed, I wouldn't expect the linking routine to activate," said Turner. "Also, we'll have to consider the possibility of a long travel time for the comm transmission to reach us."

A message appeared on Lanson's centre screen.

> *Combination not available.*

"I guess that means the other vessel is at lightspeed," said Lanson.

Five seconds later, the message appeared again.

> *Combination not available.*

Lanson suspected the messages would become a distraction, so he resized the window in which they were appearing and dragged it to the farthest edge of his right-hand screen. Now, he could see any changes, but only when he chose to look for them.

"We don't have any idea how far the Sagh'eld have to travel," said Matlock. "What if they head to one of their home worlds and it's a two-month journey?"

"We can't do much about that, Commander," said Lanson.

Nevertheless, just the thought of waiting potentially weeks was enough to make him agitated. He had another idea, which he pondered for a short while. Then, Lanson entered the *Infinitar*'s navigation system, where he adjusted the display filters so that they would show every Aral facility, rather than only those at Tier 0.

"There's a Tier 2 Aral facility called Edron approximately two day's travel time from here," said Lanson. "What if the Sagh'eld took our target there first? Maybe to rendezvous with a lifter."

"It's possible the enemy went to Edron like you say, Captain," said Matlock. "However, if Lieutenant Turner is right and the attack here on Avristol took place three or four days ago, the Sagh'eld could have arrived at the facility, loaded our spaceship into a lifter and be long gone."

"Don't be so sure, Commander," said Abrams. "Our navigational system calculates the travel time based on our lightspeed multiplier. It doesn't know the multiplier of a Sagh'eld warship."

"And our own multiplier increased with the addition of both the *Ragnar-2* and the *Ragnar-4*," said Massey. "The *Ragnar-3* was already more capable than a Sagh'eld Ex'Kaminar."

"It's certain that a transit which takes the *Infinitar* two days to complete will take the Sagh'eld significantly longer," said Abrams.

"How much longer?" asked Lanson. "Give me some numbers."

"I estimate it might take the Sagh'eld six days or more to complete a journey the *Infinitar* finishes in two, Captain," said Abrams. "And while I didn't quite pull that answer from my ass, I'm not about to vouch for its accuracy."

"I won't hold you to anything, Lieutenant," said Lanson. He smiled thinly. "If we head straight to Edron, we might just beat the Sagh'eld to the arrival. Assuming I'm right to think that's where the enemy are going."

"It's a long shot," said Matlock. She shrugged. "But there's nothing here for us. We either set a course for Edron, or we accept the loss of a Singularity class and we pick a different destination."

"Edron is sounding better by the second," said Perry.

"That it is," Lanson agreed.

He looked at the jagged opening in the bay doors above and again considered piloting the *Infinitar* outside, to find out what the Aral had built at the Avristol facility. It was a risk he didn't need to take.

"Lieutenant Abrams, we're going to Edron," said Lanson. "Target a million klicks from the planet's surface."

"Yes, sir. The coordinates have been entered. Two minutes and we'll be on our way."

Two minutes was an impressively low warmup time for lightspeed entry and Lanson was eager to find out if the number would drop farther once the *Infinitar* was linked to the other Singularity class vessels. First, of course, he had to locate those vessels and Lanson hoped that Edron wouldn't turn out to be a wild goose chase.

The digits on the timer hit zero and the *Infinitar* launched itself into lightspeed, bypassing the walls of the Avristol bay in the process. Lanson spent the next few seconds watching the status monitors for indications of hardware failure. He wasn't expecting problems and, sure enough, the readings were all where they needed to be.

For the next few hours, the crew remained at their stations. Lanson sat quietly for much of the time. He couldn't get the Ravanok out of his head. The sphere was so far beyond anything he'd ever encountered that he wondered if he'd fully grasped the enormity of having the huge vessel in pursuit. A spaceship that size would surely have capabilities far beyond anything possessed by either the Ixtar or the Aral, and Lanson wished he knew what motives drove the species which controlled the Ravanok.

Perhaps the sphere's arrival at Baltol happened purely by chance.

Lanson couldn't bring himself to believe it even for a moment. The Aral had known about the Ravanok and perhaps the latter was responsible for their extinction. An opponent like the Ravanok could have forced the Aral to ever more desperate measures to protect themselves, and it was looking steadily more certain that the Galos was the result.

After a time, Lanson told himself to stop thinking about the Ravanok and the Aral. It was becoming too frustrating to hunt for answers that weren't to be found in his head.

Suddenly remembering his curiosity about the *Infinitar*'s name, Lanson accessed the warship's data arrays. He ran a search on the word *Infinitar* to see what would come up. A single result was generated.

When he called up the file, Lanson discovered it was a book, contained within a library of other works on the data array. He knew he shouldn't be surprised, since Human

Confederation warship crews also had access to a wide variety of reading materials to keep them occupied during the long lightspeed transits, and yet he hadn't once imagined that the Aral might have a similar need for entertainment.

Lanson didn't beat himself up over this minor lack of consideration for a species he'd never met. Instead, he flicked rapidly through the pages of what appeared to be an ancient Aral myth. In the story, the Ragnar were a people who had sought immortality. In order to achieve life everlasting, they had channelled their life energies into an artifact they called *Anforos*. From these life energies, the god *Infinitar* was born.

What happened to *Infinitar*, the book didn't say, nor did it mention if the god was benevolent, vengeful, or somewhere in between.

Lanson closed out of the file and let the story sink in. While the history of humanity was filled with tales of a similar nature, this Aral myth was nevertheless powerful, even though he suspected much of the nuance was lost in the translation.

"What've you found, Captain?" asked Matlock.

"A story from the past, Commander," said Lanson.

He rose from his seat and told the rest of his crew what he'd learned. Knowing the origins of the warship's name left Lanson with a peculiar feeling. He couldn't decide if it was hubris that would lead an entire people to sacrifice themselves in the search for immortality, or if their lives were so terrible that they believed this was the only way to improve their lot.

Lanson gave a mental shake of his head. It was, after all, just a story, and he knew he shouldn't overthink it.

Tiredness threatened and Lanson headed for his quarters, having also given Turner and Massey a five-hour break from duty.

Settling on his bed, he stared at the ceiling for a time. Eventually, the soothing thrum of the engines sent him to sleep, where he dreamed of gods and sacrifice. When his alarm went off, Lanson rose, exited his quarters, and went directly to the mess area. Once there, he ate and drank quickly. For once, the soldiers were nowhere in evidence.

When he was done, Lanson returned to the bridge, where Matlock, Perry and Abrams were clearly ready for some shut-eye. Turner and Massey were back at their stations.

"Nothing to report, sir," said Matlock.

"Go," said Lanson. "Get yourselves some rest."

When the three members of his crew were gone from the bridge, Lanson settled himself in for a period of restless tedium. He hadn't slept enough, but there'd be time to catch up before the *Infinitar* exited lightspeed at Edron.

The remainder of the journey dragged, like the seconds were mired in quicksand. Lanson was an old hand at coping, and he wasn't affected by it much.

At last, with all members of the crew fully rested and at their consoles, Lieutenant Abrams called out his ten-minute warning.

Soon, the *Infinitar* would exit lightspeed a million kilometres from a planet called Tarai, where the Aral had constructed the Edron facility. There, Lanson hoped to find Sagh'eld warships.

If the enemy had a presence at Tarai, perhaps they would indeed bring the stolen Singularity class to the planet. Otherwise, the *Infinitar* would never be completed, and Lanson had a deeply held belief that the Aral warship was the key to something big, even though he didn't yet know what that might be.

Edron beckoned.

NINE

The *Infinitar* re-entered local space and Lanson immediately pushed the control bars to halfway. A surge of acceleration followed, and the Galos howl mixed with the resonant thunder of the warship's Rodos drive brought a smile to his face.

"Sensors coming up," said Turner.

The feeds showed nothing of interest, and Lanson's eyes skated across them to the windowed status report on his screen.

>*Combination not available.*

"Our target isn't here," he said. "That could be either a good or a bad thing."

"Commencing local area scans," said Perry.

"I have a lock on Tarai, sir," said Turner. "First impressions – it's another shithole."

"The universe is full of them, Lieutenant," said Lanson. "I long ago stopped being disappointed."

He gave his attention to the feeds. Tarai was made up of blues, browns, reds and whites, though it wasn't clear whether these were the colours of the surface, or caused by atmospheric conditions. With a diameter of fifty thousand kilometres, the planet was mid-sized and with little else to make it stand out from countless others.

"Local area scans complete and clear, sir."

"Keep scanning, Lieutenant Perry."

"Yes, sir."

"Reduce velocity, Captain," said Turner. "It'll help with the feed enhancement."

"Reducing velocity," Lanson confirmed.

He raised an eyebrow when he saw that the warship was travelling in excess of six hundred kilometres per second, with no apparent effort. Lanson promised himself – not for the first time – that he'd run some tests to find the *Infinitar's* limits, when the opportunity arose.

The feed enhancement didn't take long to finish and when it was done, the view of the planet was greatly improved. Lanson stared hard. According to the coordinates within the navigational system, the Edron facility was on this side of the planet, slightly north of the central belt. A few patches of blotchy grey caught his eye, but they were too indistinct for him to decide if any of them were the Aral installation.

"The atmospheric conditions are worse than bad, Captain," said Turner. "I've counted more than a dozen toxic substances, plus there's a strong wind and plenty of airborne particles."

"Do we need to reduce our range, Lieutenant?"

"No, Captain, I'm just letting you know the difficulties. If the Edron facility is here, I'll find it." A short time later, Turner announced her success. "I have sensor sight. Enhancing."

An area north of the planet's central belt sharpened and Lanson zoomed the feed. The Edron base was neatly contained within a wall, and the buildings were unmistakeably Aral in origin. In total, the base covered almost four hundred square kilometres, including a landing field which occupied a quarter of the area, and which was also enclosed by the walls.

"Doesn't look like much," said Lanson.

"The Aral built hundreds of places like this, Captain," said Matlock. "And thousands at Tier 3 and below."

"If there are enemy warships near the base, I assume you'll be able to detect them from here, Lieutenant Turner," said Lanson.

"Yes, sir. If there's anything of significant size within a thousand klicks of Edron, I'll find it."

"What about objects of insignificant size?"

"Do you mean shuttles, Captain?"

"Shuttles and anything else that'll tell us the Sagh'eld are on Tarai."

"No guarantees I'll spot ground troops or parked transports, sir."

"You have five minutes. After that, I'll consider an approach to half a million klicks."

"Yes, sir."

Turner didn't need five minutes. "I've located an object, Captain. It's twenty klicks above Edron. Size and mass estimates suggest a high likelihood it's a Sagh'eld Tagha'an heavy cruiser."

The news made Lanson's heart thud in his chest. It was the confirmation he needed that the journey to Tarai might not have been a waste of time. "Is it alone?" he asked.

"I'm unable to confirm at the moment, sir. I'll continue scanning."

"Lieutenant Perry, please assist."

"Yes, sir."

"Keep your fingers crossed that we arrived early, Commander Matlock," said Lanson. "And let's hope that Tagha'an is alone."

"Are you planning to attack, Captain?" asked Matlock. "I'm sure we can destroy that heavy easily enough with the element of surprise, but what if the enemy warships we hope are inbound arrive, detect the wreckage and then re-enter light-speed before we can stop them?"

"They won't," said Lanson firmly. He pointed at the window on his screen, which was filled with lines of the same text – *combination not available*. "If the target vessel arrives in this solar system, we'll know about it straightaway. The linking routine should activate and the Singularity vessel will head directly for us. We can't plan for what happens after that."

"Yes, sir," said Matlock. She screwed up her face, as if an unpleasant thought had just occurred. "The new vessel might be filled with Sagh'eld, Captain. We'll have to isolate them from the *Infinitar*."

"Lieutenant Perry, did you hear what Commander Matlock said?"

"Yes, sir."

"As soon as the combination is finished, I want you to lock down every door between the *Infinitar* and the linked vessel."

"Yes, sir."

With the scant preparations completed, Lanson waited to find out if his sensor operators would detect any additional warships in the vicinity of Edron.

"There're no other warships visible, Captain," said Turner after a few minutes. "We've expanded the scan area, and there's nothing within twelve hundred klicks of the base."

"High altitude scans are clear as well, sir," added Perry.

This was about as clear an invitation to attack as Lanson could imagine. "We'll destroy the Tagha'an," he said. "Once it's out of the picture, we'll have an easier time dealing with the inbound warships."

Nobody mentioned that those inbound warships might have already visited Tarai and could now be outbound. Lanson didn't let himself dwell on the possibility either.

"Lieutenant Abrams, ready us for lightspeed," he said. "Our exit point is to be just across the planet's curve from the Tagha'an. We're going to approach at high velocity and blow those bastards into pieces."

"Yes, sir, coordinates entered. Two minutes counting down."

Lanson had plenty of combat experience, though not so much with the *Infinitar*. He was feeling the nerves and he couldn't deny it. Despite the undoubted superiority of the *Infinitar*, the Sagh'eld warships retained an aura of invulnerability. A glance at the weapons panel offered Lanson some reassurance. The Aral vessel was packing the armaments, and he well remembered the destructive power of its Avantar missiles.

"Ten seconds!" yelled Abrams.

With his fingers wrapped comfortably around the control bars, Lanson readied himself for the transit. The *Infinitar*'s engines generated overlapping bass expulsions as the warship entered and exited lightspeed within the tiniest fraction of a second.

"Sensors coming up!" said Turner.

Lanson held the *Infinitar* motionless, his jaw muscles tight as he waited for the feeds to become available. A view of the outside world appeared on his screen a moment later, and the sights were as harsh and bleak as he'd expected. Ten kilometres below, the planet's surface was rugged and scarred, the rocks a variety of dull colours. The density of particles in the atmosphere added a greyness to everything, and the storm winds created rivers of dust which rushed snakelike through fissures and canyons.

"I've added a course overlay to your tactical, Captain," said Turner. "The Tagha'an is fifteen hundred kilometres from our current position."

"Acknowledged," said Lanson.

He rotated the *Infinitar* until its nose was aimed along the heading line on his tactical. Steadily, he shifted the control bars and the warship accelerated. With his nostrils flared, Lanson watched the feeds. He felt nothing of the ferocious winds outside. Even the worst extremes of weather were no threat to the mass of a warship, yet nature never gave up.

As the *Infinitar* gathered velocity, the ground sped by underneath, becoming a blur that merged the colours into a hue somewhere between a brown and a grey. Meanwhile, the wind-borne particles ahead added a drabness to the feeds, like a rain-threatened winter's dusk.

Glancing across, Lanson saw the determined set of Matlock's face. Her hands were poised over the weapons panel as she prepared to unleash hell upon the enemy. Lanson realised that the tension within him had diminished, leaving him with the familiar anticipation of a life and death struggle. Adrenaline flowed through his veins, and he felt completely in balance.

"One thousand klicks and we'll have visibility on the Tagha'an," said Turner.

Lanson increased the *Infinitar*'s velocity until the warship was racing across the planet's surface. The hull temperature sensors informed him the nose section was heating up, though not to any significant degree.

"Five hundred klicks," said Turner.

"As soon as you have a weapons lock, Commander…"

"Yes, sir. I'll turn the enemy ship into wreckage."

"Three hundred klicks."

The *Infinitar* flew across an area of the planet where competing storms met, creating thick clouds of dust that even the warship's sensors struggled to penetrate. Lanson thought briefly of blizzards he'd experienced back on Earth, where the snow had come down so heavily it was as though the rest of the world beyond his vision had simply vanished.

Shaking off the thoughts, Lanson gave his full attention to the feeds. Gaining the first strike on the Sagh'eld cruiser was vital, since he didn't want the *Infinitar* to suffer extensive damage if he could avoid it.

"One hundred klicks."

"Any time now," said Matlock.

"Enemy warship sighted," said Turner calmly.

The Tagha'an appeared on the tactical screen as a red dot, still at the same twenty-kilometre altitude and in the same position as when it had first been detected from way out in space.

"Forward and topside Avantar clusters one to three targeted and fired," said Matlock. "Gradar repeaters set to track and destroy."

Such was the velocity of the missiles that Lanson saw only the briefest glimpse of their orange propulsions, before they vanished into the distance. Hardly any time later, the warheads struck their target, and the flash of multiple detonations lit up the planet's skies.

And that was that. Such was the power of the Avantar missiles that the Tagha'an cruiser was torn apart by this single salvo, and the debris began falling towards the ground. Having built up the engagement in his head, Lanson could only stare at the star-bright fragments of the heavy cruiser as they came down. As he watched the light trails descending through the dust, he reduced velocity and set the *Infinitar* on a circular course directly above the Edron base.

"The Sagh'eld didn't launch a single missile," said Matlock. "And all seventy-two of ours detonated."

A part of Lanson didn't want to celebrate such an easy win, as if it was somehow dishonourable to emerge victorious without so much as a scratch. He knew it was foolish to think like this. The Sagh'eld had, on many occasions, inflicted similar defeats upon the Human Confederation fleet and now they'd had a spoonful of the same medicine. Lanson hoped it tasted like shit.

With the *Infinitar* travelling in a slow circle around Edron, and the debris of the vanquished falling, Lanson's eyes went to the underside feeds. He had an excellent view into the Aral base and one of the first things he noticed was the eight cargo shuttles the Sagh'eld had parked on the landing field. When he zoomed the sensor, Lanson spotted two loading vehicles travelling away from a nondescript structure of alloy.

"Those shuttles weren't visible earlier, Captain," said Turner. "They're parked right on the edge of the landing field next to that warehouse, which kept them hidden from the sensors."

"What're those loaders carrying?" Lanson wondered.

"Tech," said Abrams. "What else?"

Lanson pondered how best to deal with the Sagh'eld ground forces. Usually, he'd have greeted them with missiles, but since the enemy had shown a great interest in the Galos tech, he didn't want to risk a nasty surprise by firing upon the transports.

That was the moment Lanson remembered to check the update window on his right-hand screen. When he saw that the bottom line of text was different to all the others, he experienced a surge of adrenaline.

> *Combination request received. Combination not available.*

"It's here!" said Lanson. "The Singularity class must have exited lightspeed!"

The feeds showed nothing, but of course the Sagh'eld could have entered local space anywhere. In addition, the words of the update were different to what Lanson had expected. If the combination was not available, that meant the target vessel was being forcibly prevented from activating its linking routine.

Time was limited. If Lanson was to steal the Aral warship from the Sagh'eld, he needed to find the enemy before they realised their Tagha'an had been neutralised. When that happened, they'd take off into lightspeed and his chance to complete the *Infinitar* would be gone.

TEN

"Find those warships!" Lanson snarled.

"Yes, sir. Scanning," said Turner.

The situation was already slipping out of Lanson's control. Although the Tagha'an was no longer able to transmit a warning to the newly arrived spaceships, the transports on the landing field would certainly do so.

Lanson's experience with the Sagh'eld told him the aliens were prone to overconfidence, which made it more likely they'd have exited lightspeed near to the planet. If the enemy were within the transmission arcs of the shuttles, they'd soon learn what had transpired here on Tarai.

An idea came to Lanson and he cursed himself for not thinking of it earlier.

"Lieutenant Perry, search for a ground receptor on Edron," he said. "If you find one, request a connection."

"Yes, sir, I'm running a receptor sweep," said Perry. "Receptor found...connection requested...request accepted."

"Find out if the Aral installed monitors on the planet's surface," said Lanson. "And check for a satellite ring."

"Yes, sir," said Perry. She went quiet for a few seconds. "There's a satellite ring, but it's been disabled, Captain," she said. "However, the Aral installed hardwired surface monitor towers, one of which is tracking six targets at a distance of twelve thousand kilometres from our position."

"Six targets? Damnit!" said Lanson.

He knew he shouldn't be surprised. The Sagh'eld had committed serious resources to Ravrol, so it was clear they were aggressively pursuing their search for Aral tech. He should have better anticipated the enemy, and Lanson swore inwardly at his own failings.

"What data do we have on those six warships?" he asked.

"Size and mass estimates from the monitor tower indicate the presence of one superheavy lifter, two Ex'Kaminars, two Tagha'an heavies and one Ingosor light cruiser."

"Don't those bastards ever run out of battleships?" said Lanson in disgust.

"There's more, sir. The mass estimates of the two Ex'Kaminars differ by almost a billion tons."

Lanson's mind jumped back to one of the enemy battleships he'd encountered on Ravrol. The Ex'Kaminar had been equipped with a prototype Galos weapon – a weapon which packed sufficient punch to take out the colossal Ixtar warship *Ghiotor*. Although the discharge had also disabled the Ex'Kaminar, Lanson certainly didn't want to run into a vessel carrying the same tech.

"Captain, the monitor tower has gone offline," said Perry. "The Sagh'eld must have taken it out."

"Did it detect any positional changes from the enemy warships before it happened?" asked Lanson.

"No, sir. Oh crap."

"Tell me," said Lanson.

"The enemy warships have been picked up by a second

monitor tower, sir. They're heading our way." Perry cursed. "The second tower has now gone offline."

"Does this mean they know we're here?" asked Matlock.

"Their actions suggest a high likelihood they do, Commander," said Lanson. "Lieutenant Turner, access the ground hardware and see if you can activate the base defences."

"Yes, sir, I'm requesting a connection."

Lanson's grip tightened around the control bars. He needed something to swing the situation in his favour, since he didn't like the odds of facing the incoming enemy warships. The Edron ground launchers were exactly what he needed.

It was not to be.

"Captain, the ground defences are offline," said Turner.

Lanson wanted to curse, though with an effort he held his tongue. The Ravrol defences had been offline, as had the defences of every Aral facility he'd visited so far. The fact of it was far beyond coincidence, and Lanson wondered if the Aral themselves had shut down their weapons, or if the cause was something else.

"The enemy warships have come into range of a third tower, Captain," said Turner. "Only four vessels are detected – the superheavy and one of the Tagha'ans are no longer part of the approaching group."

"Can we take out two battleships, a heavy and a light cruiser?" mused Lanson. He smiled thinly at a sudden thought. "Maybe we don't have to."

"What's the plan, Captain?" asked Matlock.

"We have a single charge left on our negation shield, Commander. In addition, our experience at Ravrol indicates the other Singularity warships are also equipped with a negation shield."

"With only a single charge."

"Which is all we're going to need," said Lanson.

"You're going to fire missiles at the Sagh'eld transports in the hope that one of them is carrying a Galos cube?" asked Matlock, her eyes wide.

"That's right, Commander. If we set off a Galos detonation, it should destroy everything within a hundred thousand klicks, except the *Infinitar* and the warship in the hold of the Sagh'eld superheavy."

"Shit, Captain, that's one hell of a risk," said Abrams. "The enemy might well know we're here, but there's a chance they believe we're blind to their presence. If we take them by surprise, we could come out on top."

"I agree this is an engagement we might win," said Lanson. "But we're still going with my plan."

"Yes, sir."

Lanson wasn't sure he was making the right decision. However, he'd been in life-or-death situations many times before and he'd long ago learned that the best thing to do in the face of uncertainty was to choose a path and stick to it.

"The approaching Sagh'eld warships are passing over a fourth tower, Captain," said Turner. "They're within five thousand kilometres of our position. We'll be within their line of sight in less than one minute."

"Acknowledged," said Lanson. "Commander Matlock, target those Sagh'eld shuttles and the two loaders. Destroy them."

"Yes, sir," said Matlock. "Missiles targeted and fired."

Ten Avantar missiles raced from the same underside cluster. The missiles accelerated towards their targets, while Lanson watched on the feeds. Like Abrams had said, this was an enormous risk, but Lanson saw it as an opportunity to defeat his opponents without his own warship suffering so much as a scratch. A conventional engagement would definitely be messy and with no guarantee of success. Besides, if there was no Galos detonation, Lanson had a backup plan.

"Boom," said Matlock.

The Sagh'eld ground forces had no defence against the Avantar missiles, and all ten warheads struck their intended targets. Even before the blasts had faded, Lanson was certain the eight transports, the two loaders, and whatever cargo they were carrying, were utterly destroyed.

"No Galos detonation," he said after a few seconds. He didn't know whether to be disappointed or relieved.

It wasn't time to dwell on the failure of Plan A, so Lanson immediately put Plan B into action.

"When those four Sagh'eld warships are just over the horizon, I'm going to execute an instant lightspeed transit to the last known position of the superheavy," he said. "It's possible the lifter went elsewhere since we lost sight of it, so we'll have to be on our toes to find it and then crack it open before enemy reinforcements arrive."

"Breaching the superheavy without harming the target vessel won't be easy, Captain," said Matlock. "Especially considering the size of the hole we'll need to make."

"This is our last chance to recover the Singularity warship, Commander. One way or another, we have to make it work."

"Yes, sir."

"Fifteen seconds and the incoming warships will have us in sensor sight, Captain," said Turner. "They're still destroying the ground towers as they approach, but not quickly enough to prevent us receiving their updated positions."

Calmly, Lanson reached out with his left hand and tapped a fingertip on the tactical screen to indicate his intended destination, a hundred kilometres vertically above the last known position of the superheavy. Once that was done, he placed his hand back on the controls and rested his thumb gently on the ILT activation button.

"Five seconds, Captain."

Lanson counted the seconds down in his head, and when he reached two, he activated the ILT with a hard press of the button. The sensors went offline and the *Infinitar*'s engines thumped twice as they hurled the warship into lightspeed and then back into local space.

"Sensors coming up," said Turner.

"Come on, come on," muttered Lanson. He resisted the temptation to put the *Infinitar* into motion and held it in place.

"Sensors up," said Turner. "Scanning for the enemy vessels."

Lanson swept his eyes across the feeds. This area of Tarai was mountainous, and every bit as inhospitable as it was at the Edron facility. Storms there were in plenty, but no sign of the two Sagh'eld warships.

"Activating that ILT has generated a cooldown timer, Captain," said Abrams. "We won't be able to use the facility again for another three minutes."

"Is that a hard limit, or can we override?" asked Lanson.

"I'll check, sir."

"Shit! Missiles coming our way, Captain! A mixture of Zavon and Gorlans!" yelled Perry. "Enemy Tagha'an located, five hundred klicks north of our position!"

The moment he heard the warning, Lanson pushed the control bars as far as they'd go, and the force of the acceleration pressed him into his seat. On the tactical, twenty tiny red dots sped towards the *Infinitar*, while the Tagha'an which launched them was a larger dot, heading rapidly east. Of the superheavy, there was no sign.

"Gradar repeaters set to track and destroy," said Matlock. "Spine countermeasures launched."

Plenty of alloy separated the *Infinitar*'s bridge from the hull repeaters, but even so, Lanson imagined he could hear the guns pulsing as they hurled out torrents of projectiles. At the same moment as the repeaters fired, the warship's topside Spine launchers ejected dozens of seeker missiles high into the planet's atmosphere. With extraordinary agility, the interceptors turned through the air as they homed in on their targets.

"Starboard Avantar clusters one to six, and topside clusters one to three, targeted and fired," said Matlock. "The enemy warship has activated its Kraal countermeasures."

"Our onboard systems have been hit by the Tagha'an's scrambler, Captain," said Abrams. "We have not been shut down."

Despite the *Infinitar*'s clear superiority over the Sagh'eld heavy cruiser, this engagement was a reminder that, when they were not taken completely by surprise, the enemy warships were entirely capable of fighting back. The Tagha'an's Kraal guns raked into the Avantar missiles, wrecking many. In the meantime, the *Infinitar*'s own countermeasures neutralised all the incoming Zavons. Unfortunately, one of the – much faster - Gorlans slipped past the Aral warship's defences, crashing into its starboard flank.

"Damnit!" said Lanson as the enemy warhead exploded in a white-hot burst of plasma.

His mood was quickly improved by the sight of a dozen Avantar missiles detonating against the Tagha'an's midsection. The size of the blasts suggested the damage was either critical or terminal, yet the Sagh'eld heavy managed to launch a second – much smaller – salvo from its forward and stern clusters.

"Captain, the ground sensors on Edron have not detected the four enemy warships," said Perry. "They must be heading back our way."

"Just what we need," said Lanson through gritted teeth. "Where's that superheavy?"

"Got it!" said Turner a moment later. "Another of the ground towers has picked it up – the lifter is stationary, about five thousand kilometres north."

"It's preparing for lightspeed," said Lanson angrily.

The engagement with the Tagha'an hadn't lasted long, but when the margins were tight, a few seconds could easily be enough to turn success into failure. Lanson couldn't let the superheavy escape.

Fortunately, the Tagha'an had suffered greatly from the first Avantar salvo. A huge hole had been torn in its midsection, and the metals glowed white from the plasma heat. The heavy cruiser's most recent salvo of Zavon missiles had already been chewed up by Gradar fire, while Matlock had launched another thirty-six Avantars from the *Infinitar*'s rear clusters.

"Let's get that superheavy," said Lanson, banking north.

The *Infinitar* gathered velocity. Meanwhile, the Tagha'an didn't retain enough operational countermeasures to thin out the wave of incoming Avantars. Twenty of the Aral missiles evaded destruction and they struck the heavy cruiser in its already weakened midsection. The combined explosions were enough to split the Sagh'eld warship down the middle, and the two huge pieces of debris began to spin wildly, each accelerating along a separate trajectory.

"The heavy's Rodos drive modules are still functioning," said Abrams. "But their control systems have failed."

"No control systems equals no weapons," said Lanson.

The Tagha'an was defeated and he paid the wreckage no heed. One enemy warship was out of the fight, yet others remained, four of which would be closing in rapidly from the south. Lanson was determined to have a shot at the superheavy before its escort vessels could interfere.

"Captain, the lifter took out the monitor tower!" said Turner.

"I'm surprised they didn't do it sooner," said Lanson.

He felt a twinge of unease. If the lifter abandoned its light-speed warmup and headed off around the planet, the pursuit could turn into a game of cat-and-mouse, with all the guesswork and uncertainty that would involve.

He focused on the horizon, hunting for the enemy lifter, while around the *Infinitar*'s unyielding hull, the storms of Terai blew unceasing, as if the planet itself was set against Lanson and his crew.

Holding down his anger, Lanson readied himself for the next engagement.

ELEVEN

The *Infinitar* raced north, its engines producing a deep, background rumble. Fearful of overshooting the target, Lanson refrained from tapping too deeply into the warship's propulsion. It was frustrating, but the superheavy wasn't more than a few seconds' travel time ahead. Soon enough, the enemy vessel would become visible, and then the fun and games could begin.

"Sir, I've detected the lifter!" yelled Perry. "It's accelerating south-west, a thousand kilometres west of our position."

"Damnit!" said Lanson, when he saw the sensor feed. The superheavy was at a low altitude, in order to minimise the range at which it would be visible, and its already high velocity was increasing. He brought the *Infinitar* into a tight turn, intending to give chase.

"The Tagha'an transmitted details about our position and our firepower," said Matlock. "The lifter crew have decided they'll be safest if they rendezvous with their escort ships."

"And we damn near let our target slip by," said Lanson, angry that he'd been outmanoeuvred. "Commander Matlock –

attack the lifter with missiles. We need to disable it before it joins with the other warships."

"Avantar missiles locked and launched, Captain. Portside clusters one to six, undersides one to three."

Almost at once, the enemy vessel's Kraal guns began firing. The lifter's armaments were primarily defensive, and it was fitted with plenty of hull repeaters. Lines of white stabbed out, picking off the Avantar missiles.

"Enemy Zavon launch detected, Captain," said Perry. "Sixteen total."

"Gradar repeaters set to track and destroy," said Matlock. "Forward Avantar clusters one to four, targeted and fired."

The Aral missiles travelled with enormous velocity, as if they'd been fitted with additional shielding to protect them from atmospheric friction, and it was clear the lifter's targeting systems weren't quite capable enough to deal with the Avantars. The Sagh'eld vessel's many repeaters weren't sufficient to neutralise the incoming threat, and a full dozen warheads exploded against the superheavy's portside flank, near to its stern.

"A good start, but not enough," said Lanson.

He held the *Infinitar* on an intercept course. At any moment, he expected the four Sagh'eld warships to appear on the southern horizon and turn up the heat.

"All sixteen enemy missiles have been destroyed, Captain," said Perry. "I have detected the launch of another sixteen."

"Five confirmed detonations from our second Avantar salvo," said Matlock. "Starboard clusters one to four, targeted and fired. Captain, I'm waiting on reloads for the other on-target clusters."

"I'll see what I can do about that," said Lanson.

He shifted the control bars, and at the same time adjusted the output load across the warship's different engine modules.

Lanson judged it just about perfectly, and the *Infinitar* rotated smoothly around its vertical axis until its starboard clusters were on target. Now, it was travelling almost flank-first towards the superheavy, allowing Matlock to discharge another salvo of missiles.

"Two enemy Zavons about to impact," said Perry.

"Avantar missiles locked and launched," said Matlock. "Starboard clusters one to four."

"Enemy Zavons neutralised," said Perry. "That was close."

"Let's straighten up this warship," said Lanson. Again, he shifted the controls and re-balanced the propulsion output. When he was done, the *Infinitar*'s nose was aimed directly at the fleeing lifter.

"Enemy missile launch detected," said Perry. "Another sixteen."

"Topside Spine missiles launched," said Matlock. "Targeting forward Avantar clusters."

The recent Avantar detonations had left the superheavy trailing flames in its wake, the plasma light made pale by the atmospheric conditions. Lanson narrowed his eyes and did his best to gauge the extent of the damage inflicted upon the enemy warship. Not for the first time, he was left impressed by the payload of the Aral missiles. The lifter's flank was heavily cratered, and he judged the vessel's hull was almost breached in several places.

"Forward Avantar clusters one to four, targeted and fired," said Matlock.

"One enemy Zavon remains from the last wave," said Perry.

The Sagh'eld missile seemed to have a charmed existence. It twisted and turned through the Gradar streams, heading ever closer to impact. Having already witnessed his warship take a hit from the Tagha'an heavy, Lanson wasn't keen to see a repeat. He threw the *Infinitar* to portside. It was the first time he'd fully tested the warship's manoeuvrability and he was astounded by how rapidly it responded, with hardly a groan from the metals around him.

"The Zavon overshot," said Perry. "Our rear Gradars have destroyed it."

Lanson wrenched the *Infinitar* back onto course, just as the previous salvo of Avantars exploded against the lifter's portside flank and topside armour. The enemy vessel's defences had clearly been weakened and the quantity of Kraal fire was noticeably reduced.

"Enemy missile launch detected," said Turner. "Eight Zavons in total."

Sensing that the enemy's hull armour had been breached by the explosions, Lanson stared at the feeds, his teeth clenched.

"Underside Avantar clusters one to four, targeted and fired," said Matlock. "Spine missiles launched."

At that moment, the lifter pilot pulled off a move that was a tribute to the one Lanson had executed only a short time before. In a single, rapid movement, the superheavy rotated around its vertical axis, hiding its weakened portside flank and exposing its undamaged starboard armour. It was an unwelcome and infuriating display of skill, though one which Lanson reluctantly found himself admiring, particularly so because of the lifter's vast size.

"Well, shit," he said. "Now we have to do it all again."

"Zavon launch detected from enemy lifter," said Perry. "Sixteen total."

Lanson's frustration threatened to boil over into outright fury, but he didn't allow the red mist to descend. The *Infinitar* was still operating well within its atmospheric velocity limits and he pushed the controls to the ends of their guide slots. A thump in the back of acceleration followed and the warship tore after the Sagh'eld lifter. Gradar projectiles smashed a dozen of the Zavons into pieces, while Spine missiles took care of the rest.

"Captain, I've detected an Ex'Kaminar battleship to the south," said Turner. "Make that two Ex'Kaminars."

"This isn't working out quite like I hoped," growled Lanson.

Expecting Thak cannon projectiles to be heading his way at any moment, he banked the *Infinitar* hard to port, increased altitude and then banked hard to starboard. Given the relative positions of the enemy warships, Lanson had limited options for avoidance, and he hoped the enemy crews were incompetent, hungover, or preferably both.

"Tagha'an heavy detected, also to the south," said Turner. "And it's accompanied by the Ingosor light cruiser."

"Missile launches detected from all four enemy warships, Captain."

"Eight confirmed Avantar impacts on the superheavy, sir," said Matlock. "Can you give me the starboard clusters?"

"Be ready," said Lanson, rotating the *Infinitar* so its starboard flank was facing the lifter, while also maintaining the same heading and velocity as before.

"Starboard clusters one to six, underside clusters one to three, targeted and fired," said Matlock.

As the missiles sped after their target, Lanson glanced at the tactical. Red dots – missiles and warships – filled the screen in far greater numbers than he would have liked. The Gradar turrets were effective, but they'd be overwhelmed by so many inbound warheads.

"Let's see if we can outrun these missiles," said Lanson. "Commander Matlock, the Gorlan missiles have a higher velocity than the Zavons. Set the Gradar turrets to prioritise the Gorlans."

"Yes, sir."

"Captain, I'm detecting emissions from the farthest Ex'Kaminar," said Abrams urgently. "The particles aren't quite Galos, but they have similarities."

"Another Sagh'eld super-weapon," cursed Lanson. "Let's hope the battleship's crew are under strict instructions not to fire it."

"Not a chance," said Abrams.

By now, Matlock was launching missiles and Spine countermeasures as rapidly as their clusters would reload. Gradar projectiles sought out the incoming Gorlans and broke them apart, while the Sagh'eld Kraal guns did likewise to the Avantar missiles.

"The *Infinitar* is incomplete," said Lanson. "We don't have the firepower for this."

Although the warship lacked sufficient missile clusters to overwhelm so many attackers, its propulsion was magnitudes in advance of the Sagh'eld Rodos drives. The lifter was only two hundred kilometres ahead, both flanks trailing flames. Lanson intended to pilot the *Infinitar* over the top of the superheavy, so Matlock could launch missiles into the enemy's portside flank and free the Singularity warship trapped inside.

How the combination would be enacted while the Sagh'eld were causing so many problems, Lanson didn't know, though he was doing his best to come up with some ideas.

"Sir, the emissions from the Ex'Kaminar are climbing," said Abrams. "It's possible they're readying for a shot."

"A shot they can't take if we're too close to the lifter," said Lanson.

Expecting another Thak projectile to be on its way, he enacted a violent change of course, before correcting back onto the same heading as before. A second later, he repeated the left-right adjustment, just as a bright orange streak raced by, travelling at incredible velocity.

"Another one dodged," said Lanson.

Such was the *Infinitar*'s own velocity that its nose section and the tip of the topside Singularity cannon were glowing a dull red. According to the hull instrumentation, the temperature of the alloys in those places was in excess of two thousand Celsius and rising fast. Lanson wasn't concerned about the heat – yet – and he guessed he had at least another two thousand Celsius to play with before it became a critical issue.

"The enemy Zavons are having a hard time keeping up with us, Captain," said Turner. "And our repeaters are taking care of the Gorlans."

When the *Infinitar* was within fifty kilometres of the lifter, the enemy vessel banked suddenly east and climbed away from the planet's surface. Lanson altered course to follow, and the lifter banked again, this time west.

"The enemy crew doesn't want us coming too close," said Matlock.

"They must know the Ex'Kaminar crew is lining up an attack," said Lanson, his eyes wide and locked on the feeds as he attempted to predict the movements of the lifter. "The battleship on Ravrol created a detonation sphere about twenty klicks in diameter."

"So we have to stay real close to the superheavy."

"That's the plan, Commander."

It was a plan the enemy crew were determined to see fail. The lifter banked first one way and then the other, changing altitude at the same time. Lanson's reactions were good, and he had the added benefit of piloting a vessel designed to outmanoeuvre its opponents. Consequently, he had little difficulty in maintaining the pursuit.

"We've been hit by a scrambler, Captain," said Massey.

"Our onboard systems are unaffected. I don't think the scramblers are effective against Aral tech."

Lanson heard the words, though he didn't respond. He was struggling to keep on top of everything which was happening. The tactical was filled with red, he was doing his best to outguess the Sagh'eld weapons officers, and the modified Ex'Kaminar would likely discharge its super-weapon the moment he slipped up.

Having come too far to contemplate failure, Lanson kept his cool. The best efforts of the lifter crew weren't good enough, and he piloted the *Infinitar* directly over the top of the enemy vessel. In response, the superheavy increased altitude, as if to force a collision. Lanson held his nerve – the *Infinitar* was the smaller of the two spaceships by physical size, but it certainly possessed a far greater mass – and refused to change course.

His gamble paid off. Instead of colliding with the *Infinitar*, the lifter's pilot declined the opportunity and accelerated once more towards the surface. Lanson had expected the move and continued the pursuit. Now, the superheavy's portside armour was within weapons sight. The earlier Avantar detonations had created a series of huge craters, which still glowed from the heat. Several hull breaches were clearly visible, the largest being a long, narrow opening where three craters merged.

"I'm trying to obtain sensor sight into the lifter's main bay, Captain," said Turner.

"Our Singularity warship is in there," said Lanson. "Commander Matlock, finish what you started."

"Yes, sir. Targeting portside midsection Gradars."

The hull repeater projectiles thundered into the lifter's heat-softened armour, and the opening was torn steadily wider. Meanwhile, the crew of the enemy vessel did what they could to make the task as difficult as possible. The lifter accelerated and slowed, banked and climbed. Lanson stuck as close to superheavy's portside flank as he could manage.

Although the lifter was vast, it didn't provide much of a shield against the incoming missiles. The Sagh'eld warships repositioned so they had a clear line of sight on the *Infinitar*, while the lifter crew did their best to coordinate with the others.

"The Gradars aren't doing enough, Commander," Lanson growled.

"I've held off on the Avantars, sir."

"Use them."

"Yes, sir."

Lanson's mind registered a snapshot of the engagement. The enemy warships were pressing, and their missiles would likely soon penetrate the *Infinitar*'s defences. No longer could Lanson outrun the enemy warheads, because he was effectively tied to the lifter's flank. Should he choose to accelerate away, the modified Ex'Kaminar would discharge its Galos weapon. The *Infinitar* could generate one more negation shield, but Lanson was desperate to hang on to this game changer for as long as possible.

He wondered if he'd screwed up by targeting the lifter for so long. Perhaps if he'd focused on the four escort warships he'd be in a more favourable position.

Lanson's anger burned within him. The Sagh'eld were the bane of humanity's existence and had been for years. Losing to them was unthinkable. Victory wasn't yet out of the question.

There had to be a way.

TWELVE

The exchange of fire continued without cease.

"Portside Avantars, cluster four, tubes one to three, targeted at enemy lifter and fired," said Matlock. "Rear and topside clusters one to four targeted at modified Ex'Kaminar and fired. Spine missiles ejected."

The three portside Avantars launched and detonated against the lifter's armour in the blinking of an eye. Matlock had deliberately aimed forward of the largest breach, to avoid accidentally damaging the contents of the superheavy's main bay.

Lanson couldn't give his full attention to Matlock's efforts. Working on the assumption that the enemy Galos weapon would generate a blast with a twenty-thousand-metre diameter, he reckoned he needed to stay within a thousand metres of the lifter in order to dissuade the Ex'Kaminar's crew from taking an offset shot.

Given the velocities and the sizes of the vessels involved, a thousand metres felt like a hair's breadth. Lanson felt sweat prickling his scalp and the tightness in his muscles was becoming an ache that threatened to turn into a distraction.

And still Lanson didn't know how the linking between his warship and the Singularity vessel could take place with the Sagh'eld applying so much pressure.

Maybe it's time to lightspeed out of here, he thought.

Lanson glanced at the tactical. If he executed an ILT targeted to exit lightspeed a quarter-turn around Terai, it would reset the combat and – with any luck – allow him a surprise attack on the Sagh'eld. Taking out the modified Ex'Kaminar would completely alter the balance of combat.

Just as Lanson was about to select his lightspeed destination, words from Lieutenant Abrams gave him pause.

"Captain, I'm reading Galos emissions from the rearmost opening in the lifter's hull!" said Abrams.

"Are those emissions coming from our Singularity warship, Lieutenant?" asked Lanson.

"I don't think so, sir. The source isn't large like a warship, and it's badly shielded."

"A Galos cube," said Lanson.

His earlier plan to detonate any stolen Galos tech on the Sagh'eld shuttles hadn't worked out, but here was another chance, albeit in different circumstances. The doubts from before came back and this time he found them harder to ignore. Now, his mind was set on an ILT and a combat reset, rather than gambling everything on a roll of the dice.

"We're going to—" Lanson began.

He didn't finish what he'd been meaning to say. Appearing with the suddenness of death, the Ravanok exited lightspeed, a hundred kilometres directly overhead. On Lanson's control panel, the readings for the *Infinitar's* propulsion began jumping all over. This time, the engines didn't shut down.

The Ravanok sphere was a foe beyond anything Lanson had encountered before and he felt hatred welling up inside him, until it was thick in the back of his throat. Last time, the *Infinitar*'s missiles had been useless. This time, Lanson had another option.

"Commander Matlock, target the Galos cube on the lifter and hit it with missiles."

"Yes, sir," said Matlock. If she felt fear, it wasn't evident in her voice.

"Captain, the lifter's Rodos drive has shut down," said Abrams. "The same thing has happened to the other Sagh'eld warships. No, wait! The modified Ex'Kaminar is still generating power."

Without its engines to keep it airborne, the lifter commenced its arcing journey towards the planet below. Lanson matched course and velocity, while his eyes searched out the opening beyond which the source of the Galos emissions was to be found. The lifter's flank was a mess, and it seemed almost close enough to touch.

"Captain, maintain this position!" said Matlock urgently. "One of our portside clusters is lined up with the lifter's hull breach."

"Fire when ready, Commander," said Lanson tightly.

The Ravanok had only just arrived and already it had tilted the balance of combat immeasurably. Lanson wondered when the sphere's crew would realise that the *Infinitar* was not affected by the Rodos shut down. When they figured it out, they'd surely employ a different method of attack.

Lanson glanced at the topside feeds, hoping the crew of the Ravanok were so accustomed to instant success that they'd take a few moments to adapt to the unexpected. In the split second his eyes were on the feed, Lanson saw a burst of dark energy – utterly tiny in comparison to its target - strike the Ravanok.

Had it not been for the sensors, his eyes would have been

unable to discern the explosion against the material of the alien sphere's hull. As it was, he knew the Ex'Kaminar had discharged its Galos weapon, though whether the attack had resulted in any damage, he couldn't yet be sure.

"Portside Avantar cluster five, targeted and fired," said Matlock.

Twelve missiles accelerated from their launch tubes and crossed the narrow gap separating the *Infinitar* and the super-heavy. Lanson's brain hardly had time to register the detonations before the sensor feeds all went black. From a place deep within the *Infinitar*, the negation shield generator boomed like a sledgehammer striking a sheet of iron.

"That's the last charge for our negation shield gone," said Matlock.

Lanson hoped upon hope that the Singularity class in the lifter's hold had also been equipped with a negation shield. He turned towards the windowed status readout on his right-hand screen. The words there were exactly what he'd been waiting for.

> *Combination request received. Combination routine initiated.*

The sensors hadn't gone offline, they'd simply been unable to collect any data from within the Galos explosion. When the blast sphere vanished, the feeds resumed like before. The first thing Lanson noticed was that the planet was gone. No matter remained, nor any other indication bar memory that Terai had ever existed.

"There's the Singularity class, sir!" said Perry. "It's orienting itself to combine."

Lanson couldn't spare more than a glance at the target vessel. His attention was required in several places, and time was not on his side.

"The Ravanok is still overhead, Captain!" said Turner.

Lanson bared his teeth at the sight of the seemingly endless sphere. "Has it suffered any damage from the Galos explosion?" he asked.

The Ravanok was so dark, the sensors were struggling to gather data. From what Lanson could see, the sphere was untouched, though it was possible he was mistaken.

"There's no visible sign the Ravanok was affected by the Galos blast, Captain," said Turner.

"Sir, the modified Ex'Kaminar has not been destroyed!" said Perry. "Its propulsion is definitely operational and now it's —" She swore. "I don't know what's happened. The battleship is blurred, like it's out of focus."

Lanson's eyes jumped from the Ravanok to the feed of the Ex'Kaminar. The battleship was two hundred kilometres east and at a hundred-kilometre altitude. It was in motion, though its velocity was much lower than it had been only a short time ago before the Galos blast.

Clear as day, the battleship's nose section had blown out, leaving a vast crater from which debris fell like a heavy rain. In addition, the vessel's armour plating had been ruptured in several places, which Lanson guessed was a result of Avantar impacts.

"Captain, the output from our Galos propulsion is falling!" said Abrams. "It can only be an attack from the Ravanok!"

"What's the rate of the fall and can you stop it happening?" asked Lanson.

"The output decline isn't linear, sir. I think there are defensive routines in the *Infinitar*'s control systems," said Abrams. "I'll see if there's anything else I can do."

Lanson had already seen at Baltol that the Ravanok was capable of far more offensive action than propulsion shutdown attacks, yet so far, the *Infinitar* remained intact. Why the enemy had chosen this occasion to hold back, he didn't know.

Something about this opponent seemed cold and implacable, and Lanson imagined that an alien consciousness, with infinite patience, driven by motives that he would never understand, might reside with the Ravanok.

"Sir, the Ex'Kaminar...it's launched missiles at the Ravanok!" said Turner in a mixture of shock and disbelief.

Lanson continued to juggle his attention between the different events. He looked at the tactical, which showed that the battleship had launched an impressive quantity of both Zavon and Gorlan missiles at the alien sphere. Then, Lanson turned to the feeds, where he saw the Thak turrets atop the Ex'Kaminar rotating onto target. The twin barrels protruding from the Sagh'eld warship's forward turret suddenly jumped back with the force of the recoil.

A moment later, a huge shape blocked out the feeds from the *Infinitar*'s forward and underside arrays. The Singularity warship – which Lanson had been unable to watch as closely as he would have liked – had manoeuvred itself into a position from which it could link.

"The Ex'Kaminar should be within the visibility arc of the starboard midsection arrays," said Perry. "I'll obtain a lock."

Throughout the ongoing developments, Lanson felt helpless. He didn't want to interfere with the linking routine, so he left the controls alone, unsure if they'd even respond to his input. In the meantime, the *Infinitar*'s Galos propulsion output was falling, with no certainty it could be stopped anytime soon. And then there was the Ravanok. How the sphere had located the *Infinitar* and travelled to Terai so quickly, Lanson couldn't begin to guess. All he knew was that he and his crew were in the centre of a shitstorm, and he had no idea how to escape it.

"Sensor lock reobtained on the Ex'Kaminar, sir," said Perry. "It's heading straight for the Ravanok."

"Our Galos output is down to eighty-five percent,

Captain," said Abrams, his voice tight with stress. "I still haven't figured out how it's happening, so I'm no closer to a solution."

A series of faraway, thumping impacts made everything on the bridge vibrate. Clunking noises followed, and Lanson guessed the physical part of the linking routine was almost complete.

"As soon as the combination is finished, we're going into lightspeed," he said.

He reached out, intending to select a destination several billion kilometres away. Before Lanson's finger made it to the tactical display, his eyes were drawn by the sight of Sagh'eld missiles detonating against the Ravanok. Then, the Ex'Kaminar vanished, just like the planet before it.

"Did the battleship go to lightspeed?" asked Lanson.

"Negative, Captain," said Massey. "I think the Ravanok—"

"Shit," said Lanson. "And we're next."

All the distractions were out of the way, and the sphere could give its full attention to the *Infinitar*. Lanson grabbed the control bars and found them unresponsive. He cursed again. The clunking sounds had ended, so surely the linking routine was finished. Lanson darted out a hand for a second time, and he selected a location on fringes of the solar system. He didn't know the maximum range of an ILT, and he hoped the instant transit would take the *Infinitar* far enough away. However, it was already beginning to look as if no distance was far enough to escape the Ravanok.

Having chosen his lightspeed destination, Lanson repeatedly pressed the ILT button on the control bar. The jump didn't activate and he became aware of a growing pressure against his body, as if the air on the bridge were being crushed. Glancing around, Lanson found that simply moving his head had become an effort. In addition, the lights had dimmed, as though he was seeing them through a dense fog.

"What the hell?" gasped Lanson.

The pressure intensified to such a degree that he imagined his bones creaking beneath the weight of it. He groaned with the agony and knew he would soon be dead. Regardless of the pain and the closing jaws of oblivion, Lanson's finger kept on pressing the ILT button.

A rumble from the Galos propulsion signalled the *Infinitar*'s entry into lightspeed. The pressure disappeared instantly, as though death's shroud had been torn away and left to drift in the space vacated by the Aral warship. Not knowing if it would make a difference, Lanson kept his thumb hard on the ILT button, wondering if he might gain some extra time at lightspeed by doing so.

The transit was over all too soon, and the *Infinitar* dropped back into local space. After a couple of seconds, the sensors came online, and darkness filled every screen.

Lanson half-expected the Ravanok to appear at once and destroy the *Infinitar* as utterly as it had the Sagh'eld Ex'Kaminar. For the moment, the sphere was elsewhere.

He didn't expect that situation to last.

THIRTEEN

"Lieutenant Abrams – pick a destination, I don't care where the hell it is, and ready us for lightspeed."

"Yes, sir," said Abrams. "The length of the transit will be twenty-four hours unless cancelled sooner. Two minutes and we'll be on our way."

"What about the Galos drain?"

"Our propulsion output is no longer dropping, Captain!" said Abrams, not even trying to conceal his surprise. "In fact, the maximum available is back to the same level as before the Ravanok attacked."

It was a piece of well-deserved good news and Lanson was relieved that his warship hadn't been permanently hobbled by an unavoidable attack. Even so, the immediate danger wasn't nearly over. The Ravanok had already tracked the *Infinitar* across the vast distance to Terai, so he doubted a few billion kilometres was going to delay it for long.

"Captain, I've isolated the Singularity warship from the rest of the Infinitar," said Lieutenant Perry. "However, the life-form monitors indicate the vessel is empty."

"In which case, remove the isolation locks," said Lanson.

"Yes, sir."

Lanson dropped his eyes from the feeds to perform one of his regular status checks of the instrumentation on his control panel. Everything was in order, though a new option on one of the top-level menus caught his eye.

> *Void Travel*

"What the hell—" said Lanson, opening the menu.

> *Unlock?*

"Damn right," he said, ignoring the stare he was getting from Commander Matlock.

Lanson wasn't a man for careful experimentation, and he accepted the unlock prompt without hesitation. Several seconds went by and nothing happened, but then, the output gauges on the command console – every one of them – jumped to maximum and held there, while the background note of the propulsion altered from the sanguine drone of normal, to something altogether more threatening. A hard, yet exhilarating edge became overlaid upon a hum of absolute technological perfection. It wasn't loud but it made the hairs on Lanson's arms stand on end.

"Captain, an option just appeared on the navigation system," said Abrams. "It's asking if I want to initiate void travel."

"The Singularity class we just combined with must have been carrying some additional hardware," said Lanson. "Is there any indication what this void travel does?"

"No, Captain."

Lanson was more than intrigued. He had much to catch up on, and little breathing room in which to do it. He opened his mouth to ask Abrams a question, but the words died on his lips when he saw that the Ravanok had exited lightspeed less than a hundred kilometres from the *Infinitar*'s portside flank. Such was the vastness of the enemy vessel that it appeared more like a sheer wall than a sphere.

"Forty seconds on the lightspeed timer," said Lanson.

He doubted the Ravanok would allow the *Infinitar* to escape again, and forty seconds was a long time.

Lanson gave the only order which might make a difference. "Activate the void travel," he said.

"Yes, sir. Activating void travel."

The *Infinitar*'s propulsion produced a colossal, whining shriek, which rose from nothingness to an all-encompassing physical manifestation of sound. Lanson felt as though he was being squeezed through a wringer, and it wasn't just from the noise of the engines. Other forces were beating against him, and he felt with certainty he was about to die.

Lanson didn't die. The whine of the propulsion abruptly fell away and the energy of the void travel dissipated, leaving him gasping for breath and with a strange feeling he wasn't within his own body. Expecting pain, Lanson was relieved to discover that none lingered.

Raising his head, he looked at the sensor feeds. He wasn't sure if the arrays had gone offline at all, but if so, they were back now. The view outside was nothing spectacular, suggesting the *Infinitar* was somewhere in the middle of nowhere.

"Do we have any casualties?" asked Lanson, his voice stronger than he'd expected.

He twisted in his seat to check on his crew. Nobody claimed injury, though somebody groaned.

"Where are we?" said Lanson. "Where did the void travel take us?" As he spoke, he scanned his console. The propulsion readings were error free.

"We're at the endpoint of our intended lightspeed journey, Captain," said Turner. "We completed a twenty-four-hour transit in only a few seconds."

"It was a lot less than a few seconds," said Abrams. "Our navigation system has assigned the same time stamp to both the exit and re-entry. We completed the journey in zero time, or near as damnit."

"I've just spoken to Sergeant Gabriel on the comms, sir," said Perry. "He reports no injuries, though he did ask what the hell just happened."

"I'm glad everyone came through," said Lanson. "Let the Sergeant know there's an excellent chance we'll be using the void travel again at some point in the future."

"Yes, sir."

"So - we're here," said Matlock. "How long before the Ravanok joins us?"

"That's the big question," said Lanson.

He didn't know if the alien sphere would continue its pursuit, though the wise money was all on *yes*. For whatever reason, the Ravanok had an interest in either the *Infinitar* or its crew, though Lanson believed the former was more likely.

"The Ravanok made the Aral extinct," he said, repeating his thoughts from earlier. "And now it's after us."

"We have something it wants," said Matlock. "Even if we don't know what that something is."

"The best I can think of is that the Ravanok doesn't want us to complete the *Infinitar*," said Lanson. "If I'm right, I'd dearly like to know what's so special about this warship."

"The *Infinitar* is equipped with Galos engines, and the ability to cross perhaps infinite distances in zero time," said Abrams. "I'd call that pretty damn special."

"I'm more thinking about the weaponry, Lieutenant," said Lanson. "The Singularity menu."

He hadn't checked the weapons panel since the most recent combination and he turned to it now. Opening the Singularity menu, Lanson discovered that every option was greyed out like before. It was galling, but he was increasingly sure the contents of this menu would remain unavailable until all six parts of the *Infinitar* were combined.

"We're better than we were," said Lanson. "However, it would be nice to have access to the topside Singularity cannon."

"On the plus side, we've gained some additional Avantar clusters, Gradar turrets and Spine launchers," said Matlock. "According to the logs, we combined with the *Ragnar-5*."

"Leaving only the *Ragnar-1* and the *Ragnar-6* to go," said Lanson. "Let's see what we look like now."

The external sensor arrays weren't designed to view the warship in which they were installed, but they had plenty of adjustment. After a minute or so, during which Lanson directed the sensors towards the *Infinitar*'s hull, he was left with a general idea of the warship's appearance.

"We still look out of proportion," he said. "The *Ragnars* 2, 3 and 4 have formed a complete stern and most of the midsection. The *Ragnar-5* sits at the front and forms part of the nose and forward midsection. When we find them, the two missing warships will sit either side of the *Ragnar-5*."

Lanson pictured the finished vessel in his head. He reckoned it would measure eleven or twelve thousand metres from nose to stern, with a mass nearing a third of a trillion tons. The overall shape would be more hulking than streamlined, though the two missing pieces might well prove him wrong.

"What's the plan, Captain?" asked Matlock.

"We're going to Indeston," said Lanson, recalling the name of the Tier 0 facility at which he believed another of the Singularity warships would be found. "And after that, we'll journey to Landrol. When we're finished with those places, the *Infinitar* should be complete."

"I entered the coordinates for Indeston into the navigation

system, Captain," said Abrams. "It's located on a planet called Farun. I expected we'd be looking at a transit time between twenty and thirty days, but instead it's only eight days."

"We got another boost with the last combination?" asked Lanson.

"Yes, sir. A big boost."

"Eight days, or we could use the void travel," Lanson mused.

"Would that be wise, Captain?" asked Matlock. "We don't understand how the void travel interacts with our other tech."

"I accept what you're saying, Commander, however I think we'll need to find the limitations of the void travel sooner rather than later. Without it, I don't see how we're going to stay ahead of the Ravanok."

Matlock didn't offer an argument. "Then let's do it."

For a few seconds, Lanson drummed his fingers against his console, as he considered whether he wanted to depart immediately, or to stay put while he and his crew searched the control systems for anything else new which might have appeared from the combination with the *Ragnar-5*.

And we need some data on the Ravanok, he thought. *How long will it take to find us out here? The more we know, the better we'll be able to survive.*

Chancing another encounter for the sake of gathering intel was a risk Lanson didn't want to take just yet. Better to travel directly to Indeston and then Landrol and hope to complete the *Infinitar* before the sphere showed up again. It was always possible that the finished Aral warship had offensive capabilities designed specifically to combat the Ravanok.

"We'll use the void travel to go straight to Indeston," said Lanson. "Target an arrival ten million klicks out."

"Yes, sir," said Abrams. "That first transit was rough."

"I thought I was going to die," said Turner.

Lanson nodded. "I wonder if our encounter with the Galos cube on Cornerstone was what enabled us to survive." He didn't spend any time thinking about it. "Lieutenant Perry, let Sergeant Gabriel know we're about to utilise the void travel again, and tell him in advance of all subsequent transits."

"Yes, sir."

"We're ready to go any time you choose, Captain," said Abrams.

"That time is now, Lieutenant."

Abrams inhaled audibly. "Void travel activated."

The experience of the second transit was identical to the first in terms of the noise and the feeling of dislocation. However, this time, Lanson found the journey to be physically much less traumatic. When the sound of the propulsion faded, he recovered from the void travel almost at once and he was hopeful that his Galos-modified body was learning to cope.

On this occasion, Lanson was able to spot that the sensor arrays hadn't even gone offline. They'd flickered once, and then the view changed.

Lanson was rapidly coming to terms with the *Infinitar*'s new ability to travel from one place to another in what was effectively zero time and he knew how much his chances of success had improved.

It was time to locate the next Singularity warship and, with the Ravanok likely in pursuit, this window of opportunity would not be open for long.

FOURTEEN

"Commence scans!" Lanson ordered. "Lieutenant Turner, locate planet Farun."

"Yes, sir."

As he was speaking, Lanson turned to the window on his right-hand screen. The words were not encouraging.

> *Combination not available.*

Lanson advised the other members of his crew. "It looks like we've come to the wrong place."

"This is still a Tier 0 facility, Captain," said Matlock. "We should scout the place anyway."

"I agree," said Lanson, though not without some reluctance. "We've come this far, and maybe there's something worth finding here."

"Captain, I've detected an instability on our Galos propulsion," said Lieutenant Abrams.

Lanson closed his eyes for a moment. He didn't need this crap. "What kind of instability?"

"I'm not sure, Captain – I'm still getting my head around the changes to our propulsion from the last two combinations," said Abrams. "I think both the *Ragnar-4* and the *Ragnar-5* were made up almost completely from Galos modules wrapped in armour. Those modules are operating in tandem since we combined, but one of them is giving erratic power readings."

"Is this anything like what happened to the *New Beginning*?"

"Where the propulsion went crazy before finally exploding?"

"Yes, that."

"I'm not sure, Captain. The *New Beginning*'s engines showed massive power spikes because of the criticalities in its Rodos modules, and I'm not seeing exactly the same thing here. There's an instability, but it's not significantly affecting our power output."

"Figure out the cause and fix it," said Lanson.

"I'll do what I can, sir."

During the short conversation, Lieutenant Perry had completed the local area sweeps, and Lieutenant Turner had obtained a sensor lock on Farun. The feed enhancement completed just as Lanson focused his attention on the faraway planet, giving him a view which hinted at much, but gave little away.

"A gas giant?" he asked. "Or does the planet have a solid surface?"

Muddy hues of brown and red were mixed with greys and yellows. With a diameter of 120 thousand kilometres, Farun would be challenging to explore given the time pressure of having the Ravanok in pursuit.

"I can't offer certainty from this range, but I'm not currently able to detect a solid surface, Captain," said Turner. "The gas atmosphere is making the scan data difficult to interpret. It's possible there's rock underneath all the other crap. I should be able to tell you for sure once we're nearer to the planet."

"If Farun is primarily gas, then we're looking for an object that's in orbit," mused Lanson. "Perhaps Indeston is below the outer layers of the atmosphere."

"If so, locating the facility will be a real headache," said Turner.

"Only if it wants to remain hidden, Lieutenant."

"Should I run a receptor sweep, sir?"

Lanson normally preferred to have the initial sensor scans completed first, but on this occasion he was keen to make early progress.

"Do it," he said.

"Running sweep for comms receptors," Turner confirmed. "Receptors found."

"How many?" asked Lanson.

"Eight total, sir. They are not transmitting their locations."

"Pick one at random and initiate contact," said Lanson.

"Yes, sir. Request sent...comms link accepted."

"What's on the other end of the link?" asked Lanson. "Hopefully it's an AI, rather than a dumb system designed to follow protocol."

"It's a dumb system, Captain," said Turner a few moments later. "I now have access to its location, and I think it's part of a satellite network."

"Will it route our transmissions to the Indeston facility?"

"Negative, sir," said Turner. "The satellite is unable to form a connection to base."

"Why not?" asked Lanson, fighting to keep the irritation from his voice.

"The satellite is receiving an error code telling it the remote connection is unavailable."

"Which is about as generic as it gets," said Matlock.

"Try another satellite, Lieutenant Turner," Lanson ordered.

"Yes, sir." Turner wasn't quiet for long. "The second satellite is returning the same error code."

"What're the possible reasons?" asked Lanson.

"Just what you'd expect, Captain. Either the Indeston facility no longer exists, or its comms systems have been instructed to reject any inbound requests."

"There's a third possibility, sir," said Perry. "If Indeston is a mobile platform like you suggested earlier, it could have gone elsewhere."

Lanson sat back in his seat and pondered the situation. He hadn't been thinking for long when Lieutenant Abrams announced some good news.

"The anomaly on our propulsion is gone, Captain. I'd like to tell you it was something I did, but it was automatically fixed by the *Infinitar*'s control system."

"Any idea as to the cause of the anomaly?"

"The void travel is what triggered it, sir. The journey here produced some big output spikes, though given how many Galos modules we're carrying, I wouldn't have expected those spikes to create an instability."

"You have a theory?"

"Yes, sir. The Aral had clearly discovered a method of travel which is far beyond anything the Human Confederation's scientists can even dream of. I have no idea what this *void* is, or how the *Infinitar* is able to enter it. However, I keep asking myself what would happen if the Aral hadn't quite mastered void travel. Perhaps we would see anomalies such as the one we experienced only a short time ago."

Lanson had always been fascinated by tech, which partly explained why he was so interested in the Aral. The aliens were far in advance of the Human Confederation, and discovering their creations was like having a sight into a possible future. On the other hand, the more Lanson saw of technology's potential, the more he wondered if it was a thing to be feared as much as it was to be embraced.

"Is your conclusion that we should limit the use of void travel, Lieutenant Abrams?"

"I think we should be aware of the potential downsides, sir."

"I wish I could offer you and Lieutenant Massey the opportunity to study the *Infinitar's* propulsion systems," said Lanson.

"We'll do what we can with the time we have, sir."

Lanson nodded, his mind already returning to the situation at hand. He was reluctant to believe that the Indeston facility might no longer be here at Farun and he certainly didn't want to imagine it had been destroyed. Unfortunately, the words on his right-hand screen demanded he consider both possibilities.

> *Combination not available.*

"Those satellites should hold records of their last communications with Indeston," said Lanson.

"Yes, sir," said Turner. "I've already run a query on three of the satellites. Their records have been deleted."

"Well, isn't that just great?" said Lanson sourly.

"I have visibility on five other satellites, Captain," said Turner. "Plus there should be others on the planet's blind side."

"If the transmission records have been deleted from three satellites, I have little hope they'll have been left intact elsewhere."

"That's what I think as well, Captain."

"I've got an idea, sir," said Perry. "Give me a moment to check something out."

Lanson was keen to find out what trail Perry was following, and it took an effort to keep his mouth shut. Thirty seconds later, his patience was rewarded.

"Yes!" said Perry. "I think I've discovered a way to locate Indeston. Or at least to find out when it exited this solar system, if that's what happened."

"Explain," said Lanson.

"Within the Human Confederation military, most comms are sent along an encrypted tunnel and aimed directly at the receptor. This reduces the chance of interception and also allows the comms amplifiers to—"

"Skip the basics, Lieutenant. Tell me what you've found."

"Yes, sir. In order for the Aral satellites to aim their transmissions at the Indeston facility, they make slight adjustments to their orientation so their transmitters are always aimed at the receptor as it travels by underneath them."

"So Indeston is or was an orbital?" said Lanson.

"Yes, sir, and the comms satellites were designed to keep records of their positional adjustments. I guess that would help with troubleshooting if something went wrong with the calibration systems."

Lanson asked the big question. "Is the Indeston orbital here at Farun?"

"Yes, sir. The last reorientation of the westernmost visible satellite was fourteen hours ago, and the adjacent satellite reoriented a little under fifteen hours ago." Perry sounded almost breathless. "I'm missing a single variable that would allow me to give you an exact time that Indeston will appear around the planet's eastern cusp, but it won't be long – within the next thirty minutes."

"Are you able to determine the altitude at which Indeston is orbiting?" asked Lanson.

"I'll be able to give you an approximation in a few minutes, sir. Once I've checked the data."

Lanson glanced at the time, as if that would somehow tell him when the Ravanok was due to break lightspeed. The sphere would come, he was sure of it. With any luck, he'd be able to complete a rapid investigation of Indeston and then be on his way.

"Captain, I believe the facility is orbiting about a hundred kilometres beneath the planet's outer atmosphere," said Perry at last.

Lanson had already decided on his approach while he was waiting. "Lieutenant Abrams, we're going to Farun," he said. "Target an arrival place just above the planet's atmosphere."

Given the speed at which Abrams responded, it was clear he'd guessed the next order which would be coming his way. "Yes, sir. Coordinates entered. Two minutes and we'll enter lightspeed."

The seconds counted down, and Lanson tried to get a feel of what might be waiting for him at Indeston. His intuition was quiet, and, though he didn't usually make decisions based on gut feel, Lanson would have preferred a sense of what was coming.

After two minutes, the *Infinitar*'s propulsion hurled it into lightspeed.

FIFTEEN

"Run the scans," said Lanson, as soon as the sensor feeds resumed. "Find that space station."

"On it, sir."

Lanson held the warship motionless as he stared at the forward feeds. Planet Farun was a hostile place and its atmosphere contained numerous toxins in varying proportions. A wind – with a speed in excess of eight hundred kilometres per hour - blew continuously from north-west to south-east, and the dull colours which Lanson had noted earlier were now but a single shade of dirty yellow.

"Assuming the Aral wanted to keep Indeston hidden, they chose a good location for it," said Matlock.

Lanson was of the opinion that the universe was so expansive that mostly anywhere was a good hiding place. "The Aral didn't design any of their other Tier o facilities to orbit gas giants, Commander," he said. "And Dalvaron was in empty space."

"There's a reason for everything, sir," said Matlock, her eyes narrowed. "The Aral chose Farun."

"That they did," said Lanson. Maybe the reason was important, though he doubted it would have any bearing on the mission.

Twenty minutes went by, and the crew were silent, except for when they were providing updates on the warship's status. Lanson didn't like waiting at the best of times, and it required an effort to keep his muscles from tensing up. His eyes kept drifting towards the feeds, and the ever-changing movements of the planet's atmosphere. Far below, the pressure would be immense and even the solidity of the *Infinitar* would eventually succumb to the crushing gravity of the gas giant.

"Captain, I've located an object!" said Perry. "It's at the extremes of our sensor range."

"Indeston," said Lanson.

The object was huge, and it could be nothing other than the Aral space station. At a distance of almost a thousand kilometres, its outline was unclear in the murk, and Lanson couldn't grasp its overall shape.

"The space station is travelling at six-point-five-four kilometres per second, sir. It'll pass a hundred kilometres north of our position and at an altitude of minus three hundred kilometres," said Perry.

Lanson wasn't about to sit idly while Indeston came to him. He requested power from the engines and guided the *Infinitar* onto an intercept course with the space station. After a few seconds, the warship's sensor tech asserted its control over the atmospheric conditions and the target snapped into greater focus.

The design of Indeston was peculiar, though with a recognizable purpose. Viewed from the current angle, the space station was little more than a fifteen-kilometre-thick, rectangular slab, almost a hundred kilometres on its longest edge and with a width Lanson judged to be about forty kilometres. The top of the slab was flat – likely so it could function as a landing field – and with two ten-kilometre cubes at each end.

"No sign of any Aral warships," said Lanson. "Just like every other facility."

"Are those Galos cubes?" asked Matlock.

"I'm running output scans, Commander," said Abrams. "Done. The readings are low level and of a type I don't recognize. It's possible those *are* Galos cubes, but well-shielded by their casings."

"If a Singularity class was ever parked here, it's gone now," said Lanson.

He adjusted the *Infinitar*'s approach in order that he could see beneath the platform. No new features were revealed – the undersides of Indeston were completely flat.

"There must be some interior space," said Matlock. "Bays, working areas, and living quarters. What if there's a Singularity class inside? Maybe Indeston has internal shielding and it's preventing us from detecting the target vessel."

Lanson wasn't convinced, despite his eagerness to believe. "The Aral haven't shielded any of the other Singularity warships, Commander."

"We can't leave without finding out, sir."

"I wasn't thinking about leaving," said Lanson. "I was wondering how the hell we proceed from here. If the station comms won't respond, we can't request access."

"We should take a closer look at the platform, Captain."

Lanson nodded his agreement and guided the *Infinitar* closer to Indeston. Once the warship was directly over what he assumed was the orbital's upper side, he matched velocity while maintaining a distance of ten thousand metres.

Having encountered several examples of cutting-edge Aral construction, Lanson told himself he shouldn't be impressed by Indeston, and yet he couldn't fail to admire what this alien species had achieved. The *Infinitar* was huge, and yet its mass was dwarfed by that of the orbital.

"Scan for bay entrances," said Lanson, as he looked between the feeds.

The landing field below was solid alloy, and the lack of visible seams suggested that Indeston had been constructed in one piece elsewhere – an engineering feat in itself - rather than being brought here in parts and then assembled. Turning his attention to the four cubes – each clad in a much darker material than the main platform – Lanson felt sure they housed Galos tech. What role they'd originally played in the operation of the orbital, he didn't know.

"Uh, Captain, look what I just found," said Perry.

On one of the underside feeds, Lanson saw a cluster of six grey cubes – each about a metre in size – surrounding a larger cube made from a black material, which gleamed like polished obsidian. Cables linked each of the smaller cubes to the central one.

"Sagh'eld security breakers," said Lanson.

"Yes, sir," said Perry. "I'm not sure what that big cube is."

"Nothing we're going to appreciate, I'm sure," said Lanson. "It's with a bunch of security breakers, so its purpose is likely the same. Lieutenant Perry, scan for enemy warships."

"Yes, sir."

Lanson had been on edge before the discovery of the cubes and now his agitation stepped up a notch. The cubes had seemingly been abandoned on the landing field, about a quarter of the way along. Lanson wasn't fooled – the Sagh'eld wouldn't have left so much valuable hardware here without purpose.

"The short-range scans are clear, Captain," said Perry after a few moments. "I can expand the search volume, but the environmental conditions will prevent long-range detection of any hostiles."

"If we can't see them, they can't see us," said Lanson. "Do what you can, Lieutenant Perry. For once, we're in command of a vessel with better sensor tech than anything on a Sagh'eld warship."

"Yes, sir."

"What the hell are those security breakers doing here?" muttered Lanson.

"The Sagh'eld warship which deployed them might have been destroyed in an engagement with the Ixtar," said Matlock.

"In which case, there'd be a transport on the Indeston landing field," said Lanson.

"Maybe the Ravanok has been here. It took out the Sagh'eld warships at Tarai."

"That it did, Commander, and yet I was left with the impression that the destruction of the Sagh'eld was incidental to the Ravanok. The sphere wanted the *Infinitar*. It just happened to be bad luck for the enemy fleet."

Matlock grimaced and made no effort to argue. "In which case, the Sagh'eld warship which deployed those security breakers is either no longer here, or it's beyond the range of our sensors."

"What if the security breakers were successful?" mused Lanson. "That larger cube looks as if it's a new generation. Maybe it penetrated the Indeston security."

"In which case—" said Matlock.

Lanson nodded. "A Sagh'eld warship could be somewhere inside Indeston."

"I know I said we shouldn't abandon this place without searching for the Singularity class, but is this a fight we want?"

"We've got other places we could go, Commander," Lanson agreed. "However, Indeston is here and now."

"It's unlikely the target vessel is within the orbital, Captain."

"I know," said Lanson. "And yet I keep asking myself why was there a Singularity class at each of the other Tier o locations? So far, the data on our star charts has been accurate."

"What if the Sagh'eld have already stolen the target?" asked Matlock.

"Then we might be able to extract a record of when it happened from the Indeston computer systems."

"Then let's do it," said Matlock. "But we still have to figure out a way inside."

"Those security breakers must be interfaced with the orbital," said Lanson. "Either there's a physical port which is currently hidden from sight by the enemy hardware, or there's a short-range data receiver. Whichever it is, I should be able to connect to the Indeston systems."

"Are you planning to leave the *Infinitar*, Captain?"

"Not if I can avoid it, Commander. First, we'll bring our warship into close range to find out if its comms system will interface."

"And if not?"

"Then I'll head down in a shuttle. I'm the only one with Tier o access."

"Would you like me to order Sergeant Gabriel to one of our transports, sir?" asked Perry.

"Yes, do it," said Lanson.

With steady hands, he piloted the *Infinitar* vertically towards the Indeston landing field. At a thousand-metre altitude, Lanson brought the warship to a halt.

"Scan for receptors, Lieutenant Turner," he said.

"Running the scan. No receptors found."

"Let's get closer," said Lanson.

He reduced altitude yet further, until the lowest point of the *Infinitar*'s undersides were no more than a hundred metres above the platform.

"Scan again," he said.

"Scanning...no receptor found," said Turner. "No, wait! There was a flicker of a response. You'll have to take us lower, Captain."

"Lower it is," said Lanson through gritted teeth.

A short time later, he'd reduced the *Infinitar*'s altitude to only fifty metres. With the muscles in his forearms tight, Lanson held the warship stationary.

"Running the scan," said Turner. "Receptor found. Interface request accepted."

"What options do you have?" asked Lanson.

"I can request the opening of Bay 1, sir."

"Send the request."

"Request sent...and accepted."

The moment Lanson heard the confirmation, he lifted the *Infinitar* directly away from the Indeston landing field, and then brought it to a halt at a five-thousand-metre altitude.

Checking the underside feeds, he saw the dark line of a seam running the centre fifty thousand metres of the platform. Gradually, the bay doors opened, their size indicating the use of advanced technology to both move them and to keep them from collapsing beneath their own mass.

Lanson watched anxiously, wondering what he'd find within the Indeston main bay.

SIXTEEN

After a few seconds, the gap between the bay doors was wide enough that Lanson could see the floor, some ten kilometres below the opening. Any Sagh'eld in the bay would have already been alerted, though so far, he could see no sign of aliens.

"It looks as though there are some crates and vehicles at the far end of the bay, sir," said Turner.

"I've detected a spaceship, Captain!" said Lieutenant Perry urgently. "Crap, it's an Ex'Kaminar!"

The Ex'Kaminar was parked parallel to the platform's longest edge, and not far from the bay wall, which was the reason Perry hadn't spotted it immediately. With each passing second, more of the Sagh'eld battleship's flank was revealed.

"Damnit," said Lanson, though it was no longer a surprise to discover just how much progress the enemy were making in their efforts to acquire the Aral technology.

"Another damn battleship," said Matlock.

"I think we're just finding out how extensive their fleet is in comparison to our own, Commander," said Lanson. "They're halfway to defeating the Human Confederation and they aren't even trying."

"I have a weapons lock on the Ex'Kaminar, sir," said Matlock. "I'm waiting on your order to fire."

Lanson wasn't ready to give the order. He guided the *Infinitar* to one side of the opening, where it was out of the battleship's sensor arcs. "Lieutenant Abrams, scan for Galos emissions," said Lanson. "If we fire into that bay, I want to know that we aren't going to kill ourselves in the process."

"I've already run a scan of the visible area, Captain, and—"

Abrams was cut off by a shout from Turner. "Sir, the bay doors are closing again!"

"The Sagh'eld must have issued the command," said Lanson. "To keep us out."

"Should I target the security breakers, Captain?" asked Matlock. "Perhaps if they were destroyed, the Sagh'eld would lose their ability to control the doors."

Once again, Lanson was hesitant. The largest security breaker bore such a resemblance to a Galos cube, that he was wary about its potential to detonate.

Damn, the Aral tech is getting into my head. Not every cube is Galos.

"Lieutenant Abrams, scan those security breakers for Galos emissions," snapped Lanson.

"Scanning...they aren't Galos, Captain."

Lanson turned towards Matlock. "Destroy the security breakers, Commander."

"Yes, sir. One Avantar missile will do it."

The missile raced away and detonated against the Indeston landing field. Lanson didn't need confirmation that the targets were destroyed – there was no way they had survived the blast. He gave his attention to the bay doors, which were now almost closed.

"Let's take another look down there," said Lanson.

He piloted the *Infinitar* over the narrowing gap and brought the warship to a standstill, where the underside sensors had a view into the bay.

"The Ex'Kaminar is out sight again, Captain," said Turner. "I think I saw a shuttle go past the opening."

"Please confirm."

"Yes, sir, it was definitely a shuttle – a mid-size personnel transporter from the look of it."

"What's the plan, Captain?" asked Matlock.

"I'd like to destroy that battleship, Commander," said Lanson. "Lieutenant Abrams, were your scans of the bay conclusive?"

"I detected no Galos emissions, sir, but that doesn't mean there are no Galos cubes within the bay – they could be shielded."

"So we either take the gamble of bombarding the Ex'Kaminar while the doors are partially open and hope we don't set off an explosion, or we launch a limited attack on the enemy vessel to draw it from the bay," said Lanson.

"I doubt the Sagh'eld will be passive in this, sir," said Matlock. "I'd expect them to have their Thak cannons trained towards the bay doors, and it's certain the battleship will have repositioned."

An exchange of fire between opening doors was likely to be unpredictable, though at least the *Infinitar* would have the advantage of space in which to move. The worry was that the enemy retained the means to close the bay doors, in which case Lanson might be left with no option other than to blow a hole in the surface of Indeston.

"I'm bringing us close to the receptor again," he said.

"Should I launch our missiles at the Ex'Kaminar while it's still in the bay, Captain?" asked Matlock.

"Not immediately. We'll give the battleship a chance to exit the bay. If it stays put, we'll encourage it to leave."

"Yes, sir."

As Lanson piloted the *Infinitar* towards the receptor, he asked himself if he was doing the right thing. He was confident his warship could defeat the Ex'Kaminar, though at a likely cost of suffering damage in return. And yet, this was a Tier 0 site. Lanson didn't want to withdraw and allow the enemy to plunder whatever technology was available here at Indeston. This was, he told himself, about seeing the bigger picture, instead of focusing solely on recovering the final two Singularity vessels.

Having piloted the *Infinitar* down to a low altitude above the landing field, Lanson instructed Lieutenant Turner to issue a command to open the bay doors.

"The command is sent, Captain," she said.

Lanson pulled back on the controls and the *Infinitar* climbed away from the surface.

"Captain, I'm reading an energy flow through each of those four main cubes," said Abrams in warning. "The cubes are definitely shielded, but there's some leakage."

"What's the purpose of the energy?" asked Lanson sharply. He reached for the tactical, in case he needed to activate an ILT. "A weapon?"

"I don't know, Captain," said Abrams. "There's a—" He cut himself off. "The power readings have dropped back to zero. I don't know what that was about."

Lanson withdrew his hand from the tactical. He'd been hasty to believe the orbital was charging up a weapon. "The Sagh'eld might have cracked the security on the bay doors, but I can't imagine they'll have managed to override all the failsafes necessary to make a Tier 0 orbital attack a Tier 0 warship."

During the short conversation, the bay doors had opened

partway, and Lanson looked to see if the Ex'Kaminar had repositioned. The enemy vessel wasn't in view, and he cursed under his breath as he waited for it to be revealed.

"Where is it?" he muttered.

Soon, the opening was wide enough to accommodate the battleship, were its commanding officer of a mind to begin the engagement, and yet the enemy vessel remained hidden. Lanson piloted the *Infinitar* first one way and then the other, in order that its sensors could see deeper into the bay.

Eventually, the doors had opened enough that the sensors could gather a feed from almost every part of the bay. The Ex'Kaminar was no longer inside.

"Where the hell did it go?" asked Lanson, the adrenaline of anticipated combat already subsiding.

"The bay only occupies the central area of Indeston, Captain," said Turner. "It's possible that other bays exist beneath the cubes at each end of the platform. If so, there'd be plenty of room for them to accommodate a Sagh'eld battleship."

Lanson's mood was becoming increasingly foul. The Ex'Kaminar's crew clearly knew more about this Aral facility than he did, even though the alien scumbags lacked Tier o access to the hardware. This wasn't about Lanson's pride. If the Sagh'eld were making strides in their understanding of the Aral tech, it could only be bad news for humanity.

"Where did that transport go?" Lanson asked.

"I can't see it, Captain," said Turner. "If it's hiding near the bay ceiling, it'll be out of sight until we enter the bay."

Lanson wasn't ready to enter the bay yet, though he accepted it was a necessity. It seemed wisest to take stock before charging headlong into a possible engagement with an enemy warship.

The topside doors were fully open, and he spent a moment scanning the contents of the bay. Aside from the huge crates and vehicles he'd spotted earlier, Lanson saw indications that Indeston was a primary repair facility. Huge slabs of alloy were stacked in one corner and on the opposite side were dark cubes of different sizes.

"Tell me those are Rodos modules and not Galos cubes," said Lanson.

"They're definitely Rodos modules, Captain," said Abrams. "Enough of them to build two warships like the *Ragnar-3*."

"I wonder if Indeston was used for construction, rather than repair," said Lanson, reconsidering his thought from moments ago.

"All the equipment is there, Captain," said Abrams. "I'm sure the bay is fitted with the gravity field generators needed for both repair and construction."

"Maybe one of the Singularity vessels was built here," said Matlock.

"I was thinking the same thing myself," said Lanson. "But where is the warship now?"

"The records should be contained within the local data arrays, Captain," said Matlock. "Maybe there'll be receptors inside the bay we can use to remotely access them."

"We'll check it out," said Lanson. "We're entering the bay. If the Ex'Kaminar is visible in an adjacent bay, we will not engage. Lieutenant Abrams will continue his scans for evidence of Galos tech."

"Yes, sir, I'll do that."

Lanson didn't take the slow and steady approach. Instead, he dropped the *Infinitar* vertically into the bay at high velocity, decelerating at the last moment so that the vessel came to a halt with its undersides a thousand metres above the bay floor, and oriented lengthways.

"There is no sign of linking doors to other bays, Captain," said Lieutenant Perry after a few seconds.

"There was no sign of doors on the Baltol cube either," said Lanson.

"I'm running some additional scans to see if there's anything I missed, sir."

"I've located the transport, Captain," said Turner. "It's stationary on a platform near the ceiling directly ahead of us."

The alloy platform jutted out from the centre of the wall, and it was large enough to accommodate several transports. Right now, the Sagh'eld shuttle was parked adjacent to three smaller Aral craft, and room was left over for another couple of similarly sized vessels.

"I can't see any Sagh'eld troops, sir," said Turner. "It's possible they stayed on the shuttle, but they'd have to be suicidal to do that."

"I'm sure they've disembarked," said Lanson.

He felt the beginnings of unease. The Sagh'eld might well have abandoned the shuttle simply to escape into the depths of Indeston, but Lanson found himself wondering if the enemy had a specific goal.

Then there was the mystery of the apparently missing Ex'Kaminar. Lanson's disquiet increased. Whatever was happening at Indeston, he needed to get to the bottom of it, and quickly.

SEVENTEEN

"Captain, the molecular scan has not detected the presence of exit doors from this bay," said Perry. "There again, the high-precision scans failed at Baltol."

"I don't believe the linking doors we're looking for exist," said Lanson, who'd just that moment reached a conclusion about what had happened to the Sagh'eld battleship. "Lieutenant Abrams – could those power readings you obtained from the topside cubes have been an indication that Indeston was preparing to send the Ex'Kaminar into void travel?"

"If we assume those cubes are enormous Galos power generators, then there's every chance you're right, Captain."

"And if the Ex'Kaminar was transported elsewhere, might the same have happened to the Singularity warship we believe was either constructed or stored here at Indeston?" mused Lanson.

"We need access to the data arrays," said Matlock. "If we can obtain the flight records, we'll be able to follow the target vessel to its destination."

"Lieutenant Turner, see if you can interface with the orbital," said Lanson.

"I'm running a receptor sweep, Captain," said Turner. "No receptors found."

"That can't be right," said Lanson. "How the hell would a spaceship in this bay communicate with personnel on the orbital if there are no receptors?"

"I think I've found the answer to that, sir," said Perry. "Look at this."

One of the underside feeds was targeted on an area at one end of the bay near the floor. Here, the metal was charred and uneven around a shallow, one-metre crater.

"That's too small to be a missile strike," said Lanson. "It looks more like the result of an explosive charge."

"Yes, Captain, and the same thing happened at the opposite end of the bay."

"The Sagh'eld destroyed the receptors before the Ex'Kaminar entered void travel," said Lanson. "They must have identified the *Infinitar* as an Aral warship and assumed we would have access to the Indeston systems."

"We should be able to access the data arrays from a console within the orbital, Captain," said Massey.

"I'm sure you're right, Lieutenant, but that would require a deployment. It's a delay we can't afford." Lanson had another thought. "I'll bet the Sagh'eld from that transport have been ordered to secure the main control station for the bay."

"There'll be at least one other control station," said Turner. "We don't have to be in the main station to access the flight records."

"If the Sagh'eld know what they're doing, they'll be able to initiate a lockdown of the bay," said Abrams. "Once the emergency protocols are in place, they might be able to shut down the secondary control stations."

Lanson was reluctant to believe that the Sagh'eld had the knowledge to operate the orbital, and even more reluctant to accept that they might have access to the Aral systems. Then, he remembered the new gen security breaker on the landing field above, and suddenly he was not so sure anymore.

"Lieutenant Perry, get on the comms to Sergeant Gabriel," said Lanson. "Find out if he's ready to deploy."

"He is, Captain," said Perry after a few moments. "The Sergeant has the Ezin-Tor with him, and he asks if that's a problem."

Lanson remembered warning Gabriel that he shouldn't rely on the Aral cannon. However, if the soldier wanted to take it with him, Lanson wasn't going to stand in the way.

"It's no problem at all," he said.

"I'll let Sergeant Gabriel know," said Perry. "And should I order him to launch the shuttle?"

"Not yet," said Lanson. "Commander Matlock – destroy that Sagh'eld transport. If the enemy left a crew on board, I don't want them giving our soldiers a hard time."

"Yes, sir. Forward Avantar cluster 1, tube 1, locked and launched."

The missile sped across the bay, leaving an orange trail through the semi darkness. A flash of plasma followed and Lanson was sure the Avantar packed enough of a punch to destroy the Sagh'eld shuttle five times over.

When the initial blast faded, only glowing wreckage was left, and the force of the explosion had pushed the remnants of the shuttle up against the far bay wall. Lanson peered closely at the feed, worried in case the missile strike had inadvertently blocked the exit. He couldn't be sure one way or another.

"Captain, we've received a shutdown command!" said Abrams.

"Shit!" said Lanson. "Can you reject the command?"

"Negative, sir. It's come from the Indeston station, and we will lose control of the *Infinitar* in the next few seconds."

"Lieutenant Perry – order Sergeant Gabriel to deploy immediately!" yelled Lanson.

"Yes, sir. Order given and acknowledged."

One-by-one, Lanson was frozen out of the warship's onboard systems. He tried desperately to regain control, but there was no obvious way – if a way existed at all – to reject the shutdown command. Cursing, Lanson crashed his fist onto the top of the console.

"Sergeant Gabriel's shuttle has entered the bay," said Perry. "I am not frozen out of the comms – what order should I give to our soldiers, sir?"

"Tell them to locate the main bay control station and rescind the shutdown command," said Lanson. "Unless we can figure something out before they get there."

"Yes, sir."

Lanson was angry, though he kept it from his voice. "We shouldn't have fired that missile at the Sagh'eld shuttle," he said. "The orbital issued the shutdown code to ensure we couldn't wreck the bay from the inside."

"You have Tier 0 access to the Aral systems – can't you delete the shutdown code, Captain?" asked Perry.

"I might be able to do so if I wasn't locked out of my console," said Lanson. "Sergeant Gabriel will have to rescind the code from the bay control station."

"The Sergeant doesn't have Tier 0 access, Captain," said Turner. "Will the control station accept his instructions?"

"All the soldiers are on Tier 1," said Lanson. "I doubt the original commanding officer of the bay was higher than a Tier 2, so Sergeant Gabriel shouldn't have any access problems."

"If a lower-tier officer is able to rescind a Tier 0 shutdown code, wouldn't that be a security problem?" asked Perry.

Lanson didn't want to get into a discussion on the subject, particularly since he didn't know the ins and outs of the Aral security procedures. He took a stab at the answer anyway. "I'd guess that only the Indeston station's control systems can issue the shutdown code, and that the bay's main control station has elevated privileges to remove the code when certain conditions are met."

Perry didn't say anything else and Lanson was glad, since he was finding it hard to keep on top of his anger. He turned to his console. The sensor arrays were still online, though Lanson had no control over them. Consequently, the feeds were stuck in their last positions, which wasn't too much of a problem since they were already pointing in the directions where they were most useful.

Sergeant Gabriel's shuttle was visible on one of the forward feeds, and he was preparing to land on the far end of the platform from the wrecked Sagh'eld transport. Seconds later, the shuttle set down, one of the flank doors opened and soldiers jumped the short distance to the ground. Without hesitation, they ran towards the centre of the platform, where the exit from the bay was most likely found.

SERGEANT EVANDER GABRIEL'S feet thudded onto the platform outside the shuttle. Indeston's vast bay was evenly illuminated to a low level, though the source of the light wasn't evident, as if it were exuded by the walls. The vista fell somewhere between terrifying and awe-inspiring, though neither emotion was enough to slow Gabriel as he dashed along the platform.

Several Aral shuttles – angular vessels with low profiles - were parked here, and a red glow on the alloy about eighty metres away marked the position of the Sagh'eld transport. Intel on the exit's location was non-existent, and Gabriel hoped it wouldn't be hidden by the burning hot wreckage.

As he ran, Gabriel couldn't stop himself from looking to his left. The *Infinitar* was a long way distant, and yet its size was unmistakeable. Although the warship wasn't complete, Gabriel could imagine how threatening it would look once the final two pieces were in place.

Approaching the remains of the Sagh'eld transport, he came to a halt. The vessel had been well and truly obliterated by the Avantar missile. Pieces of debris had been hurled against the adjacent shuttles, while the largest piece of wreckage could hardly even be described as a shell. To the left and the right, the walls were charred from the explosion, as was the ground nearby.

"Any sign of an exit, Captain?" asked Corporal Hennessey, her face a peculiar shade of red behind the visor of her combat suit as the shimmering heat from the transport bathed her in crimson.

"I can't see one," said Gabriel.

He breathed through his nostrils while he scanned the visible parts of the bay wall. In the past, the weight of his loadout would have left him panting after an eighty-metre sprint, but now his breathing was even and his heart rate hardly elevated. Neither did he feel the additional weight of the Ezin-Tor cannon slung across his back, which he'd brought to accompany his Aral rifle.

Gabriel was still unsure if he'd made the right choice in bringing the Ezin-Tor. The gun was shockingly powerful – perhaps too much so for this mission – and it came with side effects he didn't understand. It wasn't too late for him to return the weapon to the shuttle, but he had a feeling that it might come in handy.

"Find the exit," said Gabriel, indicating that his squad should search in both directions.

The soldiers spread out, while Gabriel approached the Sagh'eld shuttle, with Private Mitch Davison alongside.

The heat coming from the wreckage would have burned them both alive had they not been wearing their combat suits. As it was, Gabriel was able to come almost into touching distance before the temperature warning on his HUD began flashing and a gentle alarm chimed in his earpiece. The bay was in vacuum, so no sounds of distressed alloy carried from the remains of the shuttle.

Gabriel might have once found the situation peculiar, but after so many years on the frontline, this almost counted as normal.

"No sign of bodies," said Davison, peering into the ruptured hull.

"I doubt there'd be anything left of them to see, Private," said Gabriel. "Besides, we both know those alien bastards exited the shuttle before it was destroyed. They'll be waiting for us."

"Sergeant, over here!" said Corporal Ziegler on the squad comms.

Gabriel jogged over to where Ziegler was standing at the bay wall, about twenty metres away and not far from the nose of an Aral transport.

"What have you found, Corporal?"

"An access panel," said Ziegler.

The soldier indicated a section of the wall which was covered in char from the Sagh'eld shuttle. Ziegler had wiped a small area clear, revealing the access panel which had been hidden beneath.

"Good spot," said Gabriel.

"I scrubbed off some more of the char over here, Sergeant,

and I found the door seams," Ziegler continued, pointing to his left.

Gabriel nodded in acknowledgement. Then, he ordered the soldiers to return from the search, and briefly addressed them.

"We're looking for the main bay control station," he said. "We don't know where it is, and we don't have a map." Gabriel thumbed over his shoulder. "Before it was blown up, that Sagh'eld shuttle would have been able to carry two hundred or more enemy soldiers in its passenger bay. Those soldiers are now waiting for us somewhere beyond this door."

"They have the numbers, but we have the exploding bullets," said Private Denny Galvan.

"Let's not pretend it's going to be easy," said Gabriel. He set his gaze on Private Stacie Wolf, who was carrying the squad's comms booster pack. "Private Wolf, I'm leaving you to deal with the comms to the *Infinitar*. Unless I have something I need to say directly to Captain Lanson."

"Yes, sir."

Comms were often a problem on missions like this, but fortunately, Gabriel and his squad had been able to interface with the Indeston internal comms systems, which would allow them to maintain contact even if there was a lot of metal in the way of the transmissions. It was a positive start.

Wary of an ambush, Gabriel waited until the soldiers were in position. Then, he placed his hand on the access panel and a door slid into its left-hand recess. Corporal Ziegler was on the other side of the door and, when it opened, he poked his head around the corner.

"An airlock. It's clear."

Gabriel smiled thinly. The easy part of the mission was over and now it was time to start climbing the slope.

"I'll go first," he said. "To make sure there're no Sagh'eld waiting in ambush."

"If I were a Sagh'eld scumbag, I'd be watching this entrance, Sergeant," said Corporal Hennessey. "You'll make an easy target."

"You're right," said Gabriel.

If he'd been in command of a full company, he too would have left at least a couple of squads to guard the entrance. Unfortunately, this was the direction in which the Sagh'eld had gone, and Gabriel couldn't afford the time to go exploring for other exits from the bay.

This was an occasion which called for the use of overwhelming force. "Private Castle, you're coming with me," said Gabriel.

"Yes, sir."

Gabriel looked at the Aral rifle in his hand. It was an effective weapon, but he was carrying a better one. Shrugging the Ezin-Tor off his shoulder, he slung the rifle across his back instead. The hand cannon had a wide barrel and plenty of heft. It was a mean bastard of a weapon and no mistake.

The preparations were done. Beckoning Private Castle to follow, Gabriel stepped into the airlock.

EIGHTEEN

The airlock space was designed to accommodate personnel only, though it wasn't small enough to be claustrophobic. Gabriel positioned himself to one side of the exit and indicated that Castle should stand farther back. The soldier's rocket launcher was balanced on his shoulder, and the business end was aimed towards the exit.

"Be ready to fire as soon as the door opens," said Gabriel.

"There'd better not be a wall dead ahead, Sergeant."

Gabriel doubted the airlock exit would be facing a wall, but he was nonetheless concerned about what he'd find on the other side. Neither Castle's launcher, nor the Ezin-Tor were designed for use in enclosed spaces.

A panel next to the exit would begin the pressurisation and Gabriel touched it with his fingertips. The entrance door closed, blocking his sight of the worried expressions worn by the members of his squad who remained in the bay. A red light glowed on the panel and Gabriel watched it closely, ready to act when it turned green. He held the Ezin-Tor in a tight grip and kept the barrel pointing at the exit door.

The light went green, and the door slid open at once. Castle was near the rear corner of the airlock and he stepped across, the coils of his launcher whining.

"Rocket out," he said calmly, before springing back towards the side wall. "Hostiles sighted."

"What're we facing, Private?" asked Gabriel, keeping himself out of sight. He heard a thump of detonation, and, by the sound, he judged that the rocket had exploded forty metres from the doorway.

"It's a big space, Sergeant. Maybe used for storage. At least three Sagh'eld were hiding behind a bunch of crates. Those ones are dead."

Gabriel cursed inwardly. He'd expected to find passages beyond the airlock – somewhere confined where a single rocket blast would clear the way. An open space offered much more of a challenge.

Although surprise was already gone, Gabriel had another trick up his sleeve in the form of the Ezin-Tor. He glanced once into the storage area. It was more open than he'd expected, with an eight-metre ceiling and a floorspace only sparsely occupied with one-metre crates in low stacks and a few loading vehicles. The right-hand wall was only a few metres away, and the far wall was a long way off. A glowing patch on the floor indicated where Castle's rocket had struck.

In this single glance, Gabriel saw no other Sagh'eld, though he heard the clunking of several gauss slugs striking the solid alloy walls outside the airlock. Given that he had an almost complete view of the right-hand wall, Gabriel was convinced the shots were coming from the left, and that was where he would have positioned his own troops.

"What next, Sergeant?" said Castle.

The choices were simple – retreat through the airlock and

fail the mission, or accept the risk of pressing on. Gabriel picked the latter.

"What next?" he asked, with a tight smile. Gabriel raised the Ezin-Tor. "This is what's next."

Hoping his reactions were better than those of the Sagh'eld, Gabriel stepped halfway from the airlock, so that only his right-hand side was showing, along with the Ezin-Tor. The storage room floor to the left wasn't any more utilised than the parts which Gabriel had already seen through the airlock door, though it still offered the enemy many places to hide.

Luck was on Gabriel's side. Straightaway, he spotted movement behind a row of crates. A slight adjustment was enough to bring the Ezin-Tor onto target and he fired the gun. The whump of discharge was instantly followed by the appearance of a huge blast of dark energy centred on the enemy positions.

Gabriel remembered the power of the Ezin-Tor, but he was nonetheless caught off guard. Throwing himself into the airlock and out of sight, he hoped he hadn't misjudged too badly.

The dark fire didn't enter the airlock, but the force of the blast did, along with a deep rumbling that had a strangely unnatural edge. Gabriel felt the shockwave like a kick in the guts and he reeled like his brains had been scrambled in a mixer. He recovered quickly and with no lingering ill-effects, which he put down to his Galos-affected body and the fact that he was partly shielded by the airlock walls.

"Damn," said Castle, shaking his head. "That sucked."

"I might not be done yet, Private," said Gabriel.

Returning to the airlock exit, he quickly leaned out far enough that he could see the left-hand side of the room. Ducking back, he listened for of ricochets. None came. Gabriel repeated the lean-out-and-back routine, only this time he left himself in view for a fraction of a second longer. No gauss projectiles struck either Gabriel or the walls nearby.

"Clear?" asked Castle.

"Maybe," said Gabriel. "If so, it won't be for long."

He couldn't afford a stalemate, nor could he delay here in the airlock. Assuming the stationed enemy guard were all dead, others would soon arrive. There'd been plenty of time for the Sagh'eld to report the attack.

Once again, Gabriel stepped into partial sight, holding the Ezin-Tor ready. He scanned the room for movement. The storage room was still and quiet. Gabriel's eyes were drawn to the place where his cannon shot had detonated. The explosion had created a fifteen-metre-diameter crater in the floor and one of similar size in the ceiling. Particles of dust fell constantly, and Gabriel guessed the alloys were still disintegrating.

"How the hell did a blast that size not kill us?" asked Castle, who'd positioned himself so he could also see outside the airlock.

"From what I've seen both of the Galos and the Ezin-Tor, the explosions they create don't channel in the way we'd expect." Gabriel didn't quite know what he was trying to say, but he continued anyway. "As if the blast spheres have a predefined magnitude that isn't affected by the place in which the detonation occurs."

Castle shrugged like it didn't matter. "Alien shit."

By now, Gabriel was halfway confident that there were no more Sagh'eld troops in the storage room. He'd left the squad channel open, so the other soldiers didn't need filling in on the details. It was time for them to enter the airlock.

"Get your asses inside," said Gabriel. "Private Castle and I will wait in the storage area."

Exiting the airlock, Gabriel sprinted towards a gravity loader about twenty metres left out of the doorway. He reached the vehicle without incident and took cover behind its high flanks. Two steps led into a basic cabin, with a single seat and control sticks. The cabin was open-sided, allowing Gabriel a view across the room. He counted three visible exits, with no indication as to which direction the bulk of the Sagh'eld troops had gone.

"Do you think the enemy will launch a counterattack, Sergeant?" asked Castle.

Gabriel had been working on the assumption that a counterattack was inevitable, but now he'd been asked the question, he was no longer so sure. If the Sagh'eld had access to the Indeston internal monitors, they'd know they faced only a small attacking force. On the other hand, if the enemy were in the dark about the numbers they faced, it would make sense for them to sit back, rather than split their forces.

"It's a hard one to call," said Gabriel.

He realised he'd been approaching the mission all wrong and he wasn't too proud to admit it to himself. The target was the main bay control room, but given the likely disparity in numbers, it didn't make any sense to attack the Sagh'eld without first gaining the intel needed to balance the scales.

Having allowed circumstances to dictate his actions, Gabriel cursed at himself for nearly falling into the trap. He was too experienced – too *old* damnit – to make that kind of mistake.

Private Castle was far more perceptive than he let on, and he was watching Gabriel closely.

"Change of plan, Sergeant?"

Gabriel nodded once. "Change of plan," he confirmed.

"We're exiting the airlock, sir," said Corporal Ziegler on the squad comms.

"Find cover quickly," said Gabriel.

"Which way are we going, Sergeant?"

"We're calling left out of this room *west* and that's the way we're going," said Gabriel.

"Is that the way to the main bay control room?" asked Private Rocky Chan.

"I hope not," said Gabriel.

"Sir?"

"Every one of us has Tier 1 access to the Aral systems," said Gabriel. "That gives us the same authority as an admiral or whatever the Aral called their highest-ranking officers. It'll certainly allow us to download a map of this facility and to obtain a live stream from the internal monitors."

"So we're looking for a console room," said Corporal Hennessey.

"That's right, Corporal. Keep your fingers crossed that the western exit will take us to one, rather than straight into the arms of a hundred Sagh'eld troops."

Gabriel broke from the cover of the gravity loader and sprinted towards the western wall. The few crates on this side of the room would offer scant cover, so he ran hard, keeping his eyes on the western exit. Belatedly, Gabriel noticed he was still carrying the Ezin-Tor. If he was obliged to make a snap shot at anything opening the door ahead, he'd likely kill himself in the process.

"Stay left, Sergeant," said Private Davison. "I've got you covered, but you're running into my line of sight."

A surge of pride caught Gabriel unawares - he should have known his squad would have his back.

"Much appreciated, Private," said Gabriel, changing course so that he wouldn't foul Davison's aim.

A few seconds later, Gabriel reached the western wall, twenty metres south of the exit door. He swiftly changed weapons so that the Aral rifle was his primary and the Ezin-Tor was slung across his back.

Given the pressure of the situation, Gabriel was obliged to take liberties with his normally considered approach. He advanced towards the western exit while the soldiers were still advancing across the room. Giving them only a moment to prepare, Gabriel activated the door panel.

"Looks clear, Sergeant," said Private Wolf, who had the best view through the doorway.

Gabriel glanced around the corner into a passage ending at a closed door about fifty metres away. He saw two other closed doors in the northern wall.

"Risky," said Corporal Ziegler, slowing to a halt on the opposite side of the doorway.

"Isn't it always?" said Gabriel.

He'd been in positions like this many times, and he knew the longer he delayed, the deeper the claws of doubt would sink into him.

"I'm going in," said Gabriel.

He sprinted into the passage, but rather than continue to the end, he stopped at the second closed door in the right-hand wall. Gabriel wasn't looking for a confrontation with the enemy – yet – and his current goal was to find a security console that would allow him access to the Indeston monitors. Behind this door, he suspected he'd find a room, rather than a passage.

A thump of his fist on the access panel had the door open. At the end of a short passage, a second, closed, door blocked his sight. Still confident this would lead to a room, Gabriel dashed to the inner control panel and operated it the moment his hand was within range.

When the door opened, Gabriel discovered that a square room, ten metres along each wall, lay beyond. A circular console in the middle of the floor had stations for three, and the lights on its top panel were illuminated at a low level.

"Clear?" asked Corporal Ziegler who'd advanced to join him.

"Looks like," said Gabriel.

A sweep of the room took only seconds and confirmed that no Sagh'eld were lying in wait.

"Corporal Hennessey, check out the first room," said Gabriel on the comms.

He was wary about summoning his entire squad into the corridor, but the main storage room was too large for them to hold, and besides, the soldiers would be better off out of sight. Ignoring the console for the moment, Gabriel waited until Hennessey had confirmed that the first door in the passage also led to a room.

"Everyone into the corridor," said Gabriel. "Watch the two exits and let's hope the Sagh'eld are elsewhere."

With the order given, he turned his attention to the Aral console. Gabriel had seen enough of the alien hardware by now that he had a good idea of how it was operated. He brought the device out of sleep and logged on without a problem.

If luck was on their side, Gabriel and his squad would soon be much-better placed to deal with the enemy.

NINETEEN

Gabriel soon discovered that, on this occasion, his luck was mixed. The console allowed him to download a map of the entire facility, which he installed into his suit databanks and then transmitted to the *Infinitar*. It came as a welcome surprise to learn that the interior of Indeston was less complex than the other Aral facilities Gabriel had explored. The orbital contained three bays – the *Infinitar* being in the largest – and numerous other cavernous spaces, presumably used for storage.

Aside from the bays and the storage facilities, the personnel areas were relatively limited, reinforcing the obvious conclusion that Indeston was primarily intended for construction, repair and resupply, rather than research and development.

Having downloaded the map, Gabriel sought and gained access to the orbital's internal monitors. The Indeston security systems were currently aware of 235 life forms in addition to the human soldiers. When Gabriel overlaid the enemy positions onto the facility map, he noted the Sagh'eld were clustered in an area less than a hundred metres away – when measured in a straight line.

Zooming the map, he spent some time familiarising himself with the enemy defences. More than half of the Sagh'eld were gathered in a large, square room – a place the map indicated was the main bay control station. The three approaches to this room comprised two passages, each of which went north-to-south, but on opposite sides of the control station. From these passages, side corridors led to the target area.

The third approach was an airlift, which stopped at eight other levels, and gave direct access to the control station. None of the Sagh'eld were in the lift or stationed on the levels above or below, which meant the enemy were either not expecting an attack from that direction, or they believed they had it fully covered with the soldiers in the main control station. Most likely, they had the lift doors jammed open so it wouldn't respond to being called from elsewhere.

"Those corridors are well defended," said Corporal Hennessey. "The Sagh'eld are spread through the side rooms, and that'll make it hard to take them out with explosives."

"And they're sure to have rocket soldiers and grenades of their own," said Gabriel. "We don't have the numbers to assault the enemy defences."

Gabriel curled his lip angrily. He and his soldiers had been given a task they had little hope of accomplishing. It was understandable why Captain Lanson had given the order to deploy, but the odds of success were worse than terrible.

"Is this orbital fitted with automated defence systems, Sergeant?" asked Corporal Ziegler. "If so, they could do the job for us."

"If they exist, they aren't accessible from this console," said Gabriel. "Besides, I didn't see any ceiling guns on our way here."

He continued studying the base map, aware that he couldn't

spend forever looking for a solution that might not exist. At some point, Gabriel knew he'd need to make a choice between ordering a suicidal attack on the enemy, or withdrawing to the *Infinitar* and letting Captain Lanson deal with the situation.

Fear of failure vied with reality in Gabriel's head and he became progressively angrier at the thought of having to run back to the warship with his tail between his legs.

Too much straight-line thinking.

The thought was enough to stir up his brain, and an idea came. Using the facility map, Gabriel traced a route through the orbital to a place from which he might just be able to launch a surprise attack on the enemy – with a little help from the Ezin-Tor.

"Listen up," he said on the squad channel. "I have a plan, and we're going to put it into action."

The details didn't take long to convey. Like the best of plans, the outline was simple and easily understood.

"Corporal Hennessey, you stay here with Private Chan. When I give the order, you'll use this console to remote lock the doors to the control station."

"Yes, sir."

Gabriel didn't delay any longer. He exited the console room and turned west along the passage. From the Indeston security monitors, he knew that no Sagh'eld lay beyond the next door. Even so, the habits of a lifetime were hard to break, and, once the door was open, he performed a visual sweep of the room. Four console stations were installed here, equally placed around the room. It was quiet.

Darting inside, Gabriel headed directly for the northern exit, though he took care to check behind the consoles as he went. He glanced at the map on his HUD again. A passage beyond this door would lead to a large open space which was directly above the main bay control station. A mere five metres of alloy separated the upper and the lower rooms.

Having opened the door, Gabriel glanced along the passage. It was empty.

"You should be more trusting of the security monitors, Sergeant," Private Wolf suggested.

"Do you remember how often control of the security monitors changed hands on Dalvaron, Private?" asked Gabriel.

"Maybe once or twice," said Wolf, the tone of her voice indicating she'd conceded the point.

Gabriel smiled without humour. "That's why I'm careful."

He entered the passage and sprinted to the end. At the far door, Gabriel nodded once to Corporal Ziegler and then struck the door panel a side-fisted blow.

As expected, a large room lay beyond the opening. Dozens of two-operator consoles were arranged concentrically around a much larger console in the centre. For several seconds, Gabriel watched and listened. The only sound was a low humming from the hardware, and the room was still.

"I'll go right," said Gabriel.

Ziegler nodded that he'd go left. The two of them darted into the room, and the rest of the squad followed. Soon, Gabriel was content that the room was empty, and he instructed the soldiers to watch the three other exits while he considered how best to enact his plan.

"Like you told us, this room is directly above the main control room, Sergeant," said Corporal Ziegler, leaning against the central console, with one foot resting on a chair. "A couple of Ezin-Tor shots targeted at the floor close to the north-east or north-west corners should create an opening above the enemy."

"It's the hardware in the control station I'm worried about, Corporal," said Gabriel.

He cursed. The situation had changed since he'd formulated his plan. A dozen of the enemy had now moved from the northern end of the room below – which was the farthest distance from the control console – and were now at the southern end, presumably in positions of cover. Killing those Sagh'eld with explosives was out of the question, since the risk of damaging the hardware was too great, meaning that a clean victory would be especially hard to attain.

The difficulties weren't lost on Ziegler. "If any of us get hit, the Galos will ensure we heal in no time."

"We can't rely on it happening, Corporal," said Gabriel. "What if the benefits we picked up on Cornerstone wear off after a time?"

Even as he said the words, Gabriel admitted to himself that the effects of the Galos were as strong as ever. He could run flat-out without needing to stop, and his muscles were able to bear the weight of his loadout without a hint of fatigue.

"If we don't take risks, this might be the end of the road, Sergeant," said Ziegler.

Gabriel didn't need reminding. There could be no holding back if the mission was to be a success.

"We'll do whatever it takes," he said. "Same as always."

"I figure we already died once on Scalos," said Ziegler with a grin. "What harm will it do if it happens again?"

Gabriel smiled in response. Swapping the Aral gauss rifle for the Ezin-Tor, he gave new orders to the squad. Not one of the soldiers objected, though they all knew what was being asked of them. Perhaps the worst wouldn't come to pass, though Gabriel doubted he'd get his wish.

The time to act had come. As one, the soldiers sprinted towards the south-west corner of the room, which was the farthest place from Gabriel's target, and with consoles behind which they could take cover.

Gabriel wasn't so lucky. Had he followed the others, his

shooting angle would have diminished more than he was comfortable with, owing to the distance. Consequently, he chose a position not far from the north-west corner, where he could stand on top of a console and fire the Ezin-Tor directly into the floor of the room.

Once everyone was ready, Gabriel climbed onto one of the consoles and looked east across the room to his target point about forty metres away. The floor was only just visible.

"Ready," said Gabriel, trying not to think about the shock-wave from the discharge in the storage room. This time, the blast wouldn't be quite so close.

Taking a deep breath, he fired the Ezin-Tor and then leapt behind the console without waiting to view the outcome. The room darkened and the shockwave from the detonation swept outwards. Hunkered down in cover, Gabriel thought he heard the shrieking of tearing metal accompanying the deep thumping sound of the blast – a sound which had the same not-quite-real quality as the last shot he'd taken. He felt the shockwave like the crashing of a wave on an angry shore, and the movement of air was savage and howling. Sheltered by the console, Gabriel was uninjured.

He didn't wait longer than a few seconds. The moment the air had stilled, Gabriel pushed himself upright and then clambered back onto the console. The room to the east was substantially affected by the Ezin-Tor blast. A huge crater had been created in the floor, with a matching one in the ceiling. The consoles around the crater's rim had either disintegrated completely or had been hurled against the walls, where they'd crumbled into pieces.

In the middle of the room, a ragged chunk had been taken out of the main console, while other consoles – farther from the centre of the explosion – had been torn from their fixings and thrown outwards. Dust swirled in the air and failing alloys sighed as they collapsed.

Remembering that the Ezin-Tor had made a crater five metres deep in the storage room, Gabriel was confronted by the decision he'd known was coming – to either fire a second shot, or to cross the room and check the crater to see if it had penetrated the main bay control room. From here atop the console, he couldn't be sure if the first discharge had been enough.

Screw it.

"I'm taking a second shot," said Gabriel.

The devastation caused by the first explosion ensured he had a clear view of where he was aiming, and he fired the Ezin-Tor into the side of the crater. Just like last time, Gabriel jumped down and kept low.

With fewer consoles in the room, he was fearful this shock-wave would cause him greater harm than the last one. The blast rumbled and the overpressured air swept across the room like a hurricane. A heavy object crashed into the far side of the console and Gabriel felt the device shudder with the impact. He curled up and wondered if he'd misjudged by taking the second shot. Other debris – dark pieces and fast moving – sped overhead, striking the wall with a sound like shattering clods of earth.

As heavy particles of disintegrating metal rattled down on him from above, Gabriel was happy to accept that the worst had passed and that he was neither dead, nor injured.

"Report," he said on the squad channel.

"I was about to request the same from you, Sergeant," said Corporal Ziegler. "All of us here in the south-west are hunky-dory."

"Glad to hear it," said Gabriel, with relief.

When he stood, dust fell away from his suit. He glanced down at the Ezin-Tor. The gun was an object that inspired both awe, and no small amount of fear within him. At the extents of his hearing, he thought he could hear the whining of its Galos power unit. The weapon had produced the same sound back on Ravrol when he'd fired it repeatedly within a short space of time, and Gabriel didn't want to think too much about how the gun had also caused him and those around him to fade out, as if they were dislocated from reality.

Distracted for only a moment by these thoughts, Gabriel strode through the wreckage towards the now much-larger crater near the north-eastern corner. The bottom of the crater wasn't yet visible, but he was sure the twin Ezin-Tor blasts had done enough.

Now it was time to face the Sagh'eld.

TWENTY

The sides of the double crater were almost smooth, as if the alloy had been scooped out with a giant spoon. A thick layer of dust slithered out of sight, like sand through an hourglass. When Gabriel made it to the edge of the crater, he noted the steepness of the sides and the seven-metre-wide opening into the room below. He judged that the first Ezin-Tor shot would have been sufficient, though it was too late to take back the second.

"Corporal Hennessey, it's time to lock the doors to the bay control room," said Gabriel, not taking his eyes from the room below.

"Yes, sir," said Hennessey. "The locks are in place."

The size of the opening was such that Gabriel could see the control station's eastern and northern walls. Sagh'eld corpses – or at least the remains of them – were numerous, and they'd been reduced to burnt lumps, or smears of carbon. Evidently, much of the energy from the second Ezin-Tor blast had channelled into the room, killing many of the enemy soldiers.

"Corporal Ziegler, check if anything's visible from the far side of the crater," said Gabriel.

"Yes, sir," said Ziegler, beginning his run around the rim and taking care not to step too close to the edge.

"Private Castle, you join him."

"Yes, sir."

Gabriel checked the map on his HUD. The Ezin-Tor had done a number on the Sagh'eld, killing them all except for a dozen to the south of the room. These enemy troops hadn't moved from their positions of cover behind the primary control console. Killing them without wrecking the hardware was going to be tough.

"I can only see corpses, Sergeant," said Ziegler. "I reckon the command console is ten metres beyond my sight range."

Gabriel had no doubt the enemy soldiers would be staying low and watchful, as they waited for the inevitable assault. Clearing them out would inevitably lead to casualties among the squad.

Something caught Gabriel's eye. Turning, he hurried towards the central console, which had been struck by two Ezin-Tor blasts, resulting in a large portion of its mass disintegrating.

"What's up, Sergeant?" asked Ziegler.

Gabriel didn't respond immediately. Running around to the intact part of the console – which had been partly shielded from the explosions – he discovered that it remained operational. He attempted to log in and his credentials were accepted.

"The hardware doesn't break easily," said Gabriel. "And the bay control console below us is even larger than this one."

"You're planning to fire the Ezin-Tor into the control room?" asked Ziegler.

"That or a rocket," said Gabriel, returning to the others.

He stared at the sides of the crater. They were steep and Gabriel doubted a controlled descent was possible, even had there been no dust clinging to the metal. As it was, anyone starting down was on a one-way ticket to the hard floor below. Gabriel sent a couple of pings from his helmet sensor.

"It's four metres from the lowest edge of the crater to the bottom," he said.

"What're you thinking, Sergeant?" asked Ziegler, his eyes narrowed, like he'd guessed that Gabriel was about to do something brave, stupid, or both.

"I'm thinking that we're running out of time," said Gabriel.

He hurried around the crater's edge and stopped at the north-east corner, near where Ziegler was standing. For a few seconds, Gabriel stared at his HUD, trying to lock the exact positions of everything into his head. The distances were tight, but he reckoned he might just make it – assuming the fall didn't kill him.

"I'm going to drop in on our Sagh'eld friends," said Gabriel, patting the barrel of the Ezin-Tor. "If this goes south, don't let the enemy get their hands on my gun."

"I'd say that gun belongs to all of humanity, Sergeant," said Private Galvan.

Gabriel sat on the edge of the crater and smiled. "And I'm putting it to good use."

Sliding himself forwards, he dropped from the edge of the crater. This was a move he knew could go wrong in so many ways, particularly if he'd misjudged and ended up tumbling headfirst through the hole.

Fortunately for Gabriel, he managed to retain a degree of control and the dust on the metal was layered thickly enough that it helped him slither down. Even so, it was difficult to stay feet first, and since his hands were gripping the Ezin-Tor, he couldn't use them to assist with stability.

The journey was short and Gabriel exited the hole, travelling faster than he would have liked. He'd oriented himself well and the first thing he saw was the main control console to the south-west. Sagh'eld troops were crouched low, their rifles aimed towards the hole in the ceiling.

Taken by surprise, the aliens didn't manage a single shot. Gabriel, however, fired the Ezin-Tor directly into the room's south-west corner. Dark energy spilled outwards from the point of impact, and a moment later, Gabriel hit the floor heavily. He attempted to roll, and he might have escaped the fall uninjured had it not been for his desire to protect the Ezin-Tor.

With an audible cracking sound, his right leg snapped between his knee and his hip. Pain lanced into his brain with shocking intensity, and he clenched his teeth against it. At the same moment, he was struck by the shockwave from the explosion. Expanding air swept him a short distance across the floor, and the energy from the blast was a bruising reminder that high-tech alien weaponry came with plenty of risks.

Protected by the dense insulation of his GK-3 Frontline combat armour, Gabriel survived the shockwave, though he felt blood dripping from his nose. Ignoring the pain from his broken leg, he struggled to free his gauss rifle from across his back, while still lying on his side. He had a good view of the room's south-western corner, the walls, floor and ceiling of which had been extensively disintegrated by the Ezin-Tor.

The control console hadn't escaped the blast. Only moments ago, it had been a circular device with a half-dozen operator stations and a thick central pillar which went up to the ceiling. However, the Ezin-Tor had obliterated more than half of the console, and the damaged pillar leaned crazily like it was about to fall.

Gabriel's first thought was that the hardware was out of action and that the mission had failed. As he was scanning for

Sagh'eld survivors, he saw faint lights on one of the console's front panels, which gave him renewed hope that all was not lost.

A figure dropped from the hole in the ceiling, landed with a thud nearby, rolled once and then sprang to its feet, an Aral gauss rifle clutched in both hands.

Gabriel recognized it to be Corporal Ziegler, and the soldier was followed in rapid succession by four more. Already, Ziegler was off at a sprint towards the control console and the others followed, two heading left and two heading right.

"Clear!" yelled Ziegler.

The remaining two soldiers dropped into the room. By this time, Gabriel was struggling to make it into an upright position, but the pain was great and his leg felt weak. Cursing, he ordered his suit to give him a painkilling shot.

"How are you, Sergeant?" asked Private Ashley Teague, the squad medic. She didn't wait for an answer and plugged a cable from her med-box into the neck port on Gabriel's suit.

"I broke my damn leg," said Gabriel sourly. "And I took some painkillers."

"The med-box will check for any other injuries, Sergeant. It won't take long."

"While we're waiting, help me over to that console," said Gabriel.

"I've got you, Sergeant," said Corporal Ziegler, who'd returned from the far corner of the room. He stooped, wrapped Gabriel's left arm around his shoulder and then straightened without apparent effort.

Having been hauled to his feet, Gabriel pointed towards the console. "We have to free the *Infinitar*."

With Ziegler's assistance, Gabriel was soon standing at one of the undamaged stations. In the few seconds it had taken to cross the room, the med-box report came back.

"A broken leg and that's all," said Teague.

"It could've been worse," said Gabriel, knowing he'd got off lightly.

"Damn right it could've been, Sergeant."

"What about the others?" Gabriel asked, touching the authentication pad on the console's top panel.

"Davison twisted his ankle, but he can walk on it."

It was all Gabriel needed to know, and he gave his full focus to the task in hand. At least, he tried to give it his full focus. A bone-deep itching, tingling and burning, all rolled into one, had started in his leg. His body was starting to heal, though the sensation of it was maddening.

Doing his best to pretend his leg wasn't irritating the shit out of him, Gabriel searched for the option to rescind the shut-down code afflicting the *Infinitar*. Opening each top-level menu in turn, he dug through the submenus, of which there were many.

"And we have to locate the flight records as well, Sergeant," said Ziegler.

"Then blow an exit hole through the south wall of this room so we can return to the ship," said Gabriel, trying to keep his voice calm.

"We've got this, sir," said Ziegler. He gave a short laugh. "I reckon you've taken Castle's record for most Sagh'eld kills in a single shot."

"I'm sure he'll give me an argument."

As it happened, Gabriel came across the flight records first. He downloaded them to his suit databank and then transmitted them to the *Infinitar*. Deciding that he might like to know exactly how much traffic the Indeston orbital had been handling recently, Gabriel opened the file. The data was in a list and easy to interpret.

"Well shit," he said. "The Sagh'eld Ex'Kaminar went to a

facility called Erion, and it wasn't the first enemy warship to make the journey from Indeston."

"How many, Sergeant?"

"Ten in total," said Gabriel. "The warship classes aren't recorded."

"What about the Singularity class?" asked Ziegler.

"That went first, though the time stamp is in a format I don't understand."

Gabriel closed the file – Captain Lanson would decide what he wanted to do with the intel, though it was already certain that a trip to Erion was on the cards, assuming all went to plan here on the orbital.

After some searching, Gabriel located the sub-sub-submenu that allowed him to order the deletion of the shut-down code. He sent the command and ordered Private Wolf to pass the information on to the *Infinitar*. Ten seconds later, Wolf gave a thumbs-up.

"Lieutenant Perry confirms the removal of the shutdown code. The self-purge routines will take a few minutes to complete, but that's nothing we need to worry about."

"Is there a reason for us to remain here?" asked Gabriel.

This time, Wolf was quiet for longer, and that put Gabriel on edge. He'd hoped for an immediate order to return to the *Infinitar*. As he was waiting, Gabriel tested his leg. The pain was almost gone, though it had been only slightly less prefer-able to the itching and tingling he was feeling now. After some experimentation, Gabriel found he could walk unaided, albeit his leg wasn't yet ready to sprint.

Picking up the Ezin-Tor, which he'd propped against the console, he spotted something different. A hinged metal plate, about an inch square, had fallen open. Gabriel thought it had probably come open in the recent fall, though he was more interested in the blue button which was in a recess beneath the now-open cover.

Peering closely, Gabriel could see no writing on the button, though a single word was etched on the underside of the metal plate.

Overcharge

"What've you found, Sergeant?" asked Ziegler.

"This," said Gabriel, pointing at the button and the writing.

"Overcharge?" said Ziegler. "I think you should push the button, sir."

"Is that right?" asked Gabriel.

Ziegler grinned. "What could possibly go wrong?"

"Maybe later," said Gabriel with a laugh. "When we're not in such a confined space."

The recess was within thumb reach of the Ezin-Tor's trigger and, since he didn't want to accidentally press the button, Gabriel pushed the cover plate back into place. It seemed to merge with the surrounding alloy, leaving no visible seam. Fortunately, the application of pressure on top of the plate caused it to spring open once more, allowing Gabriel access to the button if he ever decided it was necessary.

Closing the tiny cover plate for the second time, he turned his attention towards Private Wolf, just as she opened her mouth to speak. Having built himself up to expect an extension of the current mission goals, Gabriel was pleasantly surprised at the order he was given.

"The *Infinitar* is back online, Sergeant," said Wolf, "And we're to return at once."

Gabriel nodded and hefted the Ezin-Tor. The mission had been a success, even though he and his squad had been greatly outnumbered.

Now the only thing left to do was escape.

TWENTY-ONE

Captain Lanson kept a close watch on the feeds. Ten minutes had elapsed since he'd given Sergeant Gabriel the order to withdraw, and the soldiers hadn't yet emerged into the bay.

With the shutdown code removed, Lieutenant Perry had accessed the Indeston sensors, both internal and external. The monitors showed that Gabriel was currently in a room behind the northern bay wall. However, the remaining Sagh'eld had abandoned their positions and were actively searching for the human soldiers.

"It's going to be tight," said Lieutenant Turner.

"No, it isn't," said Lanson. "They're going to make it."

"Yes, sir."

"Lieutenant Abrams, as soon as those soldiers are back on board, I want you to activate the transit to Erion," said Lanson.

"Yes, sir," said Abrams.

Intel on the destination was distinctly lacking. Erion itself was a facility of some kind, and it was located on or near a planet named Andamar. The most interesting fact was that Erion was listed in the flight records as a Tier 0 location and, since its coordinates didn't tie up with any of the known Tier 0 locations in the *Infinitar*'s star charts, that meant Lanson and his crew were almost certainly heading to one of the places missing from the warship's navigational system.

For some time, Lanson had been working on the assumption that the Aral had sabotaged their own systems – for reasons which were not yet clear – so the existence of these Tier 0 coordinates in the orbital's flight records suggested the aliens had been less than thorough. Nothing he'd learned about the Aral made Lanson believe they were lacking in organisation, which reinforced his belief that they'd been operating under enormous duress.

Everything came back to the Ravanok. Lanson's belief in his own ability and the growing power of the *Infinitar* told him he could handle the Ixtar and the Sagh'eld. The Ravanok was something else and Lanson had no qualms about admitting the alien vessel had him scared. Losing a fight was one thing, but entering a battle with no hope whatsoever of success was one of his greatest fears.

"A couple of enemy squads have entered the storage room leading to the bay, Captain," said Perry.

"Keep watch, Commander," said Lanson. "If any of those Sagh'eld show their faces, turn them into paste."

"Yes, sir," said Matlock. "I have one of the forward Gradars trained on the airlock."

An explosion to the west of the airlock caught Lanson's attention. A section of the bay wall had been blown out and the falling particles of disintegrating metal created a grey shroud across the opening.

Through the hole created by the Ezin-Tor stepped a figure – it was Sergeant Gabriel. The soldier was receiving updates on the enemy positions from Lieutenant Perry, but he nonetheless paused to scan for dangers.

Evidently satisfied, Gabriel ran east to the place where he'd parked the shuttle, with the rest of his squad close behind. As if the Sagh'eld realised their opponents were on the verge of escape, they poured into the tunnel leading to the bay. The two squads Perry had reported earlier entered the airlock.

"Warn Sergeant Gabriel that we're about to fire one of our Gradars," said Lanson.

"Yes, sir."

The airlock completed its cycle and, though the exit into the bay was partially blocked by wreckage, the Sagh'eld became visible when the door opened.

"Have some of this," said Matlock.

A short burst of Gradar fire etched a vivid line of white across the bay. Repeater projectiles turned the Sagh'eld into biological smears and pulverised the inner airlock door.

"It must be my lucky day," said Matlock. "I now have a firing angle into the storage room."

Again, the Gradar gun hurled out a torrent of hardened alloy projectiles, which tore through the Sagh'eld who were sprinting towards the bay. When Matlock ceased fire, the Indeston monitors were tracking forty-two fewer targets than before. The much-diminished enemy forces began moving rapidly away from the airlock.

"I reckon I could squeeze an Avantar missile into the storage room," said Matlock.

"Hold fire," said Lanson, glancing across to reassure himself she was joking. "We don't want to incinerate Sergeant Gabriel and his squad."

Having been given the all-clear, the soldiers broke into a sprint along the docking platform. From this distance, they seemed to be moving at a crawl, and Lanson willed them to greater efforts, even though he was sure they couldn't run any faster.

The soldiers made it to the shuttle and disappeared inside. Less than thirty seconds later, the vessel lifted off under maximum acceleration. Gabriel was a skilled pilot and he flew the shuttle at high velocity across the bay.

"Sergeant Gabriel says he located an overcharge function on the Ezin-Tor, Captain," said Perry. "He didn't activate the overcharge, but he thought you'd want to know about it."

"Let the Sergeant know we'll talk about it later."

"Yes, sir."

Having come so far, Lanson was starting to believe the Ravanok would exit lightspeed at the perfect time to ruin his day, and he divided his attention between the bay and the Indeston external sensors. So far, the space around the orbital was empty.

"The shuttle has entered Docking Tunnel 1," said Perry.

Lanson didn't wait a moment longer. "Lieutenant Abrams, we're going to Erion."

"Yes, sir, we are," said Abrams. "I've sent the command to Indeston."

"It didn't take long for the Ex'Kaminar to enter void travel," said Lanson. "Fingers crossed we'll be out of here in next few seconds."

"I'm detecting Galos emissions, Captain," said Abrams. "They're spilling through the north and south ends of the bay."

"The topside cubes are getting ready to fire us to our destination," said Matlock.

"And let's hope there's nothing waiting in missile lock range when we get there," said Lanson.

Circumstances had pushed him into action, though on this occasion he believed it was for the best. The Sagh'eld had a heavy presence at the Erion Tier o facility – which also happened to be the place where the Singularity warship had been sent. Advance planning would have achieved nothing, so the only option was to head in, engage the enemy, and hope to come out on top.

Abruptly, the sensor feeds went blank and Lanson experienced a peculiar feeling that he was in two places at once. Everything around him blurred for a time that may have been only seconds, or might have been much longer. Then, everything settled and Lanson's anchors to reality dug in once more, leaving his body with a rapidly fading sensation that it had suffered great trauma.

"Waiting on the sensors," said Lieutenant Turner.

The feeds came online before she'd finished speaking and Lanson scanned them for signs his warship was in danger. Everything outside was dark.

Resisting the urge to accelerate from the arrival point, Lanson held the *Infinitar* in position. Sometimes heading off into the distance made for a better defence than standing still, but on this occasion, he wanted to give his sensor team the best opportunity to sweep the area around the warship, and to locate planet Andamar.

A glance at the screen to his right told Lanson that he was in the right place.

> *Combination request received. Combination not available.*

"The Singularity class is here," he said. "And it's unable to combine."

"Figures," said Matlock. "We've had it easy for too long."

"Nice joke, Commander," said Abrams.

After a tense few seconds, Lieutenant Perry completed the local area sweeps and announced them clear. Meanwhile, Lieutenant Turner was having a harder time finding the planet.

"I thought we'd have come in right on the doorstep," she said. "But I can't locate the target."

"Is Andamar elsewhere on its orbital track?" asked Lanson.

"It's possible, Captain, but I haven't yet come across a navigation system that doesn't take the basics into account. Indeston sent us to Andamar, so the planet should be here."

"Have you detected anything else, Lieutenant? A star? Faraway planets?"

"Yes, sir, I've located a star – it's three billion klicks from our position. I've also detected two other planets – the closest being two hundred million klicks nearer to the star – and I'm analysing the sensor data for three other possibilities."

"But nothing that's close by?"

"No, sir."

Lanson, having been prepared for combat, was nonplussed to discover that Indeston had sent his warship seemingly far from anything resembling a Tier 0 facility. He called up the flight records which Sergeant Gabriel had transmitted from the Indeston bay control room, and studied them carefully to ensure he hadn't overlooked anything obvious.

"The Singularity class and the ten Sagh'eld warships had the exact same arrival coordinates," he said. "Which means they exited void travel here, and then went elsewhere."

"I can confirm we're at the same coordinates as the other vessels, Captain," said Lieutenant Perry. "If the flight records are accurate, we're in the right place."

"What are we missing?" said Lanson. "There's nothing here." He drummed his fingers. "Lieutenant Turner, run a receptor sweep."

"Yes, sir, running sweep...receptor found."

"Is it Sagh'eld or Aral?" asked Lanson.

"It's Aral, Captain."

"Request a connection."

"Yes, sir. The connection request has been accepted."

"Ask for details on Erion," said Lanson.

"The receptor is only providing a single response, no matter what request I make," said Turner in puzzlement. "The response is *wait*."

"Damnit, what for?" asked Lanson, struggling to keep his cool. "And for how long?"

He didn't yet feel alarmed, though the situation was unusual. However, had Lanson been in any other warship than an Aral one, he might not have been so sanguine. Although the Sagh'eld had been able to operate with seeming impunity at other Tier o facilities, something about this place felt different – more threatening – though Lanson couldn't put his finger on what was making him think this way.

"Send another information request to the receptor," he snapped, his temper getting the better of him.

"Yes, sir, request sent," said Turner. "The response is the same as before – *wait*."

Five minutes after the arrival from Indeston, Lanson was giving serious thought to alternatives that didn't involve him sitting here doing nothing. After all, *wait* was a somewhat vague command, with no indication of how long the period of waiting might continue.

Before Lanson's impatience led him into hasty action, he was saved from further conflict with himself when a vessel entered local space less than twenty kilometres from the *Infinitar*'s starboard flank.

"What the hell?" said Lanson, the moment his brain registered the vastness of the spaceship.

The vessel had an extraordinarily strange design. The main structure was little more than a slab with rounded edges, twenty-five thousand metres in length, four thousand metres thick and six thousand high. From its visible flank, dozens of square alloy posts protruded in rows which extended from one end of the spaceship to the other.

"Avantar missiles locked and ready to launch," said

Matlock. "There are no visible armaments on the unidentified vessel."

"Hold fire," said Lanson. "Lieutenant Turner, run a receptor sweep."

"Running sweep...one new receptor found."

"Request a link," said Lanson.

The shock of this vessel's arrival had already gone, and he was near-as-damnit certain the *Infinitar* was under no immediate threat. It was clear now why the first receptor had given the command to wait – for whatever reason, this huge spaceship was to act as escort for any vessels which arrived here.

"Link request accepted," said Turner. "This is a data connection only, Captain." She didn't speak for a few seconds. "We've been asked to allow the insertion of a temporary routine into our control systems."

"What kind of routine?" asked Lanson sharply.

"There's no further information, sir."

"Could we accept the file, but isolate it until Lieutenant Abrams figures out what it's for?"

"No, Captain – I've been asked to allow the unidentified spaceship direct access to our data arrays. If I accept, the file will be transferred and then it'll attach itself to our control systems."

It was a decision Lanson didn't want to make. If he accepted the file and the nearby spaceship turned out to be hostile, then he'd effectively given up control of the *Infinitar*. On the other hand, Lanson and his crew had been transported here by a Tier 0 facility which made it likely the strange vessel had been constructed by the Aral.

"Send a name and origin query to the spaceship's receptor," said Lanson. "Maybe it's been programmed to respond to other Aral vessels."

"Name and origin request made," said Turner. "We are

looking at the *Barox-K*, sir. Its origin number identifies it as a vessel of the Aral navy."

Lanson felt better knowing this was potentially an allied spaceship, though he was still reluctant to accept the modifications to the *Infinitar*'s control system. The reality was that he had little choice if he wanted to progress the mission.

"Accept the control system file," said Lanson after a moment's hesitation.

Hoping he'd done the right thing, he waited to find out what would happen next.

TWENTY-TWO

The early signs were not good. Less than a second after Turner had accepted the file from the *Barox-K*, Lanson was locked out of the controls, and the menu options on all three of his screens became view only – he could read the text but lacked the authority to execute any of the commands.

"My weapons access level has been reduced, sir," said Matlock. "I can check our ammunition levels but not much else."

"I still have control over the comms and sensors, Captain," said Turner. "There are no problems here at all."

"What about you, Lieutenant Abrams?"

"I now only have view access to the propulsion monitoring systems, sir. I've tried re-entering my credentials, but my full rights have not been reinstated."

"This isn't like when the Indeston orbital shut us down, Captain," said Matlock. "This time we can access the control systems, just at a much lower level than normal." She smiled thinly. "There's no access level higher than Tier 0. Maybe you could re-enter your credentials and see what happens."

"I'm not sure that would be wise, Commander," said Lanson. "Not yet."

"You were expecting us to lose access?" said Matlock.

"I took the decision to accept the control system file on the basis that something like this would happen," said Lanson. "The *Barox-K* is an Aral spaceship, Commander – whatever it does should be in our favour."

"I hope you're right, sir."

"We're in motion, Captain," said Abrams.

The volume of the *Infinitar*'s propulsion increased slightly as the warship accelerated gently towards the *Barox-K*. Lanson had an idea of what might be coming, and he watched the feeds carefully.

"Lieutenant Abrams, are those flank posts on the *Barox-K* generating energy?" he asked.

"I scanned them when the vessel first appeared and they were all power neutral, sir," said Abrams. "I'll scan them again." He grunted and then cursed. "Well I'll be...those posts are now active – they're producing Galos energy."

The *Infinitar* was remotely piloted closer and closer to the *Barox-K*. A fifteen-degree rotation brought the two spaceships exactly parallel and soon the distance between them was less than a thousand metres. The rate of approach remained constant until the *Infinitar* was brought to a halt with its starboard flank as close to the *Barox-K* as was possible, without touching any of the posts.

Although the other spaceship was enormous, the *Infinitar* now had the size and mass of four Singularity class warships, and it covered much of the *Barox-K*'s portside flank.

"The *Barox-K* is here to transport visiting spaceships to the Erion facility," said Lanson.

"Why so complicated?" asked Perry.

"Because there's something at Erion that made the Aral take these extra precautions," said Lanson.

"Something way more important than anything else we've found so far," said Matlock.

"Maybe," said Lanson.

"The *Barox-K* is accelerating, sir," said Perry. "And it's bringing us along for the ride."

Lanson checked his console panel. The *Infinitar*'s velocity gauge was climbing strongly, while the propulsion output readings indicated the engines were running at idle.

"We're being held by gravity chains," said Lanson.

"Galos-generated gravity chains," said Abrams. "They're the extra-hard to break kind."

Lanson had his eyes on the velocity gauge. The *Barox-K* was faster than it looked, and it was heading towards five hundred kilometres per second. "The *Infinitar* can generate a lot of thrust, Lieutenant – especially now that our propulsion is mostly Galos."

"It would be interesting to find out if we really could be immobilised if we wanted to break free," said Abrams. "Anyway, the trouble with a Rodos gravity field generator is that its connection to the target vessel always breaks upon lightspeed entry. I wonder if Galos chains act differently."

"I'm sure they do," said Lanson. "Our scans indicate we're nowhere close to Erion, so it would make sense for the *Barox-K* to complete the journey at lightspeed."

"Then why are we travelling at sub-light?" asked Perry. "Why not initiate lightspeed warmup straightaway?"

Lanson didn't have an answer. Perhaps it was a security protocol, or something else he was unaware of. Whatever the truth, Lanson didn't spend time thinking about it. If the *Barox-K* was still at sub-light an hour from now, maybe he'd give the matter some consideration.

As it turned out, the journey at sub-light ended much sooner than an hour. When the *Barox-K* was two hundred thousand kilometres from the *Infinitar*'s arrival point, it decelerated to a standstill.

"Here comes the warmup," said Lanson.

He experienced a tingling of excitement. Although the coming destination might find him and his crew engaged with a superior force of Sagh'eld warships, Lanson felt with certainty that Erion would reveal more about the Aral. Most importantly, another Singularity warship had been sent there. If Lanson could initiate and complete the combination routine, there'd be only one warship left to find out of six. The *Infinitar* had a distinct purpose, he was sure of it, and once the vessel was complete, he'd find out what that purpose was.

Three minutes after it came to a standstill, the *Barox-K* entered lightspeed and remained there for a total of fifteen minutes, before it re-entered local space. When the *Infinitar*'s sensors came online, Lanson found himself looking at a bleak, grey planet on the forward feeds.

"That must be Andamar," said Turner. "It's one hundred thousand kilometres from our position."

"No prizes for guessing where Erion is located," said Lanson.

In the centre of the planet's facing side, an enormous hemisphere of the deepest grey was visible. The sensor overlay calculated the hemisphere's diameter at twelve hundred kilometres, and whatever lay within was hidden.

"The sensors can't pierce the hemisphere," said Turner, sounding stressed that she couldn't fix the problem.

"I reckon we're going to find out what's inside soon enough," said Lanson.

As if the words were a prompt, the *Barox-K* began accelerating directly towards the hemisphere. Having gone along with events so far, Lanson wasn't about to start rocking the boat and he watched the sensors keenly. He suddenly noticed that the hemisphere wasn't grey like he'd first thought, rather he believed it to be completely black, yet with a slight shimmer, as though it were partly in this reality and partly in another.

The *Barox-K* maintained a steady velocity, though one which ensured the journey to the hemisphere would soon be over. With five thousand kilometres to go, a short line of text appeared on one of Lanson's screens.

Welcome to Erion: Galos Storage.

Lanson read out the message to the others, in case he'd been the only one to whom it had been delivered.

"Galos storage?" said Matlock. "That would explain the need for all these precautions."

"I'm detecting a series of power spikes from the *Barox-K*, sir," said Abrams. "I don't know what's—"

He didn't finish his sentence and had no need to. The *Barox-K* had begun shimmering, just like the hemisphere and, when Lanson looked about, he noticed the bridge was affected in the same way.

"This is how we enter Erion," he said, his voice carrying a remoteness, like a comms transmission which had travelled for centuries to reach its destination.

Without slowing, the *Barox-K* plunged into the hemisphere, bringing the *Infinitar* with it. The protective barrier around Erion was hardly more than ten metres thick, though Lanson was sure it was designed to withstand an extensive bombardment.

Once inside the hemisphere, Lanson stared in wonder at the sights, albeit the *Barox-K* blocked the view to starboard. Directly below, an area of land, twenty kilometres by twenty, had been levelled and clad in alloy. Around the edge of this square were numerous huge cannons and missile launchers.

None of the weapons were visibly tracking the *Infinitar*, though Lanson wasn't yet ready to believe they were inactive.

The centre ten kilometres of the levelled square were sunken, though only by a few metres, and a visible central seam made it clear these were doors leading to wherever.

Elsewhere, Lanson noted that cubes had been placed on the surface of Andamar, separated by twelve-kilometre gaps. Each of these cubes measured five hundred metres, and it was clear that they were maintaining the outer shield.

"I've located a total of ten Sagh'eld warships, Captain," said Lieutenant Perry. "They're way off to our portside."

"Our control of the *Infinitar* has not yet been returned, sir," said Abrams.

Lanson grimaced at the sight of the enemy warships. Every one was stationary, and they were clustered three hundred kilometres north, at similar altitudes.

"Three Ex'Kaminars, three Tagha'an heavies, three Ingosor lights and a superheavy lifter," said Lanson. "Why aren't they firing at us?"

"Maybe the *Barox-K* infiltrated their control systems," said Matlock. "Given how the *Infinitar* is a Tier 0 Aral warship and we were still expected to comply with the Erion protocols, it's likely the Sagh'eld would have been subject to even greater controls."

"Why were they allowed here in the first place?" asked Perry. "And if the Sagh'eld were losing warships, why did they keep sending others?"

"I wonder if the *Barox-K*'s control systems were programmed to trust any vessel arriving from Indeston," said Matlock. "The Sagh'eld kept coming and it kept bringing them into the Erion hemisphere."

"Except it doesn't appear as if the Sagh'eld *were* trusted,

Commander. If they were free to act, they'd be launching missiles at us."

Matlock nodded slowly. "And they'd have blown a hole in those central bay doors already."

"Hull scans of the enemy vessels tell me they're all generating the exact amount of propulsion required to prevent them falling to the ground, Captain," said Abrams. "It's not any kind of proof the Sagh'eld have lost control of their warships, but their lack of action constitutes some good evidence."

"I agree," said Lanson. He turned. "To answer your question about why the Sagh'eld sent more warships, Lieutenant Perry, I'd guess they didn't know what had happened to those which had gone before. If they had a task force at Indeston, and the orbital would only send them into void travel one at a time, they could have all been neutralised by the *Barox-K* before they figured out what was going on."

"I suppose the Sagh'eld comms wouldn't have travelled from Erion to Indeston quickly enough for the first arrivals to warn the rest of the task force," said Perry.

Although Lanson was sure he'd guessed right about the Sagh'eld warships being captured, he remained wary. The ten enemy vessels had too much firepower for him to discount them as a threat.

Cursing inwardly at the uncertainty of it all, Lanson waited to see what would happen next. He expected the *Barox-K* to release the *Infinitar* at any moment, and after that, he assumed he'd be allowed limited freedom of action.

The fifth Singularity class was here at Erion, and Lanson planned to find it and complete the linking routine. Now that he was within the hemisphere, he hoped everything would be straightforward.

Lanson nearly laughed at the thought.

TWENTY-THREE

The *Barox-K* came to a halt fifty kilometres south of the levelled area, at a hundred-kilometre altitude. A message appeared on Lanson's screen.

> *Control systems partial restore complete.*

Lanson felt the control bars become live in his hands again, and he guided the *Infinitar* away from the *Barox-K*.

"What does a partial restore mean?" he asked.

"I still have no access to fire the weapons, Captain," said Matlock.

"The Aral really didn't want any accidents happening at Erion," said Lanson. "And if I'm right in thinking there's a huge vault of Galos cubes somewhere beneath those surface doors, I don't blame them."

"I have full control over the propulsion again, sir," said Abrams. "I could probably initiate a destructive chain reaction on our Galos modules if I wanted to, but that would be going too far just to make a point."

"Let's see if we can keep the *Infinitar* intact until the mission is complete, Lieutenant," said Lanson dryly.

"I've scanned the entirety of this hemisphere, Captain, and there's no sign of another Singularity warship," said Turner. "Which means it's either somewhere outside the barrier, or it's underground."

"I'm going with underground," said Lanson. "The big question is, what happens if we attempt to open the surface doors?"

"My first thought is we'd have the authority to do so," said Matlock. "However, I'm not sure the normal Aral security hierarchy applies here."

"Or it still applies, but with some additional rules," said Lanson. "Lieutenant Turner – scan for receptors."

"Yes, sir...scanning...one receptor found. It identifies itself as *Bay Door Zero*."

"Request a link," said Lanson.

"Link request accepted."

Lanson pursed his lips as he stared at the feeds, wondering how big a risk he was contemplating. The Singularity class was beneath those bay doors – he was sure of it – and yet he was reluctant to instruct them to open while he was ignorant of the Erion protocols.

"See if the *Barox-K* will respond to a request for the Erion protocol documentation," said Lanson.

"The *Barox-K* has not responded, Captain," said Turner a moment later.

Lanson cursed under his breath. He sat quietly, still staring at the feeds, and hoping something would come to him. After a few seconds, he shared the burden with his crew. "I'm interested to hear opinions."

"One way or another, we have to go through those bay doors," said Abrams. "That's what it boils down to."

"There's plenty about this situation I'm not happy with," said Lanson. "But above everything, we can't afford to come into conflict with the base security systems. Those defences surrounding the bay doors look as if they'd make short work of the *Infinitar*."

For the next few minutes, Lanson and his crew talked, though the discussion failed to produce a worthwhile outcome. As ever, Lanson began to feel the pressure of time and he wished for a mission where he had the luxury of being able to watch and plan, rather than being dragged by circumstance into premature action.

"Screw it," he said. "Lieutenant Turner, send a command to the bay doors. I want them open."

"Yes, sir, command sent."

The result was rapid and unwanted. A message appeared on Lanson's centre screen.

> *Protocol breach 019: Infinitar. Control resumed.*

"Damnit!" yelled Lanson as the control bars went dead in his hands.

"I'm frozen out of the main propulsion system again," said Abrams.

"Lieutenant Turner – find out if the *Barox-K* will tell us what happens now," said Lanson.

"Request sent," said Turner. She wasn't quiet for long. "Captain – the *Barox-K* reports it has sent a comm to base and is awaiting a response."

"Which base?" asked Lanson. "And how long is the response expected to take?"

"The *Barox-K* will not provide an answer to those questions, sir."

"Captain, assuming a Tier 0 facility will be required to handle a comm of this nature, we're looking at weeks before anything comes back to the *Barox-K*," said Perry. "And even then, it'll be an automated response, with no guarantee it'll provide authorisation to either return our control over the *Infinitar*, or permit us to open the bay doors."

Lanson had a feeling the Erion comms were Galos-ampli-fied, and he doubted the response would take weeks. Even so, he wasn't of a mind to be a passive spectator and he weighed up how much time he should allow the Aral security process to complete before he took matters into his own hands.

The decision was an easy one. "Lieutenant Abrams, you mentioned before that if I signed into the *Infinitar*'s control systems with Tier 0 access, you might be able to purge the *Barox-K*'s modifications."

"I did say that, Captain, and I've been doing some checks since then. I think I know how to get our warship back."

"If we delete the *Barox-K*'s control system modifications, won't that be seen as a hostile act?" asked Perry.

"I'm sure it'll breach a few of the Erion security protocols," Lanson conceded. "Whether it'll breach enough of them to make us a target for the surface emplacements is another question entirely."

The urgency of the situation became suddenly more apparent when the *Barox-K* accelerated from stationary, flank-first towards the *Infinitar*. Lanson didn't know what was about to happen, though he doubted this was a positive development. With no great haste, the *Barox-K* positioned itself within ten thousand metres and then, the *Infinitar* – with no input from Lanson – accelerated towards the Galos posts which protruded from the other vessel's flank.

"We're about to be tethered," said Abrams. "I think the *Barox-K* received an answer about what to do with us."

"I think you're right," said Lanson, watching as the *Infinitar* was brought to a halt almost within touching distance of the other vessel. "Lieutenant Abrams, I'm going to remotely log in to your station with my Tier 0 credentials. Let me know when you're ready to purge the control system modifications, but wait for my order."

"Yes, sir."

"You now have Tier o access, Lieutenant," said Lanson once he was done logging in.

"It's worked, sir," said Abrams. "I have full access to everything again."

"Why not re-log into your own console, Captain?" asked Matlock. "You might get your access to the controls back."

"I don't want to risk a tug-of-war, with the *Barox-K* grabbing back control and me having to re-log every few seconds, Commander. Let's get the unwanted code purged from our systems first."

A new message appeared on Lanson's screen.

> *Access permissions to Erion revoked. Prepare for return to Indeston.*

"You'll need to work fast, Lieutenant Abrams," said Lanson. "The *Barox-K* is about to eject us from the hemisphere. Once we're out, I doubt we'll get back in."

"When I said I could get our warship back, I didn't mean with a click of my fingers, Captain," said Abrams, already sounding irritated. "I have to create a special partition and run the—"

"You'd best get on with it, then," Lanson interrupted.

"Yes, sir."

Lanson expected the *Barox-K* to exit the hemisphere immediately, but it did not. Instead, it remained motionless, with its Galos chains holding the *Infinitar*.

"How much longer, Lieutenant Abrams?" asked Lanson when a couple of minutes had passed.

"I'm working on it, Captain," was all Abrams would say.

Lanson knew when to push and when to back off. He kept his mouth shut and glanced over at Commander Matlock, whose tightly clenched jaw told its story.

Another minute went by and Lanson asked himself if the

Barox-K had tied itself up in protocol knots that forbade it from ejecting a Tier 0 warship from Erion.

His hopes were soon proved wrong. Nearly four minutes after Lanson had received the message informing him that his access to Erion was revoked, the *Barox-K* began a vertical climb away from the surface of Andamar.

"If you're going to purge the control systems, now would be a good time to do it, Lieutenant Abrams," said Lanson.

"I understand that, Captain. I'm not going to be done before we exit the hemisphere."

Lanson cursed. He and his crew had escaped a few situations by the skin of their teeth, but it wasn't looking as if this would be another one. Desperately, Lanson's mind hunted for something he might have overlooked and yet he'd been through this already without success.

"What if we executed an instant lightspeed transition?" he asked. "That might break us away from the *Barox-K*'s gravity chains."

"It might, but it activates from your console, Captain," said Lieutenant Massey. "You'd need to re-log to gain access."

As Lanson's brain scrambled for a solution that continued to evade him, he realised that he'd run out of time. The *Barox-K* was approaching the opaque inner surface of the hemisphere, and in seconds it would emerge into the Andamar atmosphere. Once that happened, there'd be no returning – at least not without the considerable effort it would require to either locate the Erion protocols documentation and figure out a way to circumvent the local security, or to find a way to make the *Infinitar* exempt from those rules.

Before Lanson had come to terms with the fact that he was about to lose, the *Barox-K* came to an unexpected halt, barely five thousand metres beneath the highest point of the Erion dome.

"What the—" Lanson began, unsure if this was part of a bizarre routine the *Barox-K* was required to enact in order to eject the *Infinitar*.

What if this is a reprieve? came the thought. *What if the Barox-K has received new instructions?*

Lanson couldn't allow himself to believe, but that didn't mean he and his crew couldn't gain some benefit from this delay. "Lieutenant Abrams you've been given a second chance to purge our control systems."

"Yes, sir, and I'm still working on it. I need to concentrate."

Taking the hint, Lanson shut his mouth and kept his hands on the control bars, ready to act the moment Lieutenant Abrams was finished.

Events overtook the attempt to purge the control system. Text appeared on Lanson's screen, the words chilling him to the bone.

> *Ravanok detected. Protocol 2493 override. Infinitar: control system modifications deleted. Command transfer: Infinitar.*

Just when Lanson was beginning to think he was out of the fight, he'd been thrown back into the ring to face an opponent he had no hope of defeating.

Luckily for Lanson, he was normally at his best when the shit hit the fan. Against the Ravanok, he'd need to be.

TWENTY-FOUR

Lanson straightaway understood what the message on his screen was telling him. "The Ravanok is somewhere outside the hemisphere," he said. "I think its arrival has triggered an emergency protocol, giving us command of the situation."

"When there's war, you turn to the people with guns," said Matlock.

Requesting power from the *Infinitar*'s engines, Lanson hauled on the controls, expecting to accelerate cleanly away from the *Barox-K*. Instead, the warship responded sluggishly, and the velocity gauge crept upwards instead of racing from left to right.

Lanson spotted the problem at once. "We're still tethered to the *Barox-K*," he said.

"Yes, Captain," said Abrams. "The Galos posts are still generating energy and I don't know why."

"Conflicting protocols," said Lanson, his anger rising. "The protocol which handed over command to the *Infinitar* has not correctly overridden the protocol dictating that we should be ejected from the dome. Our control systems have been purged, but the *Barox-K* has not received an order to release the gravity chains."

"This is what happens when you replace a biological mind with a machine," said Abrams.

"All the biological minds who built this place are dead, Lieutenant," said Lanson. "And we're shackled to the flank of a trillion-ton spaceship."

As it turned out, the extra mass wasn't the impediment to acceleration he thought it might be. Lanson increased the engine output to nearly halfway and commanded the *Infinitar* to accelerate directly to portside. This time, the electronic needle on the velocity gauge surged, almost as if the warship was completely unencumbered, and the only indication of strain was an underlying drone from the engines.

Cursing his lack of prior opportunity to put the *Infinitar*'s new Galos propulsion through its paces, Lanson reduced velocity before he accidentally collided with the Erion shield.

"Lieutenant Turner, request another comms link to the bay doors receptor," he said, initiating a short burst of acceleration along a new heading, to help himself adjust to the additional inertia from the *Barox-K*.

"Requesting link."

Being tethered to the *Barox-K* caused problems beyond mere inertia. The huge vessel's proximity rendered all the *Infinitar*'s starboard arrays ineffective, as well as limiting the viewing arcs of numerous others. In addition, much of the external weaponry could not be safely fired, though Lanson was hoping to find a solution to his current difficulties before that became an issue.

In only a few seconds, it was clear to Lanson that the *Infinitar* had such a surplus of engine power that he'd have no problems piloting the warship. Having decelerated, he rotated the vessel in order that he'd have a better view of the bay doors.

"What's the delay with that receptor link, Lieutenant Turner?" Lanson asked.

"I'm not receiving a response, Captain," said Turner. "I don't think it's an issue – I reckon Erion has switched into battle mode and it's taking the local systems a few seconds to recognize the *Infinitar*'s elevated level of command."

Lanson opened his mouth to say something, but the words went unsaid. His rotation of the *Infinitar* had not only brought the surface doors into sensor view, it had done the same to the Sagh'eld warships. Those warships were currently under such an intense bombardment from the Erion automated defences that five or six were already completely engulfed in plasma.

"Hell," said Lanson, unable to think of anything more appropriate.

One of the ground launch clusters ejected another salvo of missiles, which sped across the intervening space to their target in only a split second. One of the Ex'Kaminars, which was so far undamaged, erupted into flames of such intensity that Lanson narrowed his eyes against the brightness of the feeds.

The salvos continued, with hardly a pause between them. It was clear from the colossal size of the blasts that the ground-to-air launchers were firing missiles with a payload far beyond those of the *Infinitar*'s Avantar warheads. In a matter of ten or fifteen seconds, the Sagh'eld warships were reduced to wreckage – the pride of an alien fleet obliterated by technology far superior to their own.

"The debris isn't falling," said Matlock.

Lanson had just that moment noticed the same thing. As the plasma light dwindled, a clearer picture of the destruction began to emerge. All ten of the Sagh'eld vessels had been torn apart by the high-yield missiles, but instead of beginning the long journey to the surface of Andamar, the debris had been allowed to travel only a few kilometres before being frozen in place.

The sight was bizarre and appalling at the same time. Molten alloys, burning with unwavering brightness, were interspersed with darker pieces of debris, none of it going anywhere. Lanson's eyes darted from place to place, picking out identifiable objects – a mangled Thak turret, a huge plate of armour from the flank of a Tagha'an, the nose section of an Ex'Kaminar battleship. The Sagh'eld were his enemies and yet Lanson found no joy in this.

"My link request to the bay doors receptor has been accepted, Captain!" said Turner.

"Send the instruction to open the doors," said Lanson, more sharply than he intended. The sight of the wrecked Sagh'eld fleet had rekindled his anger and it was hard to keep it from his voice.

"Yes, sir. Command sent."

The bay doors were enormous and Lanson didn't even try to estimate their mass. However, they parted without apparent strain and the gap between them widened rapidly. Lanson piloted the *Infinitar* closer and brought the warship to a standstill directly above the opening, at a ten-kilometre altitude.

"What's down there?" he wondered, keeping an eye on the underside feeds.

"Looks like a shaft, Captain," said Turner. "The visual data isn't clear enough for me to see what's at the bottom."

An update on one of Lanson's screens caught his eye.

> *Combination request received. Combination not available.*

"Damnit, the Singularity warship isn't beneath these doors," he said. "The combination isn't available."

"Maybe there's a reason, Captain," said Matlock. "What if

the target vessel is being held by gravity chains, and those are preventing the combination routine from activating?"

Lanson wanted to believe the Singularity class was here on Andamar, beneath the bay doors, but he was having a hard time convincing himself. Regardless, with the Ravanok outside the Erion barrier, Lanson had no choice other than to investigate what lay below, and hope to find something – anything – that would enable his escape from this place. However, completing the combination routine remained the primary mission goal. For now, at least.

In less than three minutes, the bay doors had opened sufficiently for the *Infinitar*, along with the tethered *Barox-K*, to enter the subsurface shaft, albeit without much clearance. Lanson's patience was not at its highest and he reduced altitude, aligning his warship with the opening as he did so.

"Captain, I've run a scan and located a new receptor," said Turner. "It might give access to the bay control systems."

"Request a link," said Lanson, his eyes unblinking as he guided the *Infinitar* into the opening.

"Link requested...link request accepted," said Turner.

Lanson had his hands full with the warship, so he didn't immediately give an order. Fortunately, the shaft dimensions matched those of the bay doors, meaning he had some margin for error. Grey alloy clad the walls, and deeper down – much deeper – the shaft entered a larger space with a metal floor. Nothing of note was currently visible.

"Query the receptor, Lieutenant Turner," said Lanson. "Find out if it's linked to a computer system that will accept our commands."

"Yes, sir."

"And instruct the upper bay doors to close."

"What if we have to make a fast exit, Captain?" asked Matlock.

"If we're getting out of here, I don't think it's going to be through those doors, Commander," said Lanson.

The shaft ended almost a hundred kilometres below the surface and the *Infinitar* entered a huge space that continued on and on in every direction, to alloy walls far away. Here, the temperatures were cold as the grave, and it was dark like a funeral shroud.

"Scan the area," said Lanson, bringing the *Infinitar* to a halt, five kilometres below the shaft exit and forty kilometres above the ground.

"What the hell was a space like this needed for?" asked Matlock.

"I don't know, Commander," said Lanson. "I'd like to say I'm getting accustomed to the wonders of Aral engineering, but I'm not even close."

"The bay is empty, Captain," said Perry, telling Lanson something he'd noted on his first glance at the feeds.

"It must have been created for a reason," said Lanson. "Lieutenant Turner, what have you learned from the subsurface receptor?"

"I've just finished querying it, Captain," said Turner, with a tone indicating the receptor had provided her some useful information. "We have a link to the main control system for the Erion Galos storage facility, and our primacy is acknowledged."

Although Lanson was pleased to know he wouldn't be having any problems with the local hardware, his positivity was tempered by circumstance.

"Does the bay control system have access to the topside sensor arrays?" he asked. "Can it tell us what the Ravanok is doing?"

"Captain, the Ravanok is currently attacking the Galos shield," said Turner. "The surface Galos generators are down to eighty-two percent."

"Can we see a feed of the Ravanok?" asked Lanson.

"Yes, sir, check your screen."

Judging by the view, the sensor was somewhere out in space, with sight of both the Ravanok and the Erion shield. The alien sphere shocked Lanson every time he saw it, and this time was no exception. Against the might of the Ravanok, even the Galos-generated hemisphere appeared tiny. A fifty-kilometre-diameter pillar of dark energy connected the enemy vessel with the Aral shield and Lanson had no doubt this was the source of the drain on the surface Galos cubes.

Having seen the potency of a one-metre Galos device, Lanson could only guess at how much energy the surface cubes could generate. For the moment, they were maintaining the shield against the enemy attack.

"We have to figure a way out of here before the surface shield collapses," said Lanson. "Is the bay controller able to provide an estimate on how long we have before that happens?"

"Thirty minutes at the current rate of drain, Captain," said Turner once she'd received a response.

"And what—"

"Sir!" Turner interrupted urgently. "When the surface cubes hit zero percent, that doesn't mean they're fully depleted. They'll have enough energy left to detonate!"

"You're shitting me? Why would—" Lanson looked to the heavens. "Why the hell *wouldn't* the Aral make them detonate? Any vessel powerful enough to collapse the shield won't have a problem with the surface launchers. Once those are destroyed, the Galos cubes stored here will be free for the taking."

Thirty minutes until detonation. It could either be an age, or the blinking of an eye, depending on what action was needed to escape from Erion. And that was assuming escape was possible. Lanson had no proof one way or another, and the clock was ticking.

When the surface shield collapsed and the Galos cubes exploded, he wanted to be far from here. Preferably in a different galaxy.

Lanson set his mind to figuring out a solution.

TWENTY-FIVE

"Ask the bay controller if we're able to bypass the Galos barrier at lightspeed," said Lanson, starting with what he hoped would be the easiest solution.

The answer was as expected. "Negative, Captain. The shield can't be bypassed, either at lightspeed, or with void travel."

"How does the *Barox-K* travel in and out?" asked Lanson.

"Apparently the *Barox-K* is carrying hardware designed to act like a key. It can pass freely through the shield, but only at sub-light."

"Interesting," mused Abrams. "Not only did the Aral discover void travel, they also figured out how to negate it."

"I imagine they had plenty of motivation," said Lanson. "What with the Ravanok hunting them down."

"I'm sure you're right, sir."

"It's something to think about later," said Lanson. "Lieutenant Turner, confirm for definite that the fifth Singularity warship was here."

"It was - until the Erion sensors detected the arrival of the

Ravanok, Captain. The warship was sent away when the emergency protocol activated."

"Where did it go and how?"

"I've obtained the destination coordinates, sir," said Turner. "And the target vessel was sent by void travel."

"I thought void travel wasn't possible through the shield," said Lanson.

"Give me a moment, sir, while I query the bay controller for an explanation."

"Go ahead."

"The surface shield actually forms a full sphere, Captain," said Turner after a short time. "When void travel is initiated, an exit hole is created, and the spaceship passes through."

Lanson smiled thinly. "Where one vessel can go, another can follow."

"The bay controller is transmitting a copy of the subsurface map," said Turner. "There are doors leading from this current bay."

"It's the void travel I'm interested in," said Lanson. "The sooner we're away from Erion, the better."

He paused for a moment and reflected on whether he was lacking ambition. Maybe the Galos storage facility offered more possibilities than he was aware of.

First task – secure the escape route, Lanson reminded himself. *Then, if there's time, look for opportunities.*

"The destination coordinates for the Singularity class are not in our star charts, Captain," said Perry. "If the coordinates are for a Tier o facility, it's possible our target warship has been sent to one of the locations which were removed from the Aral maps."

"We'll find out when we get there," said Lanson, with a confidence he was trying to believe in. "Now show me what's here at Erion."

"I've opened the map on your central screen, Captain," said Turner.

It turned out that the subsurface areas of the facility were vast and sprawling. In addition to the numerous linked warship bays, thousands of personnel tunnels had been cut through the rock like gnarled fingers, connecting rooms and storage areas, and confounding Lanson's eye as he tried to follow them from place to place.

"All these locations preceded by G1- on the map are Galos storage areas," said Matlock. "Eight in total."

"And each capable of holding more than a billion cubic metres of Galos cubes," said Lanson. "Enough to—"

He stopped himself, unsure how to finish. The one-metre Galos cube from Cornerstone had destroyed planet Lorimos, while the Galos cubes on Scalos when detonated within the local star had created a singularity with a vastly greater mass than the star itself.

If the storage rooms here on Erion were even halfway full, there'd be enough Galos to—

Destroy the Ravanok.

Lanson didn't dare to hope, but he couldn't stop himself imagining the Ravanok being torn apart in a detonation of galactic proportions, and the wreckage then being crushed into nothingness by the endless gravity of the resulting black hole.

"It looks like void travel is initiated from one of the bays three levels below this one," said Matlock, looking over. She narrowed her eyes. "What's got you thinking, Captain?"

"The Galos stores," said Lanson. "I don't care what kind of defences the Ravanok is protected by, it's not going to survive if we detonate every Galos cube within Erion."

Matlock nodded. "We'll have to deal with the Ravanok sooner or later, sir."

"I've always assumed that if we complete the *Infinitar,*

everything else will fall into place," said Lanson. "I need to stop thinking that way."

"Let's see if we can get the Ravanok off our backs," said Matlock with a half-smile.

"More than just the Ravanok," said Lanson, his eyes going to the starboard feed. "Lieutenant Turner, the bay controller should be able to instruct the *Barox-K* to switch off its gravity chains. Request that it happens."

"Yes, sir, request sent," Turner confirmed. "Ah—"

"Something wrong, Lieutenant?"

"Yes, sir. The bay control computer states it has insufficient authority to override the *Barox-K*. When the *Infinitar* was made primary, command authority over all vessels was transferred to us."

"The *Barox-K* won't—" Lanson didn't finish. He was seething, but anger wasn't going to fix anything. "More conflicting protocols," he said. "With us on the receiving end of an alien screw-up."

In a way, it was understandable. If the Aral were a largely peaceful species, their emergency protocols might rarely – perhaps never – be triggered. It was only in situations like this, where everything was heading south, that the turds bobbed up to the surface. Wide-scale testing was the usual method for unearthing these inevitable failings, but it seemed the Aral hadn't figured that out. Or maybe the Erion protocols had been created while the aliens were under extreme pressure, leading to the conflicts Lanson and his crew were now experiencing.

"Captain, there's a chance the *Infinitar* has sufficient thrust to break us free from the gravity chains," said Abrams. "However, we'd need the *Barox-K* to remain motionless, or we'll just drag it along with us."

The tethering was a pain in the ass which was in danger of becoming a major distraction. "We're not doing anything about the *Barox-K* for the moment," said Lanson. "It's slowing us down, but that's something we'll have to deal with."

Lanson soon discovered that the *Barox-K* was going to be more of a hindrance than he'd imagined. When he gave the order to open the eastern exit from the bay, he saw at once that the square-shaped aperture was too small for both spaceships to fit through at the same time.

"Room for one or the other, but not both," said Lanson, pretending he was calm.

"Since we're now the primary vessel on Erion, we could destroy the *Barox-K*'s gravity chain generators with our missiles," Matlock suggested.

"A couple of problems with that, Commander. Firstly, I don't want to find out there's another protocol conflict, such that the bay controller issues us with a shutdown command. Secondly, the *Barox-K* is using Galos energy to create the chains. I'm not sure the use of explosive force is the wisest action."

"I should learn when to keep my mouth shut," said Matlock. "I've just checked the arming range on our Avantars and we're too close for them to activate anyway."

"Going back to what you said about the use of explosives, I'm certain that not all Galos has a destructive purpose, Captain," said Abrams. "The propulsion on the *Infinitar*, for example. I've been studying the outputs and I'm convinced our engines wouldn't detonate if they were hit by a few missiles."

"I appreciate your research, Lieutenant Abrams, but now is not a good time to be conducting field tests."

"No, sir, maybe not. But if it comes to it, we might not have any choice."

"Point taken," said Lanson. "Lieutenant Turner, query the bay controller and ask if it would issue a shutdown command if we discharged our weapons."

"Yes, sir."

"Will you believe the answer, whatever it is?" asked Matlock.

"That's a good question, Commander," said Lanson, making no effort to expand on his response.

"The bay controller confirms that it will not issue a shutdown command, regardless of our actions."

It was the answer Lanson hadn't wanted, since it left him guessing. "Acknowledged," he said.

"From the look on your face, you're not about to order an attack on the *Barox-K*," said Matlock.

"Not yet," said Lanson, staring intently at the forward feed. The open bay doors had revealed a square tunnel which, after two thousand metres, exited into another large space. Nothing of interest was visible within. "If we accelerated at maximum thrust, starting at the far end of this bay, we'd be travelling fast by the time we hit the opening into the adjacent bay."

Matlock grasped the plan at once. "You're wondering if the gravity chains would break if we crashed the *Barox-K* into the bay wall adjacent to the linking tunnel at a high enough velocity."

"That's exactly what I'm thinking," said Lanson.

"Captain, just a minute ago, you were expressing reservations about firing missiles at the gravity chain generators," said Abrams. "The impact energy from a collision of the type you're suggesting would be magnitudes greater than the explosions from a handful of Avantar missiles."

"And the *Infinitar* would likely be damaged at the same time – either from an unintended impact with the passage walls, or by debris from the—" said Matlock.

"Damnit, I'm just trying to think of a way to fix this," Lanson interrupted. "Let's hear some ideas."

"We could lightspeed into the lower bay," said Perry.

"That would be a huge mistake, Lieutenant," said Massey. "The *Infinitar*'s lightspeed entry calcs can take into account a variability in our mass, but not a trillion-ton variability. Entering lightspeed wouldn't be a problem – it's the accuracy of the arrival that we'd have to worry about."

"Does that mean we definitely couldn't lightspeed into the lower bay?" asked Lanson.

"Lieutenant Massey is right, Captain," said Abrams. "I wouldn't like to think how far off-target such a transit would take us. Exiting lightspeed in the middle of solid rock would bring our mission to an end."

The options – already limited – were being whittled down to a point where Lanson was going to have to pick between a selection of high-risk alternatives. All things considered, he reckoned a Gradar attack on the *Barox-K*'s gravity chains generators was looking like the best plan out of a bad bunch, even though the repeaters almost certainly lacked the destructive power to break so much metal.

However, Lanson couldn't forget the helplessness he'd felt when the Indeston bay controller had issued the shutdown code. If the same thing happened again, he doubted there'd be time for Sergeant Gabriel to make a journey to the Erion main bay control room. Just to be sure, Lanson located the place. It was a shuttle ride and thousand-metre run to get there. Maybe it was feasible, but the margins would be tight.

"Lieutenant Turner, what is the strength of the surface shield generators?" Lanson asked.

"Seventy percent, Captain. The bay controller is predicting the shield will collapse in a little under twenty-six minutes."

Lanson had an idea, though he had to check one of the details first.

"Lieutenant Turner, if we launched a shuttle, would the

bay controller view it as an independent vessel, or would it be considered part of the *Infinitar*?"

"Once launched, the shuttle would be considered independent, Captain," said Turner, when she'd received a response to the query.

It was the answer Lanson had hoped for. "Get me a channel to Sergeant Gabriel," he said.

"Yes, sir," said Perry.

The conversation which followed was short in duration. Lanson gave orders and Gabriel acknowledged them.

When he was done speaking, Lanson cut the comms channel and waited for developments.

TWENTY-SIX

"Shuttle 1 has exited its docking tunnel," said Lieutenant Turner, five minutes after Lanson had given the order for its departure.

"Keep the sensors on it," said Lanson. He'd already explained the purpose of the launch to his crew and all eyes were watching.

Having left the comparative safety of the *Infinitar* behind, the shuttle banked west along the bay. At a distance of five thousand metres, the transport came to a halt, with its flank facing the narrow gap between the *Infinitar* and the *Barox-K*.

After a short time, the forward flank door opened, and figures became visible in the compact airlock. Lanson recognized Sergeant Gabriel – who was holding the Ezin-Tor – and Corporal Ziegler as well, who was presumably acting as anchor.

Gabriel didn't waste time. He raised the Ezin-Tor and, though the weapon gave no visible sign it had been fired, a burst of corrosive energy struck one of the *Barox-K*'s gravity chain generators.

"Come on, come on," muttered Lanson.

First came the bad news. "Corporal Hennessey is piloting the shuttle, Captain," said Perry. "The vessel has received a shutdown command. Its engines are still running, but Corporal Hennessey is frozen out of the onboard systems."

Next came the good news - the Ezin-Tor had gouged a big chunk from one of the gravity chain generators holding the *Infinitar*. Secondly, the *Barox-K* hadn't exploded.

"Has that chain generator failed?" asked Lanson, refusing to think what would have happened had the generator been made from the unstable, detonating type of Galos.

"Scanning...," said Abrams. "The generator hasn't failed, Captain, but its output has dropped off a cliff."

"That leaves twenty-eight generators still holding on to us," said Lanson.

"Yes, sir," said Abrams. "Like I told you when Sergeant Gabriel was heading for the shuttle, we won't have to break anywhere near all the generators before we can pull clear."

"Are you ready to give me an estimate of how many we need to destroy?" asked Lanson, referring to a brief argument from a couple of minutes ago.

Abrams sighed heavily. "I'm sorry, Captain, there are too many unknown variables. If you order me to pull a figure out of my ass, I'll do it, as long as you accept exactly where the answer came from."

"Sergeant Gabriel has fired a second shot," said Lieutenant Perry. "And a third."

Gabriel's aim was good, and each discharge struck one of the chain generators. The Ezin-Tor didn't quite have the punch to completely disintegrate the huge tethering posts, but it was doing a fine job of disabling them.

"The output from one of those generators has fallen to zero, and the other is at ten percent, Captain," said Massey.

"Three down, plenty to go," said Lanson.

As it happened, he wasn't expecting this to be all plain sailing, and it turned out he was right.

"The shuttle is accelerating out of position, Captain," said Turner. "The bay controller must have decided to take more direct action to prevent the attack on the *Barox-K*."

"I'm surprised it took this long," Lanson admitted. "Order the controller to rescind the shutdown code."

"That command has generated an error code response, Captain," said Turner. "Another protocol conflict."

"Time for Plan B - transmit the take-over code to the shuttle," said Lanson.

"Transmitting," said Turner. "Fingers crossed."

Lanson didn't know if the take-over code – which was a facility the *Infinitar* had in common with Human Confederation warships, and which was intended to ensure a parent vessel could always recover its own shuttles – would override the bay shutdown code.

"Corporal Hennessey reports her continued lack of control over the shuttle, sir," said Turner.

It was a setback, though one which Lanson had more than half expected. "Launch Shuttles 2, 3 and 4," he said.

"Yes, sir," said Turner. "The exits for Shuttles 2 and 4 are tight up against the *Barox-K*, so it's going to take a bit more effort to get them out into the bay."

Lanson didn't reply and continued watching the feed aimed at Shuttle 1. The vessel was now racing across the bay, heading towards the western wall.

"Ah, crap," said Lanson, suddenly realising he might have made an enormous mistake. "We can't let the bay controller pilot the shuttle into one of the adjacent bays."

"We're supposed to be command of the entire facility, Captain," said Matlock. "Order the linking doors to remain closed."

"And hope there's no protocol conflict," said Lanson. Just thinking about what a screw-up the Aral had made of their primary Galos storage facility defences was making his blood boil and he tried not to let it affect him. "Lieutenant Turner, order the bay doors to stay closed."

"Yes, sir. The command is sent."

Lanson stared at the feeds, his eyes unblinking and his nostrils flared. The linking doors stayed closed, though the shuttle continued its journey towards the western end of the bay. Having had its plan foiled, the control computer brought the transport to a halt in the farthest corner, where Sergeant Gabriel no longer had a firing angle on the chain generators.

"Pilot Shuttle 2 into position, Commander Matlock," said Lanson.

"Yes, sir, it's on its way."

Under remote control, the second of the *Infinitar*'s shuttles accelerated directly towards the first vessel. Slowing late, Matlock rotated the transport – with its flank doors already open – and guided it adjacent to Shuttle 1.

"Sergeant Gabriel says the gap is too big to jump," said Perry.

"Let me finish the fine-tuning," said Matlock, leaning close to her console. "When I'm done, he won't be able to drop his pocket change through the gap."

"The shuttles are now close enough, Commander," said Perry. "Sergeant Gabriel has transferred to Shuttle 2 and the rest of the squad are following."

Lanson wasn't yet sure if he'd made the right choice in ordering all the soldiers to the shuttle. He'd wanted to be prepared in case an attack on the physical bay control hardware was required and it was as-yet unclear if such a mission would be required. Hopefully a few more Ezin-Tor shots from Shuttle 2 would be all that was needed.

"I'm retaining control over the shuttle," said Matlock. "I'm bringing it into position."

The transport sped east under maximum thrust and Lanson anxiously watched its progress. It felt as if a conspiracy of Aral failures was working to ensure his death and he hated being powerless in the face of this enormously potent tech - tech which appeared to be governed by code written by incompetents who'd perished centuries ago.

"Decelerating and rotating portside," said Matlock. "Any second now..."

The shuttle's flank door became visible, and Sergeant Gabriel was framed in the opening, holding the Ezin-Tor at chest height.

Less than five seconds after Matlock brought Shuttle 2 to a halt, a fourth of the gravity chain generators was struck by an Ezin-Tor blast. A fifth generator followed and then a sixth.

"Corporal Hennessey reports that Shuttle 2 has received a shutdown code," said Perry.

On this occasion, the bay controller didn't delay for a moment. It piloted the shuttle away from the *Infinitar*, aiming for the same western corner as before.

"Sergeant Gabriel got off one last shot before he lost his firing angle," said Turner.

"Seven of the chain generators are now producing either zero power, or their output is so low it won't trouble the *Infinitar*'s propulsion," said Abrams.

"I'm piloting Shuttle 3 in pursuit of Shuttle 2," said Matlock.

"Captain, Sergeant Gabriel reports his concerns that the Ezin-Tor's power supply is becoming overstressed," said Perry.

"It'll have a chance to cool down during the switch to Shuttle 3," said Lanson. "A couple more shots from the Ezin-Tor and I'll attempt to break the gravity chains."

"Yes, sir."

The bay controller had clearly not been programmed with an imagination, nor to adapt its approach to problem solving. Having piloted Shuttle 2 into the same corner as before, the Aral computer left the transport stationary, fifty metres below Shuttle 1.

Commander Matlock wasn't far behind with Shuttle 3 and, as soon as Shuttle 2 came to a halt, she began positioning the transport so that the soldiers could transfer with the minimum of delay.

"If we end up using all four shuttles for this, I'll accept the need, but I won't be happy about it," said Lanson.

"We could try breaking free from the *Barox-K* before Sergeant Gabriel fires another shot," said Matlock.

"I don't think we've done enough, Commander," said Abrams. "Don't ask me to provide the calculations – this is pure hunch."

"How long before the surface shield collapses, Lieutenant Turner?" asked Lanson.

"Twelve minutes, Captain."

The margins were even tighter than Lanson had realised, and he cursed under his breath. Meanwhile, Sergeant Gabriel and his squad had transferred to Shuttle 3 and Commander Matlock was piloting it rapidly towards the *Infinitar*.

"Ready to start the shooting," said Matlock, halting the shuttle a few hundred metres away.

Gabriel fired the Ezin-Tor, shutting down one of the chain generators. Having adjusted his aim, he disabled another.

"Something's happening to Shuttle 3," said Perry. "The sensors won't bring it into focus."

"Corporal Hennessey reports the transport is still under her control," said Turner. "It has not been subject to a shut-down code."

"Get me a channel to Sergeant Gabriel," said Lanson.

"Yes, sir. He's on the bridge speakers."

"Sergeant, you're drifting out of phase," said Lanson. "What is your feeling about the Ezin-Tor? Is it good for another shot?"

"I wouldn't like to guess, Captain. If the circumstances were different, I'd have already put the Ezin-Tor aside."

"We have to be out of here in ten minutes, Sergeant – there's no time to let the Ezin-Tor cool down."

"If—" Gabriel hesitated, like he was reluctant to continue. "If I take another shot, I think we'll regret it."

Although Lanson wasn't on the shuttle, holding the gun, he heard enough in Gabriel's voice to convince him it was time to move onto the next phase of the plan.

"Hold fire, Sergeant," he said. "Commander Matlock will bring you back to the *Infinitar*."

"Yes, sir," said Gabriel, making no effort to hide his relief.

"I've recalled Shuttles 3 and 4," said Matlock. "The *Infinitar*'s autopilot system will bring them back into the forwardmost bays."

As the two shuttles headed for home, Lanson asked the question he'd been keeping on the back burner for the last couple of minutes.

"How come Shuttle 3 wasn't issued with a shutdown code?" he asked.

"I'll query the bay controller," said Turner. A short time later, she had an answer, of sorts. "The shutdown code *was* issued," she said. "The code failed, and an error was returned to the bay controller."

"What was the code?" asked Lanson, watching Shuttle 4 enter its docking tunnel. Shuttle 3 wasn't far behind.

"It was a generic failure response, Captain – like the cause was unknown."

"Maybe because Shuttle 3 has been affected by the Ezin-Tor," mused Lanson.

He didn't spend any longer thinking about it. Shuttle 3 entered its docking tunnel, leaving no reason to delay further.

The *Barox-K*, albeit only acting according to its control systems, had been an irritating pain in the ass ever since the *Infinitar* exited void travel at the Erion facility. Now, it was time to break free or die trying. Lanson smiled inwardly and readied himself for some high-velocity impact testing.

TWENTY-SEVEN

Lanson's plan was the same as the one he'd already discussed with crew. He intended to pilot the *Infinitar* at high velocity into one of the bay exit tunnels in such a way that the *Barox-K* would strike the adjacent wall. If everything worked out, the gravity chains would break and the *Infinitar* would be free.

Assuming the Barox-K doesn't explode.

The risk remained, though the Ezin-Tor attack on the chain generators had made Lanson optimistic that the *Barox-K*'s Galos modules weren't unstable and prone to detonation.

Positioning the *Infinitar* didn't take long and, when Lanson was done, the warship's nose was aimed directly at the linking tunnel to the east. The *Barox-K*, on the other hand, was lined up with the bay wall to the right of the exit.

"Is everyone ready?" asked Lanson.

He didn't wait for a response. Pushing the control bars as far as they'd go, Lanson expected drama from the *Infinitar*'s scarcely tested engines. What he got was somewhat more invigorating.

The propulsion howled and whined, and the *Infinitar* was

hurled across the bay like it had been fired from a catapult. Lanson stared at the feeds, his expression frozen in concentration.

At a velocity he had no time to check, the *Infinitar* reached the mouth of the tunnel, and the *Barox-K* struck the bay wall. The alloy plating along the full length of the linking passage rippled and then exploded outwards with the force of the shockwave. Shattered rock came after the metal, filling the way ahead with boulders, stones and dust alike.

Despite Lanson's best efforts to hold his warship on a straight-line course, the *Barox-K* acted like an anchor and dragged the *Infinitar* into a diagonal across the passage. Fighting with the controls and holding the propulsion at maximum output, he snarled with anger at the stubbornness of the gravity chains.

And then, those chains broke. Lanson knew it at once, because the *Infinitar*'s engines roared with the exuberance of release. Suddenly, the excess of available output meant he was in danger of losing control, as the warship surged deeper into the linking tunnel. Impact warnings forward and aft indicated a real danger that the *Infinitar* would become wedged in a diagonal across the passage.

"Too much debris," said Lanson, trying to make sense of the feeds.

The dust made everything indistinct, though the dark shapes dropping through the grey made him think the linking tunnel had either completely collapsed, or it was on the verge of doing so.

Determined that a few billion ton of stone weren't going to prevent him from escaping Erion, Lanson fought to prevent the *Infinitar* from becoming wedged across the tunnel, buried beneath the rock, or both. As he wrestled the controls, numerous hull impact warnings appeared on his status display.

Shit, the topside guns.

The barrels of the *Infinitar*'s main armaments were huge and designed to shrug off the effects of a few missile detonations, but the Aral had certainly not intended them to be used as battering rams. Judging by the effort it was taking to break out of the tunnel, Lanson had serious doubts the guns would be operational when the *Infinitar* emerged into the next bay.

"Captain, our Galos output has increased by fifteen percent over the expected draw from the engines," said Abrams.

"Is it a problem?" said Lanson through gritted teeth. "Because I don't need another one."

"I can't confirm, sir. I'll let you know as soon as I discover the cause."

Lanson did his best to put Abrams' report from his mind and to channel everything into piloting the *Infinitar* safely to the far side of the linking passage. From the resistance he was feeling through the controls, Lanson was sure the tunnel was completely choked. On the plus side, no matter how hard a piece of stone, it couldn't withstand the combined mass and power of a vessel like the *Infinitar*.

Bit-by-bit, the warship forced its way past the blockage, crushing the rocks and pushing through them. When freedom came it happened so quickly that Lanson was almost caught off guard. The *Infinitar* burst from the tunnel, casting debris in a fountain, and accelerating rapidly towards the far exit.

Lanson reined in the warship before it suffered a second impact. "How long left before the surface shield collapses?" he asked.

"Six minutes, Captain," said Turner.

Having expected the answer to be a lower number, Lanson didn't complain. His perception of time always misbehaved in moments of extreme crisis, leading him to believe the transit of the blocked tunnel had lasted far longer than the reality.

"I already instructed the bay controller to open every linking door between here and the void travel bay," said Turner. "We should have a clear run."

"Thank you, Lieutenant," said Lanson, pleased, since he'd forgotten to give the order himself. "You saved us some time."

With the *Infinitar* no longer chained, the short journey to the void travel bay would take less than a couple of minutes, assuming no more obstacles were standing in the way.

"East into the next bay and down three levels, Captain," said Matlock.

"I remember," said Lanson, increasing velocity again.

The eastern tunnel wasn't far, owing to the distance the *Infinitar* had covered in its rapid exit from the collapsed passage to the west. Lanson guided the warship rapidly into the next bay. The place was almost empty, barring a few stacks of alloy plating and a handful of shuttles. It was clear the Erion facility was either under-utilised, or the Aral had anticipated the appearance of an attacker they couldn't defeat, and had therefore taken their resources elsewhere.

This new bay had an exit in the south wall and one in the floor. Since Lanson's destination was down, he positioned the *Infinitar* directly above the opening and guided it into the bay below. As colossal as all the others, this bay was not so empty. A part-built warship, its hull armour missing in places and its propulsion modules exposed, was suspended in a gravity field two hundred metres above the floor.

Although it was incomplete, it was easy to imagine the sweeping curves of the finished product. In terms of size and mass, the warship would have likely been similar to the *Ragnar-3*, though in appearance it could have been designed by a different species entirely.

"All the construction vehicles are here," said Lanson, noting the swarms of lifter shuttles and the multi-armed automated handlers. "Yet the building work has stopped."

"There'll be a critical piece of equipment missing," said Abrams. "Maybe it never arrived, or maybe the Aral evacuated this place and took it with them."

It was a mystery that would remain unsolved. Without slowing, Lanson piloted the *Infinitar* into the next lower bay. He was becoming increasingly conscious of the passing seconds, and he hardly spared the contents of the new bay a glance. His mind vaguely recognized the presence of more construction materials, along with shuttles and a couple of larger vessels which might have been armed dropships, but Lanson's attention was focused almost completely on the exit tunnel.

Continuing its descent, the *Infinitar* entered the void travel bay. Lanson didn't need a second glance to be sure – each corner was occupied by a hundred-metre Galos cube, and that was all the evidence he needed. Aside from the Galos cubes, the bay was empty, though an additional – closed – door led west towards yet another bay.

"The shield's time to collapse has just dropped below four minutes, Captain," said Turner.

"Query the bay controller," said Lanson. "Find out how long it takes to prepare for and activate void travel."

"It requires thirty-one seconds, Captain."

"That gives us a couple of spare minutes," said Lanson. "I want to know if there's a facility to detonate the Galos stores here at Erion."

"I'll check, sir," said Turner. Several precious seconds passed before she had the answer. "There *is* a facility to remote detonate what the bay controller refers to as Singularity Tier

Galos, but it's not going to work for us – the Aral transported those stores elsewhere."

"Damnit!" said Lanson, clenching his fists. He was angry, but given the circumstances, he admitted to himself that getting the hell away from Erion would be a victory in itself.

"We can't change the reality, Captain," said Matlock. "It's time we hightailed it out of here."

Lanson nodded. "Lieutenant Turner, instruct the bay controller to send us by void travel to the same destination as the Singularity warship."

"Yes, sir, I'll pass on that instruction."

Turner was quiet for almost twenty seconds and Lanson got the feeling that something wasn't going to plan. "Talk to me, Lieutenant."

"We're in the crap, Captain," said Turner. "Apparently there's a protocol that disallows the primary command vessel from exiting the facility while other vessels are not yet evacuated."

Lanson could scarcely believe his ears. The Aral failings at Erion were piled so high the top of the shit heap was above the clouds. In fact, he was coming increasingly to believe that the facility's control systems had never been properly tested before the place was abandoned.

"If we lay low, whoever is crewing the Ravanok might think we've travelled somewhere else," said Matlock.

"I'm sure the enemy vessel has the means of detecting faster-than-light travel, Commander," said Lanson. "It'll know we haven't gone anywhere. It's here to destroy us, and I reckon the Erion facility is just the icing on the cake."

In truth, Lanson didn't know if the Ravanok was planning to destroy Erion. When he thought about it for a moment, he became even less sure. The ease with which the alien sphere was locating the Aral facilities suggested it could have tracked down and annihilated everything the aliens had ever built in the centuries since they went missing.

Maybe I'm wrong. Maybe the Ravanok lacks the ability to find the Aral planets, and there's something about the Infinitar which leaves a recognizable trail.

Lanson shook away the thoughts. "Lieutenant Turner, query the bay controller again," he said. "If we combined with another Singularity warship, would we still be classed as the primary vessel on Erion?"

"I'll ask that now, sir."

"Lieutenant Perry, I'm sure the bay controller can handle two requests at the same time," said Lanson. "Instruct it to return the Singularity warship back to this bay by void travel."

"Yes, sir."

Lanson waited in a state of increasing agitation. To keep himself occupied, he sent a query of his own to the bay controller. The response informed him that the surface shield would collapse in eighty seconds.

"Lieutenant Turner, Lieutenant Perry, we don't have much time," said Lanson.

"Captain, the bay controller has accepted the instruction to recall the Singularity class," said Perry. "The warmup has commenced."

"What answer have you been given, Lieutenant Turner?"

"The bay controller keeps returning a null response, Captain," said Turner. "I've rephrased the question several times and the result is the same."

"It's a situation so far beyond anything the Aral imagined, they don't even have the protocols necessary to produce a conflict," said Matlock.

"Which might be yet more bad luck for us, Commander," said Lanson. "We need the bay controller to accept we're no longer primary after we combine with the incoming vessel."

"The Singularity class will enter this bay in a little over ten seconds," said Perry.

Lanson glanced across at Matlock, who looked on edge, but still in control. He guessed his own appearance wasn't much different. "I think we can ride our luck for a little while longer, Commander."

"Here's hoping, Captain."

"Five seconds," said Perry.

Unsure where in the bay the warship would appear, Lanson watched the feeds intently. At exactly the stated moment, the Singularity warship exited void travel a few thousand metres east of the *Infinitar*.

A split-second later, the text on Lanson's screen updated.

> *Combination request received. Combination routine initiated.*

"It's happening," he said.

Turning his attention back to the feeds, he studied the newly arrived warship. The shape of this one was that of an irregular tetrahedron, more than four thousand metres in length, and a little more than fifteen hundred metres at its highest point. Aside from the *Ragnar-3* – the first piece of the *Infinitar* Lanson and his crew had captured – this vessel was the only other Singularity class that appeared as though it had been designed to operate independently of the other components.

Lanson only needed a moment to figure out where the fifth piece was designed to fit. The tetrahedron would link to the *Infinitar*'s portside, below the *Ragnar-3*, forming an angled flank and partly completing the nose section. An image appeared in Lanson's head – a picture of how the *Infinitar* would look once it was finished. The angled sides, the pointed nose, and the high stern would be the epitome of purposeful brutality.

At any other time, Lanson would have smiled. Here and now, his death was impending, and he certainly didn't want to be within this bay when the Ravanok broke through the Erion shield.

Escape was possible – if only the bay controller could find a way to resolve its coding conflict.

TWENTY-EIGHT

The moment a light appeared on Lanson's control panel informing him of contact with the other Singularity class, he gave the command.

"Lieutenant Turner, instruct the bay controller to send us into void travel," he said.

Turner was ready for the order. "Yes, sir, instruction sent." She swore. "Request denied."

"Thirty-five seconds until the shield collapses," said Perry.

"We're not going to make it," said Abrams. "Not without a miracle."

Lanson's brain raced, searching for a way out of what felt like an impossible situation. "Can we order a facility-wide stand-down?" he asked in desperation. "Then, there'll be no need for the *Infinitar* to stay here."

"Captain, the bay controller lacks the authority to instruct the stand-down," said Turner.

"Even when the damn order has come from the primary vessel?" asked Lanson, struggling to contain his fury.

"Twenty-five seconds until the shield collapses," said Perry.

"Not enough time to send us into void travel," said Massey. "It's game over."

Lanson wasn't ready to accept defeat, even though it looked inevitable. His earlier suspicions that the Aral had screwed up their protocols had now been replaced with a certainty that the base controller had suffered a hardware or software failure, making it act in an unpredictable and illogical manner. There wasn't anything Lanson could do to fix the controller – the best he could do was figure out a way to make it compliant.

An idea appeared from out of nowhere. As far as ideas went, the implementation would be fraught with risk, but Lanson was no stranger to walking the tightrope.

"Lieutenant Abrams – ready the *Infinitar* for void travel, using our own propulsion," said Lanson. "Our destination is the place from which the Singularity class was recalled."

"Yes, sir," said Abrams. "Entering the coordinates."

"Captain, we can't enter void travel with the surface shield active," said Matlock. Her expression betrayed sudden understanding. "You're planning to cancel the shield before the Galos generators blow."

"That's right, Commander."

"If we enter void travel before the combination is finished, we might leave the other Singularity class behind."

"I think there's a chance of it," said Lanson, his eyes darting to the feeds. "That's why we're going to need some luck."

The topside feeds showed a partial view of the Singularity class, which was still in the process of combining. Lanson could hear some faraway clunking sounds, but it wasn't clear how long it would take until the two vessels were linked.

"Ten seconds before the surface shield collapses," said Perry.

Lanson had waited as long as he dared, to allow the combination routine time to progress. Now was the moment to give his next order.

"Instruct the bay controller to shut down the surface shields," he said. "And do it quickly."

"Yes, sir," said Turner without hesitation. "The controller has acknowledged the order. It has not yet confirmed execution."

Lanson gritted his teeth and wished he could put a missile into the bay controller. "Has the shield been shut down?" he asked.

"The surface Galos cubes are showing zero percent, Captain," said Perry.

"And we aren't dead," said Lanson. "Not yet, anyway."

"I've received confirmation that the shield was cancelled successfully, Captain," said Turner.

"Should I activate the void travel, Captain?" asked Abrams.

"Have the control systems tie-ins with the Singularity class completed?"

"No, Captain, they haven't even begun. The physical process of linking must be still ongoing."

Lanson hadn't forgotten the combination which had taken place in the Baltol cube, and how he'd lost control of the warship for a time. He didn't want his crew to become locked out of the onboard systems just as he ordered the *Infinitar* into void travel.

On the other hand, the combination at Ravrol hadn't affected Commander Matlock's ability to pilot the warship at all. Given the evidence, Lanson reckoned it likely that each combination was different, depending on the hardware.

"Captain, we can't afford to wait any longer," said Matlock. "This is our chance – we have to leave."

Before Lanson could give the order, the sensor feeds went dark. At the same time, a dozen gauges on his instrumentation panel began jumping around crazily, while a painful, high-pitched squeal came from all around.

I left it too long.

"Lieutenant Abrams, activate the void travel," yelled Lanson. The squealing continued and it was almost intolerable.

"Void travel activated!" shouted Abrams in return.

The propulsion shrieked and the unsettled gauges went straight to one hundred percent. Lanson was ready for the transit, and he clenched his teeth. A thumping expulsion of energy swept through the bridge, and he felt a momentary separateness from his body.

As rapidly as it had begun, the shrieking sound disappeared. The squealing went on for another couple of seconds, fading rapidly and with it, bringing Lanson immense relief.

"Where are we?" he asked. His hearing had been dulled and his ears were buzzing. "Did the Singularity class come with us?"

"The sensors are online, Captain," said Turner. "I'm bringing them into focus."

Lanson shook his head clear. The sensor feeds indicated the *Infinitar* was inside a monumental bay, and it wasn't alone.

"Captain – an Ixtar warship!" said Turner.

The vessel was another colossus like the *Tyrantor* and the *Ghiotor*. At almost twenty-two-thousand metres in length, it was stationary, close to one of the bay's shorter walls and perpendicular to the *Infinitar*. Such were the dimensions of the bay that the Ixtar warship's nose and stern were each more than five thousand metres from the walls.

The *Infinitar*'s onboard systems recognized the enemy vessel and labelled it on the tactical screen. *Pembros.*

"What are your orders, sir?" asked Matlock.

Lanson felt like he'd jumped from the frying pan and straight into the fire. Perhaps foolishly, he'd hoped for a chance to take stock following the escape from Erion, but instead he'd come face-to-face with an opponent which he guessed was at least the equal of the *Infinitar*.

Preferring to run, Lanson cursed that none of the bay exits were open. In fact, no doors were visible, though he was sure they existed. An ILT out of the bay seemed like the safest option, since Lanson had no desire to activate another void travel so soon after the last one. The alternative was to open fire.

In other circumstances, Lanson might not have taken the risk. However, the pent-up anger from his time on Erion over-whelmed his desire for escape, and demanded he take direct action. Lanson could see what he believed was the enemy spaceship's disintegration cannon, mounted beneath its nose where it couldn't be fired without some manoeuvring.

"Target the enemy warship and fire," he said. "Give it everything."

"Yes, sir," said Matlock. "Forward Avantar clusters one to eight fired. Topside clusters one to four, fired. Gradar turrets set to track and destroy."

The missiles – all 144 of them – were ejected from their launch tubes. Across the bay they sped, into a storm of counter-measures. Repeater projectiles tore into the missiles, and pulses of energy knocked out their guidance systems.

Regardless, the range was so short that the enemy counter-measures were unable to completely eliminate the missile wave. Almost thirty Avantar warheads detonated against the *Pembros*'s energy shield, which appeared a split-second before the impacts and absorbed the explosive energy.

"Fire again," said Lanson, rotating the *Infinitar* so that its portside tubes were lined up with the enemy spaceship.

"Portside clusters one to eight and topside clusters one to four, targeted and fired," said Matlock.

"The enemy vessel has not fired in return, Captain," said Turner.

For a second time, the *Infinitar*'s missiles raced across the bay. This time, twenty-five exploded against the Ixtar energy shield. Lanson narrowed his eyes, wondering if he detected the first sign of weakening in the enemy defences. The Avantars were enormously potent, but he couldn't be sure one way or another how much drain they were inflicting on the energy shield.

"Fire again, Commander," said Lanson, rotating the *Infinitar* so that its underside clusters were on target.

"Yes, sir. Underside clusters one to eight, targeted and fired," said Matlock. "Why aren't they attacking us?"

Lanson didn't know. His intention had been to launch missiles at the Ixtar, to see if he could punch through their shield before they initiated a significant response. At the first sign of real danger, Lanson had planned to execute an ILT out of the bay. And yet, the enemy crew seemed content to soak missiles without firing in return.

Whatever the reason for this unexpected behaviour, Lanson didn't think he was going to like it.

"Captain, our tie-ins with the Singularity class are finished," said Lieutenant Abrams. "I'm checking to see if we have any propulsion upgrades."

"Are there any new active options on the weapons panel, Commander Matlock?" asked Lanson, rotating the *Infinitar* yet again.

"I'll check after this next launch, Captain. Starboard clusters one to eight targeted and fired. Checking weapons availability. We have additional Avantar clusters and Gradar turrets, but the options on the Singularity menu are still greyed out."

"Damnit," said Lanson, wondering when he'd get his hands on the good stuff.

The starboard Avantars detonated against the *Pembros*'s energy shield and this time, Lanson was sure the intensity of the red was diminished. Perhaps, he thought, the enemy crew had suffered a hardware failure, locking them out of their weapons. It didn't seem likely, but it would be a shame to spurn this opportunity to knock out a trillion-ton warship without taking any damage in return.

Even so, instinct was gnawing away at Lanson's guts, telling him he'd missed something of vital importance, and that the best thing he could do would be to press the ILT button on his controls and exit this place, to give himself and his crew the time they needed to discover what changes the latest combination had brought.

And yet...a free kill was too good to turn down.

As he was bringing the topside clusters to bear, Lanson heard a strange whining coming from behind. The noise was so out of place, he half-turned to see where it had come from. At that moment, a fountain of red exploded from Commander Matlock's chest. The whining sound – a gauss weapon – came again and again. Lanson felt a projectile enter his shoulder, a second hit him in the spine, and then he knew no more.

TWENTY-NINE

Lanson opened his eyes and found only darkness. He was confused and in a lot of pain. A soft groan escaped his lips and he tried weakly to move. Whatever surface Lanson was lying upon, it was yielding and shifted beneath him.

Not yet ready to attempt any greater effort, he remained still. The pain was dull, and it started from his lower back and went all the way to the top of his head, as if he'd been beaten with a club and then inflicted with a terrible hangover. As well as the pain, Lanson could feel an itching sensation which was no easier to bear.

The bridge was attacked, he thought, the memory coming back to him of Commander Matlock's surprised expression as the gauss slug burst from her chest.

How the attack could have taken him so completely by surprise, Lanson didn't know. The answer was important, but this wasn't the right moment to consider what might have happened.

With an effort, Lanson turned his head. He saw grey lumps and, when he turned a little further, he detected in his periphery the dull blue light of the *Infinitar*'s interior illumination. Breathing in through his nostrils, Lanson noticed a metallic scent, which he recognized as blood.

The exertion had been too great and, despite the pain, Lanson faded from consciousness.

Sometime later, he awoke to find the pain had lessened, though the itching hadn't gone away. He lay still, gathering his thoughts.

Where am I?

It was time to find out. Using both hands, Lanson attempted to push himself upright. The surface beneath one of his palms slithered aside and he heard a grunting sound. Repositioning his hand, Lanson tried again. This time, he found a solid surface, and, with the assistance of his knees, he made it to all fours. The grunting came again, and it was followed by a groan.

From his new elevation, Lanson discovered that he was atop a pile of bodies. Torn spacesuits were covered in blood and he saw the face of Lieutenant Abrams nearby. The man's features were sunken and his skin grey. He was either asleep or dead.

Clambering carefully to his feet, Lanson stared down at his crew. They'd been dragged off the bridge by the attackers and dumped here, in a compact room, the location of which wasn't immediately apparent. A thick trail of blood – now dried to a dull brown – led from the door to the place where Lanson and the others had been deposited.

"Is anyone awake?" he asked.

"Mmmf."

The sound had come from somewhere in the pile, though Lanson wasn't sure who had made it. He leaned in closer. Commander Matlock was visible, along with Lieutenants Abrams and Turner. Lieutenants Massey and Perry were beneath the others and Lanson lacked the strength to pull them free.

A sudden dizziness made him sit on the hard floor, with his back to the wall. He checked himself over. Bullets had entered his spine and shoulder, that he knew, but neither should have killed him instantly.

I took a headshot.

Raising his hand to his skull, Lanson felt carefully for signs of injury. Everything felt normal. His head was hurting, but it was inside rather than out.

After a time, Lanson climbed to his feet. His strength was returning, though he didn't know how long it would take to recover fully. When he'd been shot in the leg, the Galos in his body had healed him quickly. This time, he'd suffered much greater physical trauma and he guessed the repairs had been harder to enact.

"Captain?"

Commander Matlock had her eyes open, and her head was lifted.

"We were attacked on the bridge and killed," said Lanson. "The Galos brought us back."

Matlock closed her eyes. "I feel like shit."

"You're lying on top of Lieutenant Perry. I'm going to pull you clear," said Lanson, hoping he was strong enough to manage.

Grabbing Matlock's foot, he pulled steadily until she was away from the others. Returning to the pile, Lanson dragged Abrams clear, before returning to roll Perry over. Her eyes were moving behind their lids, suggesting she would soon be awake.

Lieutenant Massey wasn't so lucky. He'd been struck by what looked like a dozen or more projectiles and most of his head was missing. Blood had pooled thickly beneath his corpse, and it gleamed in the dull light.

"Shit," said Lanson, feeling like all the energy had been sucked out of him.

He stood quietly for a moment. The Galos had limits after all, and Massey had been the one to find them. He'd be sorely missed.

Steeling himself against a dozen emotions he wasn't ready to deal with, Lanson checked Lieutenant Turner, in case she'd suffered the same fate as Massey. Judging by the blood, she'd been shot in the chest, but she was breathing and there was no sign of an injury.

"How long were we out?" asked Matlock, struggling into a sitting position.

"I don't know," said Lanson. He didn't usually wear his suit helmet on the bridge and neither did the other members of his crew. Because of this, he didn't know how much time had passed.

Now that the pain was almost gone and the itching had begun to subside, Lanson became more acutely aware of the urgency. He and his crew had no guns and the *Infinitar* had been hijacked, and by whom, Lanson still didn't know.

"I need to contact Sergeant Gabriel," said Lanson.

Although he hadn't been wearing his suit helmet, his earpiece and microphone had been in place. The headset was gone, and Lanson didn't know where.

Striding across to Lieutenant Abrams, he tugged the man's headset free and put it on. The device was still connected to the internal comms and Lanson issued a voice command for a channel to be opened to Sergeant Gabriel.

To Lanson's enormous relief, he received an immediate response.

"Captain Lanson," said Gabriel.

"Sergeant, the *Infinitar* has been hijacked," said Lanson. "Have you engaged the enemy?"

"Hijacked?" said Gabriel. His tone suggested he was asking himself if this was an inappropriate joke.

"My crew and I were shot and then taken off the bridge," said Lanson. "Lieutenant Massey didn't make it. We didn't even see who attacked us."

"It was the Ixtar, sir," said Abrams, who was on the floor nearby. "They must have cracked the security on the bridge door and then they caught us by surprise. Lieutenant Massey was going for his gun and the bastards filled him full of slugs."

Lanson relayed this to Sergeant Gabriel, and then he spent the next couple of minutes in discussion with the soldier, in the hope that they could work out a plan. During the course of the conversation, Lanson learned that comms traffic from his headset had stopped about twenty minutes ago. Private Wolf was the one who figured that out.

Having thought he'd been long dead, Lanson was surprised to find he'd been out of action for so little time. Maybe he had a chance to regain control of the *Infinitar* before the Ixtar boarded with more of their troops.

That was the moment he realised how the enemy had accomplished their attack. The Ixtar had been inside the Singularity class when it was recalled to Erion and, when the combination was finished, they'd found a way onto the *Infinitar*.

"The entrance point can't have been far from the bridge, Captain," said Gabriel, once he'd heard Lanson's explanation. "And they must have moved damn quickly."

"That's water under the bridge, Sergeant," said Lanson. "We have to recapture the *Infinitar* from an unknown number of enemy troops and prevent more from boarding – assuming we aren't already too late."

"An assault on the bridge would be reckless without knowledge of how many we're facing," said Gabriel. "Though it may come to that anyway."

"The internal monitors will tell us how many Ixtar are on board," said Lanson. "Normally the presence of unknown life forms would set off an alarm, but the tie-ins for the Singularity class didn't finish until just before the attack."

"There are two miniguns above the bridge door, Captain, why didn't they fire at the enemy?" asked Gabriel.

"The automated defences are controlled by the internal monitors," said Lanson. "And the internal monitors didn't know about the Ixtar because the tie-ins hadn't finished."

He cursed under his breath. Lanson knew he'd screwed up, though he didn't want to beat himself up about it too much. The way everything had happened so quickly, along with the unexpected discovery of the Ixtar vessel in the bay, and the even more unexpected presence of enemy soldiers on the Singularity warship, made it hard to convince himself that he could have done much better.

"What's the next step for us, Captain?" asked Gabriel.

"We need to access one of the security stations," said Lanson. "That'll tell us how many Ixtar soldiers are on board, and where they're located."

"What about the enemy warship, sir? If the crew of that vessel believe they're in danger of losing control of the *Infinitar*, they'll launch an attack – maybe before you and your crew are in a position to respond."

"That's one problem out of a mountain of others, Sergeant," said Lanson. "Our first step is to access a security console. If I remember rightly, there's one not far from the mess area."

"Yes, sir, there is, and I'm on my way there now," said Gabriel. "And another thing – Private Wolf has located your connection point to the internal comms. You're about forty metres from the bridge, in one of the side rooms off the corridor leading to the airlifts in BL-10."

"That helps," said Lanson. "Pass on my thanks to Private Wolf."

"Since you're so near the bridge, I would suggest you lay low until I find out what's showing on the internal monitors," said Gabriel. He gave a bitter laugh. "The Ixtar didn't find me or my squad, and that makes me think they only have a limited force."

"I have to see to my crew," said Lanson. "Take care, Sergeant."

"You too, sir."

Lanson closed out of the channel and turned his attention to the others in the room. Matlock and Abrams were awake and alert – if not yet on their feet - while both Turner and Perry were stirring.

"When Sergeant Gabriel accesses the security console, we need to be ready," said Lanson. "Help me rouse Lieutenant Turner and Lieutenant Perry."

Fortunately, both officers were on the brink of emerging from sleep, coma, or whatever state they were in. Once they were awake, Lanson did his best to cajole them into rapid action, though he met with only partial success. He refused to become angry, since he well remembered how much effort it had taken just to open his eyes, let alone climb to his feet.

Before everyone was upright, Lanson received a channel request, which he accepted.

"Captain, I'm at the security console," said Gabriel. "There's good news and there's bad news."

"Let's hear the good news."

"There are only a dozen Ixtar on the *Infinitar*, Captain, and that includes the new Singularity class that got added to the hull. All twelve of the enemy are holed up on the bridge."

"What's the bad news?"

"It seems like my Tier 1 status allows me to access the

bridge monitors, sir. The Ixtar have a device in there with them – it's a grey cube, about a metre in size. They have it plugged into the main command console."

"A security breaker," said Lanson. "That explains how they entered the bridge so easily."

"I ran an audit, Captain, and there is no widespread breach in the control systems. The security breaker opened the bridge door, but it hasn't cracked anything else."

"You ran a—" said Lanson in surprise. "You're a man of more talents than you admit to, Sergeant."

"I've been making efforts to pick things up, sir."

"I'm glad," said Lanson truthfully. "So, we're facing twelve enemy troops who have trapped themselves in a confined space."

He pictured an assault – it would be bloody and dirty, and with no guarantee of success, at least not without the use of explosives which would likely wreck some of the control consoles. Of course, the two miniguns outside the bridge could be directed to fire at the enemy and that would reduce the risk.

"There's more bad news, Captain," said Gabriel. "The Ixtar have a second device – this one a lot smaller than the first - connected to the inner bridge door. I attempted remote access to the door security panel, but it wouldn't allow me to connect."

"What error did you receive?" asked Lanson.

"Hardware SP400 not found, sir."

"The Ixtar device must have isolated the security panel," said Lanson.

"Is there a way around that, Captain?"

"I could override the isolation command from the bridge, but that's not going to help us. Failing that, we'll have to blow open the door."

"The only weapon we have capable of doing that is the Ezin-Tor, sir, and there's no place far enough away to fire it, without both the weapon and the person holding it being incinerated and then disintegrated."

Lanson tried to convince himself that nothing was insurmountable and that there was always a way. With the Ixtar security breaker attempting to subvert the warship and the enemy troops safe behind a three-metre blast door, he was going to have to come up with a plan, and it needed to be soon.

THIRTY

Lanson had already suggested what might be the solution, only moments earlier. "I can override the bridge door from the bridge, but it doesn't have to be the *Ragnar-3*'s bridge," he said. "Sergeant Gabriel, can you call up the warship map?"

"Yes, sir, I'm looking at it now," said Gabriel. "The newest Singularity class linked diagonally upwards from the *Ragnar-3*'s bridge, and one of the connecting posts contains an airlift. That must be how the Ixtar came onboard so quickly. Their entry point was at BL-92."

"Does the Singularity vessel have its own bridge, Sergeant?"

"Yes, sir."

"And how far is it from the top of the airlift?"

"Not far, Captain. Maybe fifty or sixty metres."

Lanson's brain was beginning to add some polish to the rough edges of his initial plan. "That new warship looked as if it was designed to operate independently of the other Ragnars. Maybe its bridge is equipped for crew operations, rather than being automated."

"We could order a switchover from the *Ragnar-3*'s old bridge to the new one," said Matlock, who was also in the comm channel. "When that's done, we can isolate the old bridge and we'll be back in control. The Ixtar won't be able to hijack the *Infinitar* again, unless there's another fully equipped bridge that we don't know about."

"And if the enemy start looking for that bridge, I'll make sure they run into trouble," said Gabriel with an edge of malice.

"We have a plan," said Lanson. "And we need to get moving. Eventually, the Ixtar breaker will crack the control systems encryption, and I don't want to end up in a security conflict with the enemy hardware." He swore as he remembered another problem. "Neither do I want a flood of enemy reinforcements boarding the *Infinitar*."

The thought of losing it all brought Lanson's anger back from the place it had been hiding. He took strength from it and the adrenaline began flowing through his veins.

Lanson faced his crew. "We're leaving. Now. Who needs help to keep up?"

It turned out that his officers were ready to go, or at least they didn't say otherwise. Striding to the single exit door, Lanson turned to check that nobody was unsteady on their feet. His eyes drifted to Lieutenant Massey's corpse, over by the far wall. The man had deserved better than this.

Lanson thudded his hand onto the access panel and the door opened. The passage outside was nondescript like all the others, but thanks to Private Wolf, he knew exactly where he was. Lanson also knew how to reach location BL-92, which was an empty room one level above the bridge.

Heading starboard out of the room, Lanson jogged along the passage. He didn't make any attempt to be careful, since the Ixtar were all on the bridge and he was in a hurry.

Halting at the first intersection, Lanson turned to see how his crew were coping. Their suits were covered in blood and their faces likewise. Nevertheless, he saw only determination in their eyes.

Without a word, Lanson headed aft. BL-92 wasn't far and he arrived at the steps leading to the upper level where the airlift was to be found. The stairwell was narrow and he ascended quickly, before emerging into another corridor, identical in appearance to the last. His body was free from pain and itching, and his breathing wasn't laboured from the climb. Lanson took it as a sign that he was fully recovered from the usually irrevocable condition of death.

The door to BL-92 was five metres along the corridor and Lanson ran to the access panel. Waiting for a moment until Lieutenant Turner had exited the stairwell, he opened the door. Room B-92 was unremarkable. Somehow the newest Singularity class had linked to this area of the *Infinitar* and left no obvious trace of it happening. A single airlift was accessed from the wall opposite the door, and its access panel glowed pale green.

"Are we waiting for Sergeant Gabriel?" asked Matlock.

"No," said Lanson. "There's another security terminal near the *Ragnar-3*'s bridge and he's heading that way. Once the Ixtar lose control over the *Infinitar*, there's a chance they'll abandon the bridge and go looking for someplace else they can screw things up for us."

"At which point, they'll run into our soldiers," said Turner, with satisfaction.

"And this time, it'll be the Ixtar on the wrong end of a nasty surprise," said Matlock, unconsciously putting a hand on her chest where the gauss projectile had exited.

First, we have to reclaim our warship," said Lanson.

He called the airlift and the doors opened immediately.

The lift car would have been a tight squeeze for twelve Ixtar, but it had plenty of room for five humans.

"Going up," said Lanson, selecting the only other available destination from the lift panel.

The doors closed and the car ascended with a groaning sound that wasn't quite right. Still, the lift came to the upper level without failure and the doors opened. Outside, the passage was so cold that Lanson's breath steamed, and the chill was enough to sting his exposed skin.

"The life support has either malfunctioned or it was deliberately set to keep the temperatures low," said Lanson.

"If the air quality isn't good, we're in trouble," said Matlock.

Lanson didn't want to die from hypoxia halfway to the bridge so, reluctantly, he instructed the lift to descend to the lower level again.

"Sergeant Gabriel, we don't know if there's a breathable atmosphere in the upper level," he said on the open comms.

"I'll send Private Chan over to you, Captain," said Gabriel. "The environmental sensor in his suit will know if the air is good."

"If it's not, my crew and I will need to find replacement suit helmets," said Lanson. He had a spare in his quarters and there were other suits hanging in the nearest armoury, but the journey there and back would take near enough ten minutes.

Since Lanson didn't want to call upon another of Gabriel's soldiers, he decided to send Lieutenant Perry instead. Carrying five suit helmets would be a pain in the ass, but Lanson couldn't afford to commit a second member of his crew.

Perry dashed from the room and, two or three minutes later, Private Chan arrived. The soldier offered a greeting without slowing his march to the lift car. In moments, the lift doors were closed, and Chan was on his way up.

"The air is breathable, Captain," said Chan on the comms. "I'm sending the lift car down to you."

"Thanks," said Lanson. "Did you hear that, Lieutenant Perry?"

"Yes, sir, I'll head straight back without those helmets."

"We aren't waiting – you'll have to make your own way to the bridge."

"Yes, sir."

The lift arrived and Lanson entered the car, along with the others. Soon, he exited into the upper passage, where Private Chan had chosen to wait, his Aral gauss rifle in both hands.

"It's cold here, sir, you'll have to move fast." Chan's face twisted. "If you can't get the temperatures up, there's a chance you'll have to withdraw to the lower level."

Lanson nodded. The cold was biting and, though his suit protected his body, thanks to its inner layer of gel which had sealed up the bullet holes, his head was exposed.

"The Galos might keep us safe," he said.

"If you can take the pain, sir," said Chan.

Lanson didn't comment. The Singularity warship's bridge was no more than a short sprint from here and he broke into a run towards it. Movement seemed to magnify the cold and Lanson felt it burning on his face and scalding his lungs as he inhaled.

Thirty metres along, the passage – which was gloomy and narrow – continued aft, while an intersection led starboard. Lanson took the turning and followed the next passage five metres into a compact room. An airlift was accessed from the left-hand wall, and he came to a halt at the access panel.

"This goes straight up to the bridge antechamber," said Lanson, tapping his knuckles on the lift door.

He called the lift and stepped into the car as soon as the door opened. The others, including Private Chan, hurried inside and Lanson instructed the lift to ascend to the upper level.

In the few seconds it took to complete the journey, Lanson looked around at the members of his crew. Frost had formed on their hair and eyebrows, and they stamped their feet in a vain effort to keep warm.

The lift came to a halt and the party exited into a square room, barely four metres by four. Steps led down through the right-hand wall, while the bridge door was directly ahead. Just like on the *Ragnar-3*, two miniguns had been installed into the ceiling. Lanson's heart jumped at the sight of the automated defences, but he needn't have worried. The guns weren't even pointing towards the lift, and they didn't move.

"Inactive," said Lanson with relief.

Approaching the bridge door, he stretched his hand towards the access panel, hoping the Ixtar hadn't done anything to damage the backend security system.

"Captain, stay to one side," said Chan urgently. "Let me check the bridge is clear. Just in case."

Lanson signalled his acknowledgement and waved his crew into the left-hand corner of the room, where they wouldn't be visible once the door opened. Keeping himself out of sight, he activated the door panel. With a quiet hum, the door slid into its left-hand recess.

Private Chan watched for a moment and then darted inside. "Clear," he confirmed.

"Let's go," said Lanson.

Emerging from cover, he entered the bridge. In terms of size, it was smaller than the one on the *Ragnar-3*, and shaped like a wedge. While the rear ceiling was three metres high, it sloped to only two metres at the front, where the command consoles were located.

"This is the same hardware as on the *Ragnar-3*," said Lanson, heading along the aisle between two of the consoles.

"Same number of stations, same everything," said Abrams. "Just with less headroom."

Lanson dropped into the left-hand command seat. The Ixtar had left a fist-sized device, fitted with a small screen, plugged into the top panel. As he pulled out the wires, Lanson looked at the screen. Predictably, the text was unintelligible.

He turned in his seat. "Is everyone ready?" he asked. "Once we log on here, there's a chance it'll create an alarm on the *Ragnar-3*'s bridge consoles."

"I should be able to cancel that alarm, Captain," said Turner. "If I'm quick enough, the Ixtar might not even notice it go off."

"What are your intentions if we successfully regain control of the *Infinitar*, sir?" asked Matlock. "Once the Ixtar realise what we've done, their warship will attack us."

"I know," said Lanson. "What we're going to do is leave the enemy in control while we spend a few minutes checking to find out if the *Infinitar* has any new capabilities. Once we're ready, we'll take back our warship and deal with whatever is out there."

"While the *Ragnar-3*'s bridge is primary, we won't have any operational control, Captain," said Matlock. "We'll have view access to the external sensors, weapons and propulsion, but that's all."

"This is what we have to play with, Commander."

"Yes, sir."

Time was passing. Lanson flexed his fingers and prepared to log on.

THIRTY-ONE

"We'll all authenticate at the same time," said Lanson. "Lieutenant Turner, cancel that alarm as quickly as you can."

"Yes, sir."

Lanson spoke a three-two-one countdown and then he logged himself into the console. The usual menus appeared, though several were greyed out and inaccessible.

"Alarm cancelled," said Turner. "Hopefully I managed it before the Ixtar noticed."

"Let's find out if they're showing any signs of agitation," said Lanson.

Calling up the lifeform map, Lanson discovered that twelve Ixtar remained on the bridge, their movements giving no indication of alarm. Unfortunately, forty more of the alien scumbags had docked in one of the vacant shuttle bays and were making their way forwards. The only positive was that the *Infinitar*'s two empty bays had been farther aft than the occupied bays, meaning the enemy had a longer journey to the *Ragnar-3*'s bridge.

"Lieutenant Turner, let Sergeant Gabriel know the bad

news," said Lanson.

"Yes, sir."

The bridge door opened and Lieutenant Perry entered, frost glistening in her hair. She headed for the station next to Lieutenant Turner and took the empty seat.

"Sign in and be ready," said Lanson.

"Damnit, the life support controls have been handed off to the *Ragnar-3*'s bridge," said Abrams. "We'll have to stay cold until we've switched the primacy of the two bridges."

Lanson swore inwardly. The cold was becoming more than just an impediment – it was a constant pain on his skin and he felt as if the tear film over his eyes was always on the verge of turning into ice. Reaching up, Lanson rubbed his hair, and a sprinkling of tiny crystals fell onto his console.

"I need to know what changes have been made to the *Infinitar*," he said. "We've completed three rapid combinations without having the opportunity to discover what is new. Lieutenant Turner – is anything showing on the external sensors?"

"I'm putting the feeds on your screen, Captain," said Turner. "We're in the same bay as before, and the *Pembros* hasn't gone anywhere."

Lanson checked the feeds. Aside from the enemy warship, the sensors – which had a wide enough viewing arc to see most of the bay – weren't picking up anything new, aside from two Ixtar shuttles which were heading towards the *Infinitar*. It didn't take a genius to guess that both transports were packed with soldiers.

"If those shuttles are even halfway full, they'll hold enough enemy troops to overcome the *Infinitar*'s internal defences," said Lanson. "We can't let them dock."

"They aren't in much of a hurry, Captain," said Turner. "Besides, the *Infinitar* only has one spare docking bay, so they'll have to move things around."

"That's not going to take them forever," said Lanson, staring at the enemy shuttles and wishing he could blow them to pieces. He raised his voice. "We don't have long, folks. As soon as the first enemy shuttle is preparing to dock, I'm going to swap the primacy of the two bridges and then isolate the one on the *Ragnar*-3. When that happens, there's a high chance the Ixtar warship will commence an attack."

"Sir, as soon as we have primacy, I'll be able to kick the Ixtar out of the internal comms," said Perry. "They'll have no way to communicate their loss of the bridge - either to their own warship or the other Ixtar on board the *Infinitar*."

"That might buy us some time," said Lanson. "It's possible the *Pembros*'s crew will waste a few seconds trying to re-establish comms."

"More than possible, Captain," said Matlock. "The Ixtar won't want to lose the *Infinitar* – they'll be reluctant to open fire unless they're certain it's necessary."

"Let's hope you're right, Commander," said Lanson.

"At their current velocities, the two inbound transports will be ready to dock with the *Infinitar* in a little over four minutes, sir," said Turner.

"Acknowledged," said Lanson. "The primacy switchover should only take a few seconds, so we have a short time to figure out what's changed with our warship."

His eyes returned briefly to the feeds, where the Ixtar transports were making steady progress across the bay. Their lack of haste was perhaps a hopeful sign – an indication that the enemy felt their position was secure.

"Captain, you'll remember that just before we activated void travel to escape from Erion, the sensors went blank and we heard that squealing sound," said Abrams. He was talking quickly and that usually meant he had plenty of information to convey.

"I remember."

"At that precise moment, a whole bunch of our Galos modules began generating enormous energy. I've checked the audit logs and there's an entry for something called *deconstruction repulse*, with a duration I believe exactly matches the squealing sound."

"We were attacked," said Lanson.

"Yes, Captain, I'm certain that's the case. The Ravanok fired an instant-kill weapon into planet Andamar and we survived because the deconstruction repulse activated."

"The Aral must have been familiar with disintegration weapons," said Lanson. "They figured out a way to make them ineffective."

"I'm not finished handing out the presents, yet, Captain," said Abrams. "The newest Singularity warship is also packed full of Galos and the moment the combination was finished, those modules began generating what I'd have once called an incredible amount of energy, but in terms of this Aral tech, it's probably not even straining the hardware."

"What's the purpose of the energy generation?" asked Lanson.

"The energy is being channelled into our hull, sir, and a status indicator has appeared on my monitoring tools, showing that *harden armour* is active."

Lanson checked his own readouts and saw the same indicator. "Harden armour," he said. "I wonder how effective it is."

"It's powered by a crapload of Galos, sir," said Abrams. "It's going to be good."

"Now we're getting somewhere," said Lanson. "The *Infinitar* has always seemed vulnerable, given how much effort the Aral put into its construction."

"We've never experienced the finished article, sir," said Matlock. "And we're still missing one piece."

"Two minutes and the first shuttle will dock," said Turner. "The Ixtar transport that's already in Bay 3 is preparing to depart under remote control, so there'll soon be two vacant bays."

"Acknowledged," said Lanson. "Commander Matlock, is there anything new in the Singularity weapons menu?"

"No new options, sir – nothing hidden, nothing buried six menus deep, just the same ones as before, and with the same *missing component* error."

"I hope we won't be disappointed when we complete the final combination," said Lanson.

"I have a feeling we won't be, Captain."

"Me too, Commander."

"Captain, I've found something else in the propulsion control software which I haven't seen before," said Abrams.

"What is it, Lieutenant?"

"I'll put it up on your screen, Captain. It'll be easier than giving you a description."

A diagram appeared on Lanson's screen, showing five blue rectangles. Each rectangle was further divided into numerous squares, and some of the rectangles contained more squares than others. Each square was linked by numerous straight lines to other squares, and many of the lines ended where a sixth rectangle would be.

"This is the *Infinitar*," said Lanson.

"Yes, sir – or at least the five components we've located so far."

"And those blocks are our Galos modules?"

"Yes, Captain. If you zoom in, you'll see that they're all labelled *Stabilised Galos*."

"I remember you saying there might be different types," said Lanson.

"Now I'm certain of it," said Abrams. "The stores at Erion

were Singularity Tier Galos. I reckon that's the real dangerous type – like the cube we found on Cornerstone."

"When the final combination is completed, all these lines between the different stabilised Galos blocks will be joined to other modules," said Lanson.

"Yes, sir."

"What happens then?"

"I haven't the damnedest idea, Captain, but I'm interested to find out."

The excitement of discovery, along with the nervous anticipation of coming action had made Lanson briefly forget about the cold. The growing intensity of the pain soon reminded him, and he hoped it wouldn't affect his reactions when the inevitable combat started.

A final check of the lifeform monitors showed Lanson that the newly arrived Ixtar soldiers were making rapid progress. He guessed they intended to reinforce the *Ragnar-3*'s bridge, but once the primacy was swapped, they'd probably begin a sweep through the warship's interior, hunting for the culprits.

"Twenty seconds and the first of the enemy transports will dock," said Turner.

Lanson couldn't delay any longer. "Switching primacy," he said, entering the command into his console. Owing to the nature of the request, Lanson was required to authenticate again, which he did immediately. "Primacy successfully switched," he confirmed. "Isolating the *Ragnar-3*'s bridge."

"I have full access to the sensors, Captain," said Turner.

"Closing the external bay doors," said Perry.

"I'm back in control of the propulsion," said Abrams.

"And same with the weapons, sir," said Matlock. "I'm targeting the *Pembros*."

"Hold fire for the order, Commander."

"Yes, sir. Are we planning to stay in the fight whatever the cost?"

"Hell no – only long enough to find out how much damage our Galos hardened armour can soak," said Lanson. "If we're losing, I'll activate an ILT."

Matlock smiled. "Sounds like a plan."

"I have ejected the Ixtar from the internal comms, sir," said Perry. "They have no way to contact their warship."

A glance at the lifeform monitor showed a marked change in activity from both groups of Ixtar. Those on the bridge were now moving around more, while the forty enemy soldiers had come to a halt, presumably as they tried to figure out what had gone wrong with their comms.

"Turn on the automated defences," said Lanson. "That'll give them something extra to think about."

"Automated defences activated," said Matlock. "That should make it interesting for the enemy if they try to enter or exit the *Ragnar-3*'s bridge."

"I'll keep Sergeant Gabriel informed of developments, Captain," said Perry. "Is he to engage the Ixtar, or lay low?"

"Order him to stay out of sight for the moment and keep a watch over the enemy movements."

"Yes, sir."

Lanson exhaled, and the air steamed in front of him. So far, everything was going to plan. The enemy warship hadn't yet reacted to events onboard the *Infinitar*, but they'd soon realise something had gone badly wrong.

"It's too cold for combat," said Lanson. He instructed the life support to increase the temperature on the bridge. "So let's warm things up."

Lanson didn't wait until he was comfortable. He set his focus on the sensor feeds and smiled grimly.

It was time to fight.

THIRTY-TWO

"Commander Matlock – commence the attack," said Lanson.

"Yes, sir," said Matlock. "Portside Avantar clusters one to eight, fired. Topside clusters one to four, fired. Gradars set to fully automatic."

In a repeat of the earlier engagement, the *Infinitar*'s missiles accelerated across the bay, whereupon many were destroyed by the *Pembros*'s defensive gauss turrets. Two dozen Avantars evaded the countermeasures and detonated against the enemy vessel's shield.

Unlike last time, the Ixtar fired back. Missiles spilled into the bay in huge numbers, to be met by a withering hail of Gradar projectiles.

"Launching Spine interceptors," said Matlock. "I think the range is too short for them to be effective."

The tiny, highly manoeuvrable missiles burst from their topside launchers. A dozen or so registered targets and banked sharply towards them. The rest of the Spine wave failed to lock on to the Ixtar missiles, and these crashed fruitlessly into the bay ceiling.

Lanson couldn't do anything to stop the remaining enemy missiles from exploding against the portside of his warship. The sensors on that flank turned white and he narrowed his eyes against the intensity.

"We have suffered twenty-nine impacts, Captain," said Lieutenant Turner.

"Give me a damage report, Lieutenant Abrams," said Lanson. "Those were high-yield warheads."

"There are no warning lights anywhere, Captain," said Abrams. "That's a positive sign."

"Check and confirm."

"Yes, sir."

Lanson didn't ask questions. Despite the reassuring sound of *harden armour*, the enemy warship wasn't firing blanks. He glanced at his own readouts and the damage report window was all green lights.

Leaving Abrams to provide confirmation about the defensive system's effectiveness, Lanson rolled the *Infinitar*, so that its underside clusters were on target. A final adjustment also brought half of the rear clusters into play.

"Underside clusters one to twelve and rear clusters one to six, fired," said Matlock.

"Don't stop," said Lanson, rolling the *Infinitar* again.

He was beginning to get a feeling of déjà vu, since the engagement was progressing so similarly to the one which proceeded it, ignoring the fact that the enemy was now fighting back. The underside and rear launched Avantars exploded against the Ixtar vessel's shield, and, just like before, Lanson found himself looking for signs the opposing warship's defences were weakening.

Such was the feeling of repetition that he couldn't help but glance over his shoulder, as if part of his brain feared another Ixtar hijack squad was about to enter the bridge.

Damnit.

Lanson's anger was directed at himself, for allowing the engagement to be so predictable. He didn't want an extended slugging match with this enemy warship, since the Ixtar likely had an entire fleet. The *Infinitar* wasn't going to survive a war of attrition.

"The enemy vessel is rotating, Captain," said Lieutenant Turner. "They're going to try firing their disintegration cannon at us."

Lanson had been waiting for this and he requested maximum power from the *Infinitar*'s propulsion. The vast amount of thrust and the resulting acceleration almost caught him off-guard, and he brought the warship to a halt, not far from the bay's north wall. Meanwhile, the Ixtar spaceship stayed in the same place as before, rotating so that its nose followed the *Infinitar*. In response, Lanson reduced altitude sharply, causing the enemy vessel to adjust.

"Captain!" yelled Abrams. "I've confirmed we took zero damage from that last missile attack. A visual on our hull shows markings, but nothing significant."

It was the news Lanson had been waiting for. Abandoning his efforts to evade the enemy disintegration cannon, he instructed the *Infinitar* to accelerate diagonally upwards. The enemy warship launched another salvo of missiles. Some were pulverised by Gradar fire, others were not. Plasma explosions engulfed the *Infinitar*'s nose.

Ignoring the flames, Lanson held the warship on course. A loud creaking sound, like the *Infinitar*'s hull was under immense pressure, came from all around, and the power needles on Lanson's console swung left and right like pendulums on fast-forward.

"We were hit by a disintegration attack, Captain," said Abrams.

"So I gathered," said Lanson. "Now we're going to hit the Ixtar with a different kind of weapon."

Having expected the *Infinitar* to crumble harmlessly into pieces, the enemy crew made no effort to escape the incoming collision. Protected as he was by the life support system, Lanson felt the impact as a gentle thump, and heard it as the sound of faraway thunder.

The reality was more dramatic. In the moment before the two warships smashed together, the Ixtar vessel's protective shield appeared. Unfortunately for the enemy, their technology was not potent enough to absorb such a colossal impact. In the blinking of an eye, the ovoid of red energy faded and then disappeared altogether.

With its velocity not noticeably affected, the *Infinitar* crashed into the Ixtar vessel's underside, just behind its nose section. The *Pembros*'s armour crumpled, and surface emplacements were crushed by the enormous mass of the *Infinitar*. Watching the sensors, Lanson took enormous satisfaction from the fact that his own warship's armour remained intact.

The moment Lanson saw the velocity gauge hit zero, he commanded his warship to accelerate stern first, directly away from the Ixtar vessel.

Matlock didn't hesitate. "Forward Avantar clusters one to eight, fired!" she yelled.

The distance between the two warships wasn't great, though it was sufficient for the Avantar warheads to arm. With its energy shield depleted, the Ixtar vessel's hull was struck multiple times. The combined explosion was huge and Lanson saw huge pieces of debris being torn free.

"What's our status after the impact, Lieutenant Abrams?" asked Lanson.

He didn't wait an answer, since he couldn't afford to hesitate and besides, the sensor feeds showed little visible damage to the *Infinitar*. Pushing the controls as far as they'd go, Lanson aimed for the burning section of the Ixtar vessel's hull.

"No significant damage, sir!" said Abrams, a split-second before impact.

Once again, the *Infinitar* smashed into the opposing warship, only this time it struck where the enemy hull armour had been weakened by the Avantar detonations. Although the sensor feeds showed a chaotic mix of light and shapes, Lanson sensed his warship coming to a halt. He held the propulsion at maximum and then, with a lurch, the velocity gauge began to climb.

Knowing that the bay wall was close, Lanson hauled back on the controls. The *Infinitar* came to a stop, and he caught a glimpse on the rear sensors of the damage inflicted upon the enemy vessel. A huge chunk of its nose and underside had broken away, along with countless smaller pieces of debris. In addition to the massive hole in its hull, the structure of the Ixtar warship had been visibly affected by the collision. Armour plates had rippled all the way to the vessel's centre midsection, and many of them had partially ruptured along their seams.

"They're going to ILT out of here," said Matlock.

"If they can," said Lanson.

Determined to inflict another humiliating strike on his opponents, Lanson instructed the *Infinitar* to accelerate flank-first towards the Ixtar vessel. The enemy crew didn't activate an ILT. Instead, the *Pembros* accelerated sluggishly towards the bay floor.

Such was the power of the *Infinitar* that Lanson had no problem catching up and impacting with the other warship. Damaged armour was torn free, and it rained down towards the bay floor.

Sensing the kill, Lanson prepared to put some distance between himself and his opponent, to see if he could quickly finish the engagement with missiles. As he pulled back on the controls, a grey veil of dust suddenly covered many of the feeds. Unsure of the source, Lanson piloted the *Infinitar* stern first away from the Ixtar vessel, hoping he'd soon be clear of the dust.

"Someone tell me what happened," he ordered.

"I'm adding filters to the sensors, Captain," said Turner. "They'll improve our visibility."

Turner was good when danger threatened and even better in a crisis. In moments, the feeds had improved sufficiently that Lanson could make out the Ixtar vessel directly ahead and accelerating vertically.

Before Lanson could give the order to fire, the dust thickened and then thickened again, until visibility was once more reduced to only a few thousand metres. Movement on his console brought Lanson's attention to the output gauges, which were once again showing huge spikes.

"A disintegration weapon," said Lanson.

The first impact with the Ixtar warship in the bay had knocked out its disintegration cannon, so the attacks had to be coming from elsewhere. Emboldened by the *Infinitar*'s new defences, and by the weakened state of his opponent, Lanson decided it wasn't yet time to run. He piloted the warship through the dust, on an intercept course with the *Pembros*.

"This next sensor filter should...oh crap," said Turner.

The addition of the new filter improved the quality of the feeds enormously, such that Lanson was able to see that numerous disintegration holes had been made in the bay ceiling. The *Infinitar* was directly beneath one of the openings and through it, Lanson could see rows of Ixtar ships, high above the planet's surface. Each of these vessels was similar in size and mass to the others which Lanson had encountered so far, being approximately twenty-thousand metres in length and a trillion tons on the scales.

Aside from the equivalence in sizes, each vessel was different in design. Some were almost graceful looking, with V-shaped wings, while others were brutish, their hulls studded with angular turrets.

However, it wasn't the Ixtar fleet which most caught Lanson's attention. At just that moment, the Ravanok sphere appeared, motionless on the edge of space, like a malevolent singularity ready to devour anything in its path.

"We need void travel," said Lanson. "Right now."

"Entering the coordinates, Captain," said Abrams. "One moment."

Lanson held his thumb over the activation button on his right-hand control bar, willing Abrams to be quick. The Ixtar didn't seem too happy at the Ravanok's arrival, and their warships began accelerating in different directions. Dark blue energy weapons detonated against the sphere's hull and gauss fire thundered into its armour.

"Done!" yelled Abrams. "Go!"

Before Lanson could press the button, every one of the sensor arrays went completely blank, and the output gauges displayed scarcely believable numbers. His thumb squeezed the void travel activation button and the *Infinitar*'s propulsion boomed and shuddered, as though it had been pushed to its limits and beyond.

The sensor feeds resumed and Lanson found himself staring into cold, dark, and reassuringly empty space. How long it would remain empty, he didn't know, but he was confident he and his crew had at least some time to take stock and recover before the Ravanok caught up.

"The Galos output levels have fallen back to their usual

levels, Captain," said Abrams. "I don't think they had much more to give."

"Any anomalies resulting from the void travel?" asked Lanson.

"No, sir. Not this time."

"Judging by the numbers showing on the life form monitors, the *Infinitar*'s automated defences have taken the Ixtar troops by surprise," said Matlock.

"I'll speak to Sergeant Gabriel in a moment," said Lanson. "If there's any mopping up needed, he's the man to do it."

He tipped back his head and closed his eyes. Recent events had seen Lanson and his crew successfully unite five parts of the *Infinitar*, leaving only one to go. However, the Ravanok appeared determined to prevent the Aral's creation from realising its final, intended form.

And now, from the glimpse Lanson had been afforded through the openings in the disintegrated bay ceiling, it was apparent that the alien sphere and the Ixtar weren't friends.

Answers, as ever, were elusive. One thing was sure – Lanson had to find the last piece of the *Infinitar* and then, he could turn his attention to the Infinity Lens. Perhaps there was more to the Lens than he knew about.

The biggest problem was going to be surviving long enough to find out.

———

Sign up to my mailing list here to be the first to find out about new releases.

ALSO BY ANTHONY JAMES

Survival Wars (Seven Books) – Available in eBook, Paperback and Audio.

1. Crimson Tempest
2. Bane of Worlds
3. Chains of Duty
4. Fires of Oblivion
5. Terminus Gate
6. Guns of the Valpian
7. Mission: Nemesis

Obsidiar Fleet (Six Books – set after the events in Survival Wars) – Available in eBook and Paperback.

1. Negation Force
2. Inferno Sphere
3. God Ship
4. Earth's Fury
5. Suns of the Aranol
6. Mission: Eradicate

The Transcended (Seven Books – set after the events in Obsidiar Fleet) – Available in eBook, Paperback and Audio

1. Augmented
2. Fleet Vanguard
3. Far Strike
4. Galaxy Bomb

5. Void Blade
6. Monolith
7. Mission: Destructor

Fire and Rust (Seven Books) – Available in eBook, Paperback and Audio.

1. Iron Dogs
2. Alien Firestorm
3. Havoc Squad
4. Death Skies
5. Refuge 9
6. Nullifier
7. Scum of the Universe

Anomalies (Two Books) – Available in eBook and Paperback.

1. Planet Wreckers
2. Assault Amplified

Savage Stars (Seven Books) – Available in eBook and Paperback

1. War from a Distant Sun
2. Fractured Horizons
3. Galactar
4. Fulcrum Gun
5. Laws of Ancidium
6. Empires in Ruin
7. Recker's Chance

Forged Alliance (Eight Books – set after the events in Savage Stars) – Available in eBook and Paperback

1. Dark of the Void
2. The God's Titan
3. Vilekron
4. Ascendant of Berongar
5. The God's Reckoning
6. Shadows of Kilvus
7. Endurus
8. Flint's Justice

Guns of the Federation (Seven Books) – Available in eBook and Paperback.

1. Xaros – Jungle Planet
2. War Vessel of the Ax'Kol
3. Voltran Unchained
4. Darkness on Sagitol
5. The Andos Vector
6. Repulsor
7. Death Never Wins

Printed in Great Britain
by Amazon

27231723R00148